WHAT ARE FRIENDS FOR?

LIZZIE O'HAGAN

REVIEW

First published in Great Britain in 2020 by
HEADLINE REVIEW
An imprint of HEADLINE PUBLISHING GROUP

1

Cataloguing in Publication Data is available from the British Library

ISBN 978 1 4722 7503 5

Typeset in Bembo Std by CC Book Production
Printed and bound in Great Britain by Clays Ltd, Elcograf S.p.A.

HEADLINE PUBLISHING GROUP
An Hachette UK Company
Carmelite House
50 Victoria Embankment
London EC4Y 0DZ

www.headline.co.uk
www.hachette.co.uk

To Grace –
For all the adventures we've shared
and the ones still to come.

Prologue

Becky: I'm quite small actually, like 5ft1. Why? How tall are you?

Adam: Eight and a half inches.

Becky: Huh?

Adam: ;)

Becky has gone offline

Giorgio: Hi, I'm Giorgio.

Becky: Hi, Giorgio, your name is actually on your profile, but hi.

Giorgio: Your photo is lovely.

Becky: Not too bad yourself.

Giorgio: Ah yes. Took that one in '82. A full head of hair then!

Becky has gone offline

Emma: Hey.

Tom: Hey, Emma. How are you?

Tom: You have gorgeous eyes btw!

Emma: I know. You told me on our date.

Emma: And again the morning after.

Tom: Oh Emma! I'm so sorry. I remember now, the artist, right?

Emma: Nope. The officer.

Tom: Any chance you'd believe me if I told you I'd lost your number?

Tom: Have you got Mum a birthday present yet?

Lucy: Tom, stop using Tinder as our primary source of contact.

Lucy: It's weird.

Tom: But you never answer your phone.

Tom: Besides, you swiped right too.

Lucy: Thought it would freak you out.

Tom: Same. Guess you've always learned from the best.

Lucy: Not when it comes to dating.

Lucy: Now piss off.

Chapter One

Eve

Shit. What was that?

I hear a crash from the next room. My heartbeat picks up pace. It's probably just Buster. But as fat as he is, can a cat really make that much noise? And my flatmate Becky will definitely still be in bed, refusing to surface before 7 a.m. My mind sifts through the options.

One: switch on the kitchen light, let the murderer know I'm standing, Lycra-clad and defenceless, in the next room. Two: swing open the door, wok in hand, and jump-lunge into the living room for maximum surprise. Or three: crouch in the corner of the kitchen, swipe to my Headspace app and lose myself in some guided meditation whilst a thief takes us for all we're worth. Which to be fair isn't all that much.

Slowly I push the door into the living room ajar and peer into the darkness. A meow screeches between my feet and a ginger blur flies past as another thump fills the space before me. Not Buster then.

'Oh *crap*,' I hear a man whisper from the darkness. My heart quickens, my breathing follows, and suddenly I'm not sure which is worse: getting murdered in my gym kit or having a panic attack in front of a complete stranger. Breathe, Eve, just breathe.

The stranger fumbles, a light switch clicks and the living room is flooded with light. Well, I say flooded, but three out of five bulbs have broken in the last two years and we still haven't got round to replacing them. So not so much flooded as *dampened* with light. *Note to self: dampened with light. Could make good copy. Maybe local nature piece?* My heart thumps, so does the stranger, and I'm back in the room. Well, kind of. Peering into it at least. In the low light, I trace the man's movements, trying to place a face I'm almost positive I've never seen before. He stumbles across to the sofa, reaching behind its cushions and retrieving a black leather belt. My life flashes before my eyes. But wait, why would a murderer do that? Through the gap in the door, I watch him thread the belt back through his trouser loops, hands shaking, symptoms clear: *here we have the hung-over man.*

I breathe a sigh of relief so heavy I'm sure it's audible, but Becky's latest conquest carries on regardless. I allow the door to creak open a little further as he spots one shoe on the window ledge. A little further as he almost stumbles into our boarded-up fireplace to retrieve the other. What the hell did they get up to last night? Further still as he reaches behind the TV, pulling his shirt from the floor and shoving

4

his tattooed arms into the sleeves. I push the door wider as he finds his jumper balled up beneath the coffee table and stand in the doorway, arms folded, eyes glued to my best friend's date, trying my best not to laugh. Buster appears by my side, the Watson to my Sherlock, as I clear my throat.

'Can I help you with anything?'

'*Shit!*' Becky's date jumps out of his inked skin as he turns from what he thinks is the front door. Clearly, he doesn't remember that you enter our basement apartment from the back. The front door's as redundant as the fireplace, and the microwave, and the . . . Jeez, I wish our landlady wasn't so sweet that we don't have the heart to tell her that her house is a hovel. I watch as the tall, dark but sadly not as handsome as he thinks he is guy looks me up and down, all six foot one of me.

'Cute cat.' He looks down at my feet as he walks towards the door. Buster growls. 'Tell Bex to call me?'

I nod. Even though she hates being called Bex. Even though I know she's not going to call.

I slam our back-front door shut behind him. Mostly because it needs a good thump. A little because I'd like to give him one too. I look down at my watch. Thirteen thousand steps. Thirteen minutes past the hour. And about thirteen new article ideas to type up before they disappear from my memory, forced out by some mediocre piece the newspaper wants me to focus on instead. I walk back through the kitchen and across the living room, Buster still following.

5

I know better than to think it's because he loves me. It's almost breakfast time.

'Eve.' I turn to see a mess of dark hair and pink pyjamas sprawled on the sofa. 'I snuck out as soon as I heard him leave.' Becky lifts her head to look at me, her normally olive skin almost as white as his was. She sits up properly, her black hair cascading down her back, her gesticulating arms thrown out in display. 'I woke up like this.'

I laugh. Unlike the countless millennials who take hours to perfect the 'I just woke up like this' look, when it comes to Becky, I believe her. She hugs a large cushion to her stomach, almost engulfing her entirely. It's embroidered with an elephant, its swirling oranges and pinks a nod to its Indian roots. It's one of countless elephants and sparrows scattered around the place, a reminder of the day we met, when Becky found me crying in the toilets of Oceania after he-who-shall-not-be-named called me 'Eve the Elephant' and she branded her tiny self 'Becky the Bird' in solidarity.

'I'm *so* hung-over.' She grabs my arm like a lifeline.

'Sorry, babe, I need a shower.' I look down at my watch: 7.15. I'm not going to have any laptop time at this rate. I don't wake up at 5 a.m. to get to work in a rush.

'But I need you to shower *me* with love.' She looks up at me, all puffy puppy-dog eyes.

'Don't you need to get ready for work too?' I ask, almost scared she'll say yes. She's a mess. And I'm guessing the parents of the children she teaches would agree with me.

'Please,' she pleads. 'Eve, it was terrible. I need my therapy.' She groans.

6

'Okay. I'm going to shower, and then I've got a few things to write whilst I have breakfast. You can give me the bullet points then.' Becky smiles, mission accomplished. 'We need to talk to Matilda about the mould, too.'

To be fair, we try to talk to our landlady about all the things that are wrong with the flat. She just force-feeds us Victoria sponge and loveliness and we suddenly feel bad for whatever basic human right we were arguing for in the first place.

'I'm kind of starting to like it.' Becky smiles. 'Feel like we've got a jungle vibe going on.'

I pick up a sparrow cushion and fly it across the room towards her.

'Fine, *fine*.' She holds her hands up in surrender. 'Mould and Matthew, both on the agenda.'

Matthew, I think, rushing towards the bathroom. At least this one has a name.

I grab my towel and switch on the shower radio, letting the news wash over me as I exfoliate at speed. *Note to self: research female police officers working on sexual harassment cases.* I race out of the shower into my room – the bigger of the two despite the fact that I rarely have visitors – and switch on the iron. Becky says I'm the only woman in her late twenties who actually owns an iron. *Note to self: research the decline of ironing amongst the millennial generation?*

I blow-dry my hair whilst sitting in my towel, eyes scanning yesterday's *Metro*. I fold down the 'Guilty Pleasures' pages for Becky, then moisturise my hands, circulating my wrists over and over whilst I do. I'm not sure whether the

7

repetitive strain is getting better or I'm just getting better at ignoring it. Either way, it's not like I can type any less; it's part of the job. I put on make-up, the same as every day: enough to look pretty, not so much that I look like I've tried. Hair in a ponytail, I tuck my now crisp white shirt into dark jeans. Done. I race back into the living room, blood pumping, anxiety surging, wishing I had time for another run. An hour in the morning is usually long enough to keep my anxiety under control; the fresh air on my face, the sound of my feet hitting the pavement. It's the only reason I sneak out and back into the house before dawn.

The bundle of Becky is right where I left her.

'Eve?' I ignore her, heading to the kitchen and returning with two bowls of granola topped with yoghurt and fresh berries. The only food I ever make her.

'You don't happen to have a full English in there, do you?' She sits herself up again.

'You get what you're given,' I quip, but Becky is already tucking in. I flip open my laptop. 'Right, we have approximately eight and a half minutes. Shoot.'

'It started well,' Becky begins as I begin to type up my first article idea.

'It always does . . .'

'He looked better than his photos and the bar he picked was really cool.'

'Shoreditch, right?' I ask, not looking up from my laptop.

'Yeah,' Becky says slowly. 'How did you know?'

'Arm tattoos, skinny ripped jeans, floppy brown fringe,' I recount. 'It's textbook.'

'Wow, you were born to be a journalist,' Becky laughs.

I usually think that too. I just wish work would give me a chance to be a *proper* one.

'Okay, so yeah – cool bar, cool boy. But then he just talks about himself all night, so, *so* self-obsessed.'

'What do you think of this top line?' I say, thinking out loud.

'Eve, we're talking about *me*,' Becky objects, the irony not lost on either of us. Thankfully, I know she's joking. Becky may love the drama, but she's far from self-obsessed. She's got the biggest heart I know. Which might be why she's always trying to give it away to someone. Anyone.

'So why did you bring him home?' I ask, ideas saved, laptop stashed.

'Did you *see* him?' Her eyes widen along with her smile.

'Yeah.' I move across the room to stuff three notebooks into my bag. 'A *lot* of him actually. He was okay.' I shrug as best I can whilst reaching behind the TV to unplug my phones. There are no missed calls, no messages on either. 'Not good enough for you, though.' I look over at her. 'So no second date?' I ask, already knowing the answer. She wouldn't have pretended to be asleep this morning if another date was on the cards.

'The sex was good,' she muses. 'But you know I'm looking for more. So no. Thank you, next.' She clicks her fingers, channelling Ariana. Which for someone sharing her height isn't all that hard. 'I've got another first date lined up for tomorrow night.' She smiles, but I can tell it's not just the hangover wearing her hope thin. She's been at this online dating game for a while now. 'What are you doing tonight?' she asks, her tired eyes struggling to keep up with my movements around the room. I have three minutes until I need to leave for work.

'Becky, you're not sitting on my book, are you?' I've run out of places to look.

She reaches beneath the blankets she's burying herself under and fishes out my thumbed copy of *Far From the Madding Crowd*.

'For a girl who eats ideas for breakfast,' she looks down at Buster, his furry face now hidden in my discarded bowl, 'you sure read that book a lot. I don't know why you like it so much.'

What's not to like? The writing. The romance. The three guys fighting for the heart of one girl. I know better than to say that out loud, though. It's easier for Becky to think romance isn't on my radar and I don't have time for it right now anyway. I don't even have time for this conversation.

'I read an article that said rereading books is relaxing.' I shrug. Becky's brow is still furrowed in confusion. 'And then I read another saying that being relaxed makes you more productive.'

She cracks a smile so warm it can't help but whisper: *there's my friend.*

'And I sure as hell need relaxation today, with the shock your near-naked guest gave me this morning,' I add.

Becky groans, throwing a hand to her forehead, mortified afresh. 'I'm so sorry, Eve,' she says, and though she laughs through her self-inflicted pain, I know she means it. 'Let me make it up to you. Dinner, Ciao Becca, tonight. My treat.'

'Becky, your parents *own* it, we eat there all the time and we've never paid them a penny.'

'And you think they'd do that if I wasn't their beloved only daughter?'

'Well, no . . .'

'So *technically* it's my treat.'

I laugh. Becky's parents are the best. Sometimes, though, I wish hanging out with them didn't remind me that mine are the worst. I reach down to take the bowl away from Buster – not happy. Then again to kiss Becky on the head – also not happy.

'Remember you can always text me to stage an emergency if your next date is a dud,' I shout back to her from the kitchen. God knows I've had to do it before.

'Thanks, babe,' I hear her smile. 'But next time don't go so *big*, okay? Almost killing off my Uncle Frank in a car accident nearly gave me a heart attack.'

'You don't even have an Uncle Frank.' I open the back door. 'And what can I say? I don't believe in doing things by halves.'

'Evelyn,' she sighs, forcing herself to stand and tracing my steps across the room to lean on the door frame into the kitchen. 'You don't believe in doing anything but completing the whole fucking circle then lapping it ten times before breakfast.'

I laugh. Walking out into the sunlight, I hear her sigh behind me.

11

'Sometimes I think I have more in common with you, Buster . . .'

I turn back to see her stroking my fat cat, who has found his way back to my bowl in record time. Maybe she does, but that dogged determination to get exactly what he wants? That he shares with me.

Chapter Two

Max

I wake up to the high notes of Sam Smith's 'Stay With Me' not so much floating as forcing themselves through my bedroom wall.

I'm not even joking when I say my best friend Tom sounds like a girl. And never have lyrics been more ironic. As Sam and Tom cry out that they're no good at one-night stands, I can't help but snort into my pillow. The fact that Tom is singing this morning is because he is impossibly good at them, or trying to be at least. They say the best way to get over someone is to get under someone else, don't they? I don't really buy that, but Tom's certainly been giving it a good go recently.

I was in bed, halfway through the film *Lion*, when I heard him come in from his date. From his drunken crashing around the kitchen, I'd say he'd had a good night, but I'd take the orange and pinks of India's skyline and a multilayered love story over a pint on the common and a quickie at some stranger's house any day. Plus, if Dev Patel can go from the gangly kid in *Skins* to that powerhouse of a protagonist, well, there's hope for us all.

I stretch my limbs to reach the four corners of my bed as Tom soars up an octave before his singing stops altogether and I hear the sound of our sticky bathroom door being thrust open and slammed shut again. When you've been living together for as long as we have, you learn to read each other's movements. This one screams: *shower's free, dude*.

I force myself out of bed, replacing my bed sheets for a towel, wrapping it around my waist. Walking down the corridor, my mind runs through the thousand things I have to do today. Tom might get to rock up to work late, but I've waited too long for this step-up in the charity not to give it my best now.

Just as I open the door to the bathroom, I hear the shower turn on – and it sure as hell isn't Tom going in for round two. *Shit*.

As the steam starts to dissipate, I'm left like a deer in the headlights, blindsided by the fully naked figure of what I assume is Tom's latest date, from her dampening hair, past her bare back to her tiny waist and, well, *beyond*. I stare on, fixed to the spot, as she reaches for the shampoo, singing under her breath, serenading the shower tiles. Any second now she's going to turn around and see me standing here. Me, in just a towel, watching her, in even less. *Shit*.

I hear the door shut behind me. No, no, no, NO. It's the kind of old wooden door that expands in the heat. Tom and

I know to do our three-minute bathroom routines after we get out of the shower just to give it time to cool down. I yank on the doorknob, trying to use enough force to open it but not enough to make a noise. It's jammed shut. This is bad. Please don't turn around, *please* don't turn around.

I look round the bathroom for a towel, a loofah, anything, just to cover my eyes so she can see I'm trying not to perv. There's nothing. *Nothing.* Not for the first time, I wish we didn't live like such *boys.* She's not even brought a towel in with her. I bet Tom hasn't told her he has a flatmate. Great, now she'll be even more thrilled when she turns off the shower to meet me for the first time. I can't imagine it will bring her much comfort to know that her being here is as much of a shock to me. Thanks for the heads-up, Tom.

With nothing left for it and the steam evaporating any hopes of a better idea, I take off my towel, holding it as a wall between the two of us. Then I hear it. The scream.

'*Aargh!*' she cries, and even though I knew it was coming, I can't help but join in.

'What's the matter?' I feel a gush of cold air as Tom pulls the bathroom door open to be greeted with my bare arse, me holding a towel out like a father about to swaddle his child. 'Mate, what the fuck?!'

I turn around so that the towel is facing Tom, and now my arse is facing her whilst his *everything* is staring at me. He's as naked as the girl behind me, every part of him so big that he has nothing to hide. Not that he's even trying to.

'Tom, what the hell?!' she yells at both of us.

'This is not okay!' I shout at Tom. It's not the first time

his lack of communication has led to an unwanted run-in, but this is by far the worst.

'You can say that again,' the woman cries from behind me.

'Ruby, meet Max.' I catch the glint in Tom's eye and I can tell he's trying not to laugh. 'Max, meet Ruby.'

She screams again as I push past Tom, wrapping the towel around any last shred of dignity I have.

Which right now isn't all that much.

'Why can't your dates use a damn lock?' I walk into the living room to find Tom, long legs crossed, sipping a freshly brewed coffee with one hand and holding a book in the other.

'It's no big deal, she's probably already forgotten.' He grins, but we can both hear her ranting into her phone from his bedroom. I'll be on some kind of blacklist in no time.

'I wish *I* could forget about it.' I accept the coffee cup Tom points to on the side.

'I'm sorry, Max,' he says into his book, trying his best not to laugh. 'Maybe I should have messaged you to let you know we'd come back here instead. It was late and she didn't want to scare her housemate by bringing some stranger home.'

'How considerate of her.' I narrow my eyes in his direction before noticing what book he's holding; it's one of my favourites. 'Dude, are you even reading that?'

'I thought it would make me look sensitive.' He peers over the top of it to see my rolling eyes. 'Didn't know he could write, though.' He shrugs.

'Thomas Hardy?'

'Yeah, the hard one from *Peaky Blinders*? He can act, he's got that face and now he churns out this *Madding Crowd* thing. The guy's got it all.'

I'm mad at him for letting me scare Ruby like that, but I can't help but laugh. Literature isn't one of Tom's strong points.

'Dude, *Far From the Madding Crowd* was written in 1874, a hundred or so years before your Tom Hardy was even born . . .'

'*And* the dude can time-travel.' Tom laughs too. 'So it's proper old then,' he continues as I feel the caffeine hit my system and my startled heart begin to settle. 'I don't know why you like it so much.'

The writing. The romance. The fact that all three guys know they're willing to fight for the heart of one girl. I can only imagine what it's like to know you've found something worth putting it all on the line for.

'Tom, this is *not* acceptable.' Ruby storms into the living room, now thankfully fully clothed. 'I'm there grabbing a quick shower and your housemate thinks it's okay to let himself in, *nakedly* watch me shower and then offer me a towel as if that's totally normal . . .'

'Classic Max.' Tom shakes his head, amusement written over every inch of him. 'Here I am trying to look sensitive and you're holding a bloody towel out for the girl. Give a guy a chance, bro.'

I risk sacrificing my coffee to punch my best friend on the arm, my clenched fist just hitting hard, dense muscle. Tom doesn't even feel it.

'Look, I'm so sorry Ruby.' I turn to Tom's date, still standing, arms folded, in front of us. 'I had no idea you were in the shower, I had no idea you were even in the *flat*.'

Ruby looks from me to Tom and back again. Tom sips his coffee. I can tell he doesn't really like her. If it was Yvonne, he'd be up by her side staging a united front by now. Ruby seems to relent, collecting her coffee from the side. Tom's made it in a keep cup that must have come back with her last night; to her it might look thoughtful, but to me it's another clear sign: *anyway, last night was fun, you mustn't be late for work now.* Ruby doesn't take the hint, coming to sit next to Tom.

'So you're not some pervert?' She looks at me, softening.

'No, I promise.' Even though I can tell Tom isn't keen, I wouldn't want her to leave feeling disrespected. 'No one has a claim to a female's body but the person who inhabits it.'

'You quoting that Hardy guy?' Tom looks at me, darting his eyes back to the book.

'Nope.' I take another sip of coffee, embarrassed again. 'That one was just me.'

'Good.' Ruby snuggles into Tom's side, and he looks at me desperately over the top of her head. *Help.* 'I've only got room for one peeping Tom in my life.'

'Anyway,' Tom says slowly, starting to unpeel himself from Ruby's grip, 'it was really great to meet you but I should be getting ready for work . . .'

'Yeah, I had a really good time.' Ruby gets up too, gazing hopefully up at him. Even at around five foot eight, she looks small beside him.

'Me too.' Tom nods, moving not so subtly towards the front door.

'Like *really* good,' she repeats, pressing a hand to his broad chest.

'Me too.' He nods again. She's baiting but he's not biting.

'Like *maybe we could do this again* good,' she says, as Tom takes another step towards the door with her hand still against him, shepherding her out.

'Yeah, sure.' He bends down to give her a peck on the cheek. It's a brush-off, but she still smiles at the chivalry. It's painful to watch. Still, no one really goes on those dating apps for love, do they? What did she expect? 'Last night was fun,' Tom says, as I mouth the lines behind my mug. 'You mustn't be late for work now.'

'Good date?' I ask as Tom thrusts a hand to his hung-over head. He groans. Tom is a great conversationalist when he wants to be, but sometimes takes a little prompting. Usually in the morning. Usually hung-over. As a personal trainer, he spends most of his time teetotal, so when he does let himself drink, it's a t-total disaster. Tom doesn't appreciate this joke.

'Okay, let's make it easy,' I coax as he fills up his coffee. 'Marks out of ten.'

'Not like you to grade a woman, Max.' Tom shakes his head.

'I'm not saying grade *Ruby*,' I object. 'But I need to get to work and want to know you're okay before I do – so grading the *date* it is. So, conversation?'

'A strong two and a half.'

Ouch. That bad?

'Attraction?'

'Four and a half.'

'But you had sex?'

'Five and a half.' Tom either ignores my question or doesn't realise it's there.

'The AL?' I ask. The Awkwardness Level was something that came up often enough during our grad scheme at the bank that we deemed it worthy of abbreviation. To be honest, the highest AL ever registered was around the time we both quit.

'High.' He nods. 'She's a nice enough girl—'

'Woman.'

'Sorry, woman. She just didn't get my pulse racing . . .' The sex *must* have been mediocre. '. . . didn't keep me on my toes like . . .' He doesn't need to finish his sentence for me to hear it: like Yvonne. His ex-girlfriend. The one he realised he had given his heart to around the time she broke it into a million pieces.

'It's okay, mate.' I sigh, standing up to gather my rucksack, packed ready for work. 'There's someone out there who's perfect for you.' I smile. 'And she won't shag another PT like Yvonne did.'

Tom's laugh shakes off any sombreness. That's one thing I love about Tom. It's never too soon to laugh.

'You're right.' He smiles, but there's a hint of sadness within it. For all his bravado, I can tell he's getting worn down and worn out by all these online dates. He's been on loads lately and it's still not filling the cracks Yvonne left. 'I feel like I need another shower after all that.'

'And I need to get to work.' I nod, opening the door to leave.

'But Max,' Tom stands in the doorway as I step out onto the busy pavement, 'who's going to hold my towel?'

That's one thing I hate about Tom. It's never too soon to laugh.

Chapter Three

Eve

Becky: Matthew just messaged. What should I do?

Eve: Who?

Becky: From this morning.

Becky: Shoreditch?

Eve: Sure-ditch him already.

Becky: Were you just setting yourself up for that?

Eve: Yup.

Becky: Well played, my friend.

Becky: That's why they pay you the big bucks.

Eve: Ha! Now who's the funny one?

Looking up at the iconic News Building thrills me every time. Sometimes in an 'I can't believe I actually get to work here' way. Other times in an 'I can't believe I actually *have* to work here' way. Anxiety and adrenalin shoot through my body, tingling all the way to my fingertips. *Note to self: you are good at your job; one day people are going to see you are good at your job. No, correction: today is the day they are going to see you are good at your job.*

Breathing deeply, I channel some calm against the back-drop of suits striding into the building, forcing my heart to match the click of my heels as I walk confidently into my day. *Note to self: fake it till you make it.* A buzz fills my back pocket. Becky with more post-date updates. But she'll have to wait. Right now I need to get my head in the game. The 'allow me to introduce you to your future features editor' game.

As I walk out of the lift and onto our floor, hardly any heads look up from their hot desks or hot drinks. After decades of people looking at me – or rather, *up* at me – as I walked into classrooms, parties, even sodding doctor's appointments, it still surprises me how invisible I am here.

'Eve!' Makena beams at me as I plonk myself down at the desk beside her and begin to sift through my post. At least one person appreciates me here. I went into journalism to write stories that matter, only to have my status as a tall blonde female steer my long legs in the direction of the Thursday supplement. After all, Thursday is the new Friday, and my oh my, what would women do with their weekends if they weren't told what shade of lipstick was hot to trot this week? I tried to tell our features director that lipstick didn't technically trot. He politely told me to trot the hell on. And I would, if I didn't get my perfectly framed teeth sunk into something meaty soon.

'You're early,' I say. Our desks, like our outfits, stand in contrast to one another. Mine: neat, minimalistic, utilitarian. Hers: cluttered, colourful, a little too much.

'And you're late,' she grins, looking at her designer watch dramatically. Unlike me, Makena was born for fashion. If only she could get to write something serious about it. Instead, we were both stuck covering quick trends and click-bait.

'I know, my morning got off to a weird start. Beck—'

'I know.' Makena guesses my excuse before I can even say her name. 'She told me.'

I've told Becky countless times that it would be more efficient to share her dating dilemmas in the group chat. But then she wouldn't be able to *talk* about them countless times.

'He sounded like a good one.' Makena shakes her head, glancing down at her phone. She's been dating someone for weeks, and is still none the wiser as to whether *he's* a good one.

'Trust me,' I sigh, switching on my monitor, 'he wasn't.'

My phone buzzes again as I rest it next to my post, an angry water bill demanding my attention from the top. *Note to self: tell Becky to stop brushing her teeth in the shower.*

'I don't know why you still get your post delivered here; you've been at your flat for such a long time.'

'Have you tried to find our front door?' I look at Makena and laugh. We both know she has. And not always success-fully. Not always soberly.

I scan the emails in my inbox. PR mail mergers mingle with junk as my eyes make a beeline for internal senders. It's our weekly staff meeting this morning and I don't want

24

anything taking me by surprise. I want to appear in control, ahead of myself. So that they might just let me get ahead.

'Women are standing up, but are they standing *over there*?' I read the top line of my pitch to Makena; I've been planning to present this story for weeks.

'Tell me more,' Makena says.

'The piece will look at the advancements in equality we've made over the past decade but will also dig deeper into whether women are being siloed into speaking only to and for other women in the process. Speaking engagements – but only at women's conferences. Senior leadership roles – but only at women's magazines . . .'

'Some people like women's magazines,' Makena objects, eyebrows raised.

Becky: Matthew still has my lipstick in his back pocket. Should I go get it back?

I look down at the messages coming through from Becky, her lipstick laments perfectly timed as if to back up Makena's point – some people *do* like women's magazines. Ever since I introduced the two of them, they've been in cahoots.

Eve: Absolutely not.
Eve: I'll get you another one. They send loads of samples.
Becky: Man, I love your job.

At least that makes one of us.

25

'I know that.' I look up from my phone and back to Makena. 'But equality is about choice, right? It might not be *sit down, shut up* any more, but is *stand over there* any better?'

'Eve, it's a great idea.' Her face can't help but fall. 'But they're not going to go for it.'

'I know,' I sigh. It's too close to home, but I have to keep trying, to keep pushing. 'I'm going to keep speaking up,' I tell myself and Makena at the same time, heart hammering. 'To the whole room. Even if they're not listening.'

Makena forces her smile wide. I know my chances of being heard here are slim, but I have to keep trying. My phone buzzes again, shaking us both from the thought.

'That guy still messaging Becky?' Makena asks, in no hurry to start work.

'Yep.' I nod as I return to my inbox, an email Everest to climb.

'Least someone is communicative,' she sighs, looking down at her phone. 'Boy dramas,' she shrugs, her maybe man still blowing cold and *but–omigod–he's–so–hot*.

'Is nobody immune?' I laugh; it's my turn to be dramatic. Clicking open an email, I find what I'm looking for: the agenda for this morning's meeting.

'You are,' Makena points out.

I wouldn't say immune. Quarantined perhaps. Keeping myself a safe distance away until I have the time to invest in something real. I don't do things by halves, and it's not like I have the time right now anyway. I look at the clock on my computer, counting down the minutes until the meeting.

Fifty emails in fifteen minutes after being up since 5.15. You can do this, Eve. You can do this.

'Did you hear the rumour?' Makena pushes her feet off her desk, wheeling her chair closer to me. Clearly she has other ideas for the next fifteen minutes.

'This better be good.'

'Oh it is,' she says, her hushed tone laced with glee. 'Angela is pregnant.'

'No! Angela who is thirty-four, has been married for three years and has been talking about babies for two? Alert the media.' My words drip with sarcasm.

'Eve.' Makena raises her eyebrows again. *Note to self: book eyebrow appointment.* 'You're missing the point.' But I never miss the point. 'What will Angela need now?'

'Elasticated waistbands?'

Makena rolls her eyes, then lowers her voice again. 'Maternity cover.'

Maternity cover. I taste the two words on my tongue. Angela Baxter, features editor – not just of the supplement, but of the whole newspaper – is going to be taking months off work, maybe more. This is my chance to step up. To keep her seat warm whilst showing everyone I deserve my own place at the table.

'Think I stand a chance?' I can't help but ask. Even if I don't, I have to go for it.

'For sure.' Makena nods. 'If they hire internally, I'd say it's between you and—'

'Taren,' I say, now my turn to fill in the blanks. I follow Makena's gaze over to his six-foot figure, leaning against the doorway into the commercial director's office; he certainly knows who holds the purse strings. Although for a man who spends his winters skiing in the Alps and who summers in Monaco – for a man who *summers* full stop – is it really that surprising?

'I work twice as hard as Taren,' I say, not meaning to sound so childish. 'And surely hiring a woman would be better for their diversity quota?'

'Babe.' Makena looks me in the eye. 'I'm a young African woman who's just spent her weekend writing a piece on the world's largest tub of mayonnaise. Trust me, they don't care.'

Becky: Okay, I told him I don't need the lipstick.

Becky: And he replied: *you might not miss your lipstick but I'm missing your lips.*

Becky: That's cute, right?

Eve: No, it's creepy.

Becky: I thought it was sweet.

Eve: It sounds like he wants to sever them and store them in a jar.

Becky: You're being ridiculous.

Eve: May I take this opportunity to remind you . . .

Eve: YOU DON'T EVEN LIKE HIM.

Becky: Good point. So what should I reply?

Eve: How about you don't?

Becky: But I need to say something.

Eve: Just hold on for a bit. I'm going into the pitch meeting.

Becky: Pitch, please.

Eve: You don't have to say that every time.

Becky: Fine.

Becky: Just give them hell.

Give them hell, Eve. Just give them hell. I follow Makena into the board room and we stand around the edge of the table in its centre. Standing is meant to make the meeting shorter, but it just makes me feel taller. And it means Taren and I are standing eye to eye. Which is pretty ironic given the circumstances.

'Hello, hello,' Richard, the 'big boss', says to no one in particular. 'First on the agenda is . . .' He looks around the room for someone who actually knows what's on the agenda.

'Gareth,' I prompt.

'Gareth,' Richard repeats as if he's plucked the name from thin air.

We turn to Gareth as he pitches at speed. The story: an investigative piece on the radicalisation of a schoolgirl from south London. How it relates to our readers: current issue, strong personal narrative, locally sourced. What adverts might run alongside: higher-education courses? Local MP event? Everyone nods. It's a good piece for the newspaper. It's a piece I'd love to write.

'Up next is . . .' Richard looks round again.

'It's me.' Taren puffs out his chest. How can two small words carry so much weight? Like, *it's me* you want. *It's me* for features editor. *It's me* for prime minister.

Taren works on the sports supplement, but everyone knows he wants to be a director. A features editor on the

29

newspaper would be a good next move for him. But it would be a good next move for me too.

'The idea I had was for a . . . well, it's the one I told most of you about last night, when we were watching the game?' In reality, 'most of you' amounts to about three people. But they're the three that matter most. 'We were in the pub last night . . .' He smiles at us. It doesn't help that his pitches are set against a backdrop of swoons. Why do women lose their minds when there's a good-looking man in their midst? Makena's is on this not-so-new guy. Becky's boy dramas are still buzzing through my phone. But I have to keep my mind here, in this moment, in this room: if I keep pitching my ideas, keep my head in the game, they'll have to let at least one through the net. It's the law of averages, right?

'Great, yes. Let's run with that on Friday.' Richard's voice rings through my thoughts. Did Taren even present his idea, or did the late-night schmooze session suffice? Well, that's fine. Taren can play his game. But I'm not going down without a fight. *Note to self: get into football?*

'Great, great meeting, all,' Richard says.

What? No, wait. I have something to say. Makena shoots a smile my way: *maybe next week?* But no, I've worked hard on this. And if we don't run it now, someone else will run it soon.

'Richard, I have a—'

'It'll wait until next week, Eve.' Richard smiles, and all thoughts of running the story turn to thoughts of running away. Heart hammering, hands clammy, my legs start shaking beneath me; all classic symptoms that I need to grab my trainers and force these feelings into the pavement, strong and steady beneath my feet. The perfect stress relief. But it's not like I can do that here.

Just breathe, Eve. Breathe, I tell myself as I hurry from the meeting room to the bathroom. This is okay, I remind my reflection in the mirror. I can present my story next week. But that's what they said last week and the week before that and the week before that. I'm good at my job, aren't I?

I've never been a relationship girl. So if I'm not a smash-it-at-work girl, then what the hell am I? It's fine. If I don't get a step up, I'll step out, into something else, something new. *But you said that last week, and the week before that, and the week before . . .*

Sitting on the closed toilet lid, I swipe to Headspace. I might not be able to run, but I can still escape. *Breathe in, breathe out. In, out. In, out. In . . .*

Buzz. Buzz. *Buzz . . .*

Becky: Okay, it's out with Matthew.

Breathe out.

Becky: And it's in with Connor.

Breathe in.

Becky: He seems nice from his profile. There's just one *tiny* thing wrong with him.

Breathe out.

31

Becky: When I joked about him not having a third nipple or a mum who's actually an aunt or a girlfriend hiding in the closet, he said 'the girlfriend thing is complicated'.

Becky: What do you think that means . . . 'the girlfriend thing is complicated'?

Breathe in.

Eve: I think it means he has a girlfriend.

Becky: But not like a *proper* one.

Eve: Becky, you don't want him to have *any kind* of one.

Becky: I know, but he's cute. And he's nice. And I'm starting to think that's like gold dust on these dating apps.

Becky: I can't expect every single thing to be perfect.

Eve: No, but you can expect him to be perfectly *single*.

Becky: I just want to meet a nice guy. Is that too much to ask?

And I just want my work to mean something. Is that too much to ask too?

Eve: No, it's not.

Becky: How did your pitch go, by the way?

It didn't. But I don't want to talk about that right now . . .

Eve: We just need a new game plan.

Eve: Leave your phone alone for the rest of the day.

Eve: Let's look at your profile over dinner. A few tweaks and we'll try again.

We'll try a-fucking-gain.

I gaze up at the sign of Ciao Becca, such a contrast to how I began my morning. Where the News Building stands tall, ambitious, intimidating, the restaurant at the end of our street is small, warm, welcoming. As I push open the door and see Becky sitting at a checked-cloth-covered table, messy hair in her hands, a pocket-sized parent on either side, I can't help but feel out of place. But crossing the restaurant, I feel the buzz of the News Building begin to fade away as I settle into the only other place I truly feel at home.

'*Ciao*, Eve!' Becky's dad gets to his feet as he sees me arrive. He wraps his arms around me, which due to our height difference pretty much has him nestling his head in my chest. But there's nothing creepy about Leonardo Amato.

'Eve.' Becky's mum stands to join us and for a moment I am in an Amato sandwich.

'*Eve.*' Becky echoes her mum, her tone less of a welcome, more a plea for help.

'Our little Becca is having a bit of a breakdown,' Sofia explains.

'Another one,' Leonardo mouths behind her. I can tell from his rapper hand, thrust forward as he says it, that he's channelling DJ Khaled, but I know better than to laugh. When Sofia is in the restaurant she insists on playing nothing but traditional Italian music. But when Leonardo is left to his own devices, everyone knows he switches to the charts.

'I just want to meet someone great, fall in love, live happily ever after . . .' Becky sounds like a Disney princess. Before they became *Tangled* and *Brave*. 'Is that too much to ask?'

'Not at all, sweetheart.' Leonardo takes his seat beside her and I sit opposite. 'These things just take time.'

'Not for you guys,' Becky sobs back. 'You were like Romeo and Juliet – just set in Italy.'

My eyes shoot to Leonardo, who grins. Sofia shakes her head. Now isn't the time to tell Becky that Romeo and Juliet actually *is* set in Italy.

'You fell in love as babies.' Well, teenagers, but it's not the time to point that out either. 'You knew you were made for each other, and you swanned to England to get married and then made the *best* decision of your life . . .' We all know she means her. I laugh at her dramatics, but to be fair, I think Becky is the best decision they made too.

'Yes, but the course of true love never did run smooth.' Sofia thinks she's quoting *Romeo and Juliet*, but I can tell from Leo's expression that he knows it's *A Midsummer Night's Dream* too. 'We lost our families over it; you know your grandparents never approved.' The fact that Sofia doesn't refer to them as her parents only makes their distance more palpable. Leonardo was from a poor family; Sofia was seemingly a princess – which to be fair might be where Becky gets it from. 'So love, yes, but a love that cost us our parents.'

'I'd *love* to be so in love that I'd be willing to lose my parents,' Becky says with a little grin.

'Fine.' Leonardo laughs, their relationship strong enough to take even the harshest of jokes. Unlike me and my dad. Not that we had that much to laugh about anyway. 'Just make sure he's worth it. And don't trade us in for one of your men with the face tattoos.'

'Men?' Becky looks at him incredulously. 'There was only one.'

'That's one too many,' Sofia says as we all laugh. The woman has a point. 'And before you trade us in, ask yourself, "Who is going to make my carbonara for me now?"' That, Sofia, is another very good point. 'Two plates, I assume?'

'Three, please.' Becky smiles at the thought of her mum's cooking. 'One for me, one for Eve and one for my misery . . .'

'Oh *please*.' Sofia rolls her eyes. We know Becky wants to meet someone, but now she's acting up for our entertainment. 'Two carbonaras coming right up.'

'How was the pitch?' Becky asks.

'It's all in hand,' I say, not wanting to deal with the disappointment right now. My palms start to sweat. It didn't happen. But my idea was good. I'll have a chance to share it one day. And if the rumours about Angela are true, there may be a perfect place for me to step into soon.

'Eve?' Becky raises her eyebrows. 'Don't make me bring in the big guns.' Her eyes dart across the restaurant to her parents. The three of them have a habit of getting the truth out of me, probing my defences until they finally crumble.

'Okay, well there wasn't really time to pitch it today,' I say, trying to stay positive.

'Again?' Becky asks. 'They should be listening to your pitches *first*.'

I smile at my best friend, feeling warmed by her support. But enough about me. This evening is about one thing only: pimping Becky's profile. At least I can add some value there.

'Now let's see this profile.' I push away the pitch as Becky connects to the seriously patchy Wi-Fi and Sofia materialises with our plates.

'Ooh, let me see.' She gestures at Becky's phone.

'Mum, this restaurant isn't going to serve itself,' Becky jokes, moving her phone away and looking around the now crowded room. I dread to think how many covers they've lost as we sit in this corner night after night, covering every topic known to man – well, usually men. Sofia moves away and Becky fixes her attention back on me. 'It might not be a problem with my profile. It might be a problem with me.'

'It's a problem with your profile,' I say, not even entertaining the thought. 'Let's have a look. What kind of guy do you want to attract?' I ask. Even though I already know.

'Tall, dark, handsome.' Becky starts to rattle off her list. 'Kind, intelligent, talkative.'

I scroll down her profile of soppy essays, mirror selfies and bikini body shots.

'Well, with this,' I hold out a photo of her in a cut-out bikini that belongs only on *Love Island*, 'you're going to attract stupid men who are only after one thing.'

'I paid good money for that bikini,' Becky moans, stuffing

a forkful of pasta in her mouth. 'Well okay, wise one, what do *you* suggest?'

She looks at me, eyebrows raised. She knows I've never made a dating profile. Apart from a few drunken snogs in the Lockside, the last real date I went on was at uni. I've spent all my time since then becoming independent, completing internships, writing stories. That's all we need to do here: tell a really irresistible story.

'You're wonderful,' I say. 'Your family is wonderful.' My heart jolts with jealousy at the thought. 'We just need to get that across on here.'

One by one I delete the bikini shots, then I look through Becky's camera roll. There's a photo of her in this very corner of the restaurant, the light hitting her just right. One of her posing near Camden Lock. Another of her lifting a glass of champagne in the air in my favourite bar, bubbly personality clear to see.

'Right, that's that part done,' I say. 'Now for the questions. Man, there's a lot of them on here. What's your favourite way to unwind?'

'Watch movies at home and eat cheese on toast with you?'

'Ah *fanx*.' I give her my best teenager response; I've never been great with compliments. 'But if you want to attract someone you can have a connection with, I suggest we go a little deeper. Favourite type of movie?'

'Funny ones?'

'How about French? It makes you sound sophisticated and complements the cheese.'

'I've never really watched one.'

'Oh, they're great.' I grin, trying to remember how many times I've watched *Amélie*. 'Might prompt a romantic trip to Paris?'

'Well why didn't you say so.' Becky laughs. 'Write it down.'

'Done,' I say. 'And how about we tweak cheese on toast to cheese and wine? What's your favourite type of cheese?'

'Grated?'

'Becky, I'm being serious.'

'So am I.'

'Well now it's Camembert – and Malbec's your wine of choice.' She mouths the word back at me. 'Now, music. What's your favourite band?'

'Calvin Harris?'

'That's not a band, Becky.' I know she would love to date a musician – I mean, who wouldn't? Best get some instruments in there somewhere. 'How about the Coronas?'

'I thought we put down Malbon?'

'It's *Mal-bec*,' I say. 'And not Corona, *the* Coronas – they're a band.'

'Never heard of them. What are they like?'

'They're a cool indie rock band,' I explain with a smile. 'I saw one of their really early gigs in a pub in Dublin. Must have been thirteen. Dad took me over there for Paddy's Day.' Becky's eyes widen at the mention of my dad. I haven't seen or heard from him in years. I've not really talked about him much in that time either. 'I guess taking a thirteen-year-old to a pub was a bit of a sign, right?' This is why I don't let myself think about him. It's impossible to savour the good without the aftertaste of bad. 'Anyway, the band are really good. Niche, and it might prompt a backstory.' She can have that one for free. 'I'd leave out the dad with a drinking problem, though.'

'Sounds good.' Becky's smile is a little sad. 'Are you sure you don't want to reach out to him?' she asks as I see Sofia's diminutive figure bustling across the restaurant.

'Becky, why on earth would I need to hear from my parents when I have a family like yours?' I say as Sofia arrives to top up our pasta. 'And you're about to have a husband like this . . .' I hold up the phone to show a green-haired rocker with a piercing through the bridge of his nose. Another awful match soon to be a thing of the past.

Sofia smiles at me, reaching a hand to my arm. 'At least this one doesn't have a face tattoo.'

Chapter Four

Max

Tom: Dude, she wants me to meet her family.

Max: Who?

Tom: Ruby!

Max: Going to go?

Tom: No!

Max: But you are going to *tell* her you don't want to see her again, right?

Tom: Of course.

Tom: Was going to leave it a day or two. Soften the blow so it's doesn't seem so sex-and-go.

Max: Sounds good.

Tom: Yeah, apart from she wants to come round tonight.

Tom: Says she's forgotten her bra.

Max: Just tell her she can't.

Tom: She said she's passing by.

Tom: Told her we were out.

Max: Are we?

Tom: We are now. I'll message you the details.

I look up from Tom's messages. He doesn't need to send me the details; it'll be the same pub we always go to. Part of me is annoyed – I've just got into a really good book, *In Search of Lost Time* by this French novelist I've wanted to read for ages; another part thinks maybe it's a good thing. The guys at work are always telling me I need to get out more. Looking around the office, at the heads-down hive of activity, I could tell them the same. But that's what I love about the team here: no one is scared of putting in the hours, pushing up their sleeves, getting stuck in.

'Max, can you just help me with this copy?' I follow the voice back to the face of Heather, our head of communications.

'Heather,' I say, pleased to see her. 'You know you don't need my help.' Heather has just come across to us from a senior position at Cancer UK. She's been in her line of work for decades; she could write a press release or solve a media scandal in her sleep.

'I just want you to give it a once-over to check I've got the tone right. You know, from someone on the ground.' Her eyes seem to scan down to my shoes, the soles of which have walked every inch of the care homes the patients we help find themselves in. She may be an expert in media, but I guess I've become something of an expert in coming alongside people living with dementia. I'm not sure Heather

41

knows that being *on the ground* isn't technically in my job description. I just struggle to see how you can fund-raise for causes you don't actually care about. Surely the people you're trying to reach would see through you in a heartbeat?

'Sure thing, leave it with me.' I smile at her as she stifles a yawn. 'You do know you can always join me on a visit sometime?'

Heather smiles back but looks a little weary at the thought. She's in her sixties, wears a wedding ring and has grown-up children; apart from that, I don't know anything about her – except that she works really hard and my suggestion is making her feel a burden I didn't mean for her to carry.

'Thanks, Max,' she sighs. 'That would be nice when I have the time.'

'No rush.' I take the printout from her hands. 'How was your weekend?'

'Busy.' She isn't saying much, but I can tell she wants to share more.

'Oh yeah?'

'Yeah.' She exhales. 'I'm pretty much a full-time carer at the moment.' I nod, inviting her to go on; creating a safe space. It's what we do here.

'My husband,' she goes on. 'He's fighting cancer.'

'Oh, I'm sorry to hear that.' I offer her a little smile. Hopefully not in that pious head-tilt sympathetic way, the one that makes worn-out family members want to punch you in the face. Heather smiles again, in a way that tells me this is the first time she has confided in anyone here. 'When do you need this for?' I ask, tapping the papers in my hand.

'End of the day?'

'You got it.' I nod.

'Thanks, Max.' She beams. 'You're the best.'

'Just doing my job.' She begins to walk back to her desk. 'And Heather?' She turns to face me. 'You're doing an incredible job too.'

'Thanks.' Her face dimples and she stands a little taller. 'I needed that.'

No fewer than five colleagues come up to ask for my help before I've even grabbed a coffee. This new role has definitely upped the ante, increased my visibility here. And man, it feels good. I never get those managers who say they're too busy to help: isn't that the point? Most of the time it's just pointing people in the right direction anyway.

'One flat white for you, Maxy.' Paddy slams a takeaway cup on my desk.

'Thanks, dude. I owe you one.'

'Great. In which case, that means I only owe you five.'

'Who's counting?' I shrug. 'What I *am* counting is how many times you call me Maxy.'

'Still not sold on it?' Paddy asks, working his way through his emails. 'I think it makes us sound like a double act. Maxy and Pads, putting the fun in fund-raising . . .'

'Dude, it makes us sound like a sanitary product.' I shake my head. 'Stick to the projects.' I nod him back to his screen.

There are a number of projects we centre our campaigns around, but now I've got the opportunity to come up with something new. At the same time as managing Paddy's projects and Tom's *In Search of Lost Bras* love life.

'Hello?' I pick up the phone as soon as it rings.

'Max?' A sweet voice says my name. I recognise it instantly.

'Amy. How is she?' I swear I can hear her sigh at the end of the line. Amy works at one of our care homes. I used to try and divide my spare time equally between them, but that was before I fell for Peggy, the woman who stole my heart. She's feisty and intelligent, knows all the best books, all the best films, tells all the best stories. Oh, and she's eighty-four.

'She's good today, yes,' Amy says. 'Don't you care how *I* am?' She laughs down the line.

'Of course, sorry,' I say, clicking open a new email at the same time. 'How are you?'

'I'm good, thanks for asking.' She's kind enough to pretend my question's off the cuff.

'How are *you*? What did you get up to this weekend?'

I think of my walk around Tooting Common, my coffee and cake in Mud with nothing but my book. I can imagine Amy would be more impressed by a weekend like Tom's.

'It was pretty chilled,' I reply, really wanting to know about Peggy. How she seems in herself, whether there's any change in her colour, whether she's eating properly.

'How's Peggy's weight?'

'You can't ask a woman that.' Amy laughs again. 'But yeah, it's stable. Are you visiting tonight?'

'Great, great,' I say. 'Yeah, I . . .' Dammit, Tom's saga, the forgotten bra, his witness-protection programme. 'No, actually. I have to hide out in a pub with Tom.'

'Sounds horrible,' Amy says, as bubbly and sarcastic as ever.

'You've not been to the pub,' I reply. 'Tell Peggy I'll see her soon.'

'We can't wait.'

As I hang up, Paddy is looking at me, shaking his head.

'Oh Maxy, Maxy, Maxy,' he tuts.

'What?'

'For a clever guy you can be a bit of an idiot.'

'Why?' I ask, panic setting in. 'What have I done?'

'That Amy chick.' He pauses. 'She fancies you.'

'How do you know? You weren't on the call.'

'We're Maxy and Paddy . . .'

'Stop it,' I say. Amy doesn't fancy me.

'I can read you like one of your long, boring books . . .'

I walk into the Castle a little confused. And not just about the Amy thing. Tom and I usually bag the table for two in the front window. Sometimes they'll even reserve it without us asking. Between me and Yvonne and his many dates, I'm pretty sure Tom has gained some sort of squatter's rights here. But not today. Our table is empty. Scanning around the pub, I see his broad figure sitting in a booth, muscular arm reaching along the back of the bench occupied by a petite brunette. Across from him sits a pretty blonde woman cradling a glass of wine, a pint standing before the only space at the table. A drink and a date I assume is reserved for me. Thanks for the heads-up, mate.

'Here he is now.' Tom holds his free arm out to me. 'This is Max.'

The petite brunette says hello, and then the blonde. I stand for a second, not knowing what's going on, whether Tom knows them from the gym and is just saying hello.

'Well sit down then . . .'

I slip into the booth beside the blonde – my date for the evening?

'This is Dani.' Tom gestures towards the brunette, as if that explains everything. 'And Kimberly.' The pretty blonde smiles up at me. 'Dani and I matched on Tinder earlier this week,' he explains.

I do a quick calculation. I swear this is his fourth date in as many nights.

'And Kimberly—'

'Just got stood up,' Kimberly says, taking another gulp of her wine. A really big gulp.

'It's a funny story actually.' Tom looks at me as my eyes try to warn him, darting across to Kimberly: *it doesn't sound very funny, dude.* 'Dani messaged me earlier today to check we were still on for tonight.' Now it's his turn to warn me: *I forgot about it, bro, just play along.* 'And I say, *of course* we are, and I come into the bar and slide into a booth next to *Kimberly* by accident.' He laughs as if that isn't the most awkward thing in the world. 'Then Dani turned up, and I was like, *of course* it's you.' He laughs again. So not only did he forget he had a date, he forgot what she looked like. I know he's trying his best to get over Yvonne, but this is getting out of hand.

'My date never showed.' Kimberly necks her wine. Oh man, I feel bad for her.

'So I told her not to worry and that I'd invite you along.' Tom beams, as if he hadn't invited me to the pub this morning; as if *my* being here was the afterthought.

'Well in that case . . .' I look to Kimberly's empty glass and stained-red lips. 'Another?'

'*Dude*,' I hiss at Tom as soon as we're at the bar and out of earshot. 'What the hell?'

'I'm sorry, I'm sorry,' he says. 'I know it looks bad . . .'

'That's because it *is* bad.'

'But I just see so many faces at work and online that everyone kind of looks familiar after a while.' He brushes a hand through his hair, picking up his freshly poured pint. 'But they seem really cool.' Kimberly seems really *drunk*. 'And I guess it could be worse, right?'

'How?'

'At least Ruby isn't here . . .'

Tom gets to his feet to head to the toilet, leaving me alone with the girls. Shit, shit. Okay, I can do this. Just keep the conversation going. I refocus my attention on Kimberly, who is telling me about her master's dissertation. To be fair, she's struggling to focus herself.

'What a unique lens to view anthropology through,' I say, as she views *me* through the bottom of her glass.

'I'm glad someone thinks so,' she says. I read between the lines: *you're the only one.* She looks so sad, and not just because

47

she's finished her fifth glass of wine. This is the problem with online dating. It makes people feel distant, disposable; so removed from the realities of life that you forget the people on the other side of the screen have real feelings.

'I can't believe I got stood up,' she sighs.

'Nor can I,' I smile. No one deserves to be messed around. Time is precious, especially in this city, especially at this life stage. 'I'm going to be really honest with you,' I begin; it's what this other guy should have been. 'I'm not really looking to date anyone at the moment . . .' well, I'm not looking to date anyone online. It's not really where age-old love stories are born, and I should know, I've read most of them. 'But you clearly have so much to offer a guy – make sure you offer it to a good one.'

She grabs my hand and looks into my eyes and for a moment I think she's going to kiss me. But then she starts to cry, at first just a little bit, and then a bit more, and then a lot. Oh shit, she's crying a lot.

'You really do.' Dani reaches her hand across the table to rest on ours. 'I know I don't know you, but you seem like a lovely girl. It's obvious Tom would rather be here with you.'

'But you're gorgeous,' Kimberly tells her, and now Dani's eyes start to well. Oh crap, oh crap. Please don't cry, *please* don't cry.

'You both are,' I say, our hands still resting in the middle of the table. 'And fun and interesting.'

Oh shit, this was meant to *stop* the crying.

'And you both deserve guys who can't wait to meet you on your dates.' I look between them, their wide eyes still on me.

'You're right,' Dani says. 'I've been dating guy after guy like I'm just after someone, anyone – but I deserve someone special.'

'You do.' I nod as she cries even harder. 'You both do.'

'So what have I missed?' Tom appears by our table to see both girls sobbing and clutching my hand. 'Told them about your grandma?'

'I'm leaving.' Dani gets to her feet defiantly, looking at Tom with tear-stained eyes.

'Me too.' Kimberly steadies herself enough to stand. 'Thanks, Max.'

'Yeah, thanks, Max,' Dani says, giving me a hug before tottering away.

'Thanks, Max?' Tom turns to me, his voice spiked with sarcasm. 'What the fuck was that?'

'I don't know.' I shrug as I slide back into the booth, feeling more than a little bamboozled. 'I just encouraged them a bit, told them they were special.'

'Oh Max.' Tom shakes his head. He hardly looks heart-broken. 'It's not your fault,' he says. I might believe that if I hadn't just made two grown women cry. 'I keep finding these desperate . . .'

'Insecure?' I suggest, searching for a better word.

'Vulnerable . . .'

'Sensitive?'

'. . . women who just want to find a husband. I want to meet someone strong, someone with something about them . . .' He means someone like Yvonne.

'Give me your phone,' I say, thrusting my hand out. 'If you

49

keep attracting the same kind of girl, maybe it's something to do with your profile.'

With no better ideas and absolutely no desire to go home and risk a run-in with Ruby, Tom obliges. I swipe through his three photos: all at the gym, all topless, all barely fitting in the frame. Man, the guy is huge. No wonder I don't really get a look-in. I scan down his answers: the only thing small about him: *Eating. Biking. Gym.*

'Favourite book: *Men's Health* magazine?' I raise an eyebrow.

'Just being myself, mate,' Tom replies, taking another swig of his beer. Before Yvonne, he was confident that was enough.

'Yeah, I get that . . .' I don't want to depress him further. I've already ruined two people's nights; let's not make it a hat trick. 'But this isn't you, not really. The answers, the photos . . . It's all a bit shallow.'

'I'm not shallow,' Tom objects, draining his pint.

'You're not, not at all,' I assure him. He's not, but this profile makes him sound as deep as a puddle. 'But why don't we give a bit more detail, paint you as a three-dimensional guy, find you a three-dimensional woman?'

'That's how I like 'em,' Tom laughs. 'Okay.' He nods.

'So your favourite book,' I begin. 'Needs to appeal to the kind of woman you want to meet.'

'What's Margot Robbie's favourite?'

'I think she's taken.'

'Okay, how about that thing I was pretending to read this morning; what kind of woman would that attract?'

'Smart,' I say, sure of it. 'Complex, layered . . .'

'Like onions?' I know Tom is trying to quote *Shrek*.

'No, we're *not* putting that as your favourite movie,' I say before he even has time to suggest it. 'Your favourite writer is Thomas Hardy, and now your favourite movie is . . .' I scan mentally through my shelves back home. '*Lion*.'

'The one where the kids go through the wardrobe?'

'Bro,' I shake my head, 'you're better than that.'

'Fine, *Lion*. I'll watch it as a refresher.' He nods.

'Favourite way to spend a day?'

'Gym.' He nods again. It was before Yvonne, anyway.

'Okay, okay.' I put one hand up in surrender. 'That can be how you *start* your day. But then you like to spend your afternoons going for long walks around Tooting Common and having a coffee and cake in Mud with nothing but your book.'

'I do?' Tom grins. 'I do,' he confirms with confidence. 'You sure this is going to work?'

'If it's not broken, don't fix it?' I say, as we both recall the shit-show that was this evening.

'Oh, it's broken all right.' Tom laughs, but I know he's tired of this, tired of swiping through shallow women who could never measure up to what he had with Yvonne. Well, what he *thought* he had with Yvonne. She broke his heart. But hopefully this – pimping his profile to attract the perfect woman – will fix it.

Chapter Five

Eve

Buster stalks along the back of the sofa, wild, majestic against the background of mould. He pounces on a sparrow cushion, then an elephant one, and then nestles into Becky's lap, confident that he's the king of the jungle – or of this one, at least.

'Right, when are we going to attack these walls?' I ask Becky, who's swiping on her phone. She's hardly moved all day.

'I'm busy,' she says.

I open my laptop. Her busy looks a lot less frantic than my chilled. I've already been for a run, read the weekend newspapers and written an article. But we've got another hour or so before we're meeting the girls for drinks; there's still time to attack the marks climbing like damp ivy up our walls.

'You've been "busy" all day,' I say, looking down at my first paragraph afresh. If we're not going to spruce up our living space, I may as well freshen up this copy. It's only been an hour since I wrote it, but it's already feeling tired; or maybe that's just me.

'Hey, put your air quotes away.' Becky yawns. I'm not sure why *she's* tired: she's still in her pyjamas and it's almost 6 p.m. 'I'm busy trying to find a good guy.' She looks at me accusingly. Ever since I helped her revamp her profile, her swipe-right traffic has seemingly slowed. I've tried to tell her it's a quality-not-quantity thing, but what do I know? I turn back to my article.

'I need to move.' Becky jolts to life and Buster bolts for cover. 'I need to get out.'

'I invited you on my run.' I try to remind her she has options, even though I'm pretty sure she thinks I've edited them away. 'You used to like the idea of running together.'

'I did.' She nods, making her way to her bedroom. 'I do,' she shouts from within it as I hear her wardrobe doors open. 'I like the *idea* of running with you . . .'

I know what she's getting at: our ideas of running together are miles apart.

'I had visions, Eve, *visions*,' she says, like I've dashed her dreams; ever the dramatist. 'Of us running side by side, the wind in our hair . . .'

'In slow motion?'

'. . . running all the way to the high street, all the way to our favourite coffee shop . . .' Our favourite coffee shop is approximately one kilometre away. '. . . laughing over our lattes in Lycra . . .'

I repeat her alliteration under my breath. *Note to self:*

laughing over our lattes in Lycra. Good copy. Human interest feature?

'That's kind of nice,' I say, opening a new document, scribbling the sentence down.

'That's what I thought.' Becky materialises holding up two very short skirts.

'I meant your sentence.' I nod to the skirt on the right.

'But you just want to go fast and get sweaty and . . . well, I'm not about that life.'

'Hey, less of that.' I point to the long-sleeved black top she's silently showing me. It'll offset the shortness of the skirt, and if there's anything working on the Thursday supplement has taught me about style, it's balance. Which is ironic, given that the newspaper cares little for balance in every other area of women's lives. 'We've put on your profile that you enjoy some light exercise.'

'Heavy on the light,' Becky quips. 'I'm not sure it's working. I got loads more matches before your edit.' She sits back down on the sofa, her make-up bag now in her lap, looking across to the laptop on mine.

'That's because you were half-naked, remember?' I laugh. 'Quality not quantity.'

'Well right now I'm getting neither.'

'Let me have another go,' I suggest. I'm in need of inspiration, and swiping through strangers' profiles always sparks some sideways thoughts.

'Sure thing.' She chucks her phone onto the cushion next to me. Stashing my screen, I look at hers. Yes, there are fewer matches, but at least the guys who swiped right seem

54

to be moving in the right direction. At least they're wearing clothes. I scroll down the screen, mentally editing each profile as I go. Maybe if the journalism career doesn't work out, I can provide some kind of dating app service? Not that I have a proven track record with my current client. I look from Becky – applying her eyeliner with precision – to her potential suitors on the screen. 'Oliver, thirty-four, consultant, nice green eyes, seems to have friends, five foot three.' I read his credentials out loud.

'Too short,' Becky says.

'Coming from you?'

'We can't both be short, we'll look like hobbits.'

'Speaking of hobbits . . .' I display the next digital date before her. 'Tony, twenty-eight, teacher, incredibly hairy face.' And visible through his flip-flops, incredibly hairy feet.

'*Ew*,' Becky rolls her now perfectly made-up eyes. I watch as she brushes her hair, taming it into place with a pink satin headband. Her eyes fix on me for a moment as I look up from the screen. 'Are you sure you don't want your own profile?' she asks. 'You look like you're enjoying it.'

I shake my head. 'I just find it therapeutic,' I explain.

It's not like I don't want a boyfriend one day; I just need to get my career in place first. There's too much I want to do, too much I want to achieve. And, well, relationships just seem to make everything so complicated.

'Are you sure?' Becky presses, entirely unconvinced.

Yes, I may want a partner in the future. A family even. But it's not like my own family worked out that well. I don't want to get it wrong. I don't have the time or the energy to hold it all together again. If I swipe right, I want the time to *get it* right.

'Yes.' I nod. 'Honestly, it's like my Headspace app, just with guys.'

'Datespace?'

'That's quite good actually.' *Note to self . . .*

'Eve, not everything has to be an article idea.'

I move across the living room to our stack of shoes by the redundant front door. I find one biker boot and search for the other: why the hell do they not just stay together? Becky joins me and finds her shoe boots nestled next to one another in the mess: the perfect pair. Some people are meant to come in twos.

'Why don't you just try it, see if you can find some guy who likes Coronas and Malbon too?' I can tell from Becky's raised eyebrows that she's pulling my leg, but not with the *try for a guy* thing. That she's been saying for years. But then the course of true love never does run smooth, right? It takes time, time I don't have. And so many fears resurfacing every time I get close. I push the thought from my mind.

'We're going to be late.' I give Becky a playful push in the direction of the door. Buster follows her, weaving within her legs.

'Sorry, dude.' She picks him up and holds him at arm's length, not wanting him to leave fluff on her black top. 'No boys allowed,' she says before picking up her phone.

No boys allowed. But looking from Becky's screen to her

teeny-tiny skirt and huge hopeful grin, I know this is one rule made to be broken.

I see them as I follow Becky across the busy bar. Makena is clutching a glass of white wine, which glows against the backdrop of her bright orange top, her braided hair tied up with a blue headscarf. Lola sits with her pint of Camden Hells, a brew as cool and local as she is. Makena stands to throw her arms around me, as if she didn't see me yesterday and the day before that, and the day before that . . .

'I've missed you,' she whispers into my hair like some long-lost lover before her laughter fills the bar. Heads turn to follow the sound. It's hard to ignore Makena.

'I've missed you too.' I pull away to look into her eyes. It's our classic 'work wife' charade. Joking that we spend so much time in the office we may as well be married. But then Makena has been as distracted as Becky of late with her maybe-man.

'Well I genuinely have missed you.' Lola pushes her way to embrace me.

'Me too.' I grin down at her. She's actually pretty petite, not that any of us notice that with Becky the Bird in our midst. 'Sorry, I've been so busy with . . .'

'Work.' She finishes my sentence with a smile.

Okay, I get it. I'm at work a lot. But I always make time for our spontaneous Saturday nights out, provided they're scheduled at least a week in advance.

'How's today been?' Lola beams across at me as we take

our seats at the table. She's dressed in vintage ripped jeans and an oversized white T-shirt, with a simple gold chain holding a shark tooth. If I wore that, I'd look like an off-duty pirate. Lola looks like she's on a break from the studio or from designing the next big thing. Bearded hipster types flock to her thinking they've got her down, got her number. Then they find out she's an accountant and realise they've got her number – or *numbers* – all wrong. In any case, it's not like she's available; she's been with her boyfriend Benj for years.

'Good, thanks. Running, reading, writing . . .' I reply cheerily, as if this isn't how I spend every Saturday. As if there aren't fleeting moments where I wonder whether I'm getting weekends all wrong. Where I wonder whether Becky, doing nothing but swiping left, swiping right, isn't getting it right. At least she puts herself out there, actually believes in love.

'Always so productive,' Lola groans, as if I make the rest of them look bad.

'Compared to you,' I say, not meaning to sound so defensive. If my friend's pace is a samba, mine would be the bass. Steady, reliable, never missing a beat. But I like my beat, I'm good at it. 'In bed with Benj all day?'

'I swear you think people in love don't do anything other than swan around on clouds of stardust.' Lola laughs and I join in, even though it's far from what I know to be true: people in love lie to one another, they break each other's hearts, they ruin everything.

'You don't?' Makena feigns shock. 'Then why the hell am I on these dating sites?'

'We don't,' Lola confirms, trying not to smile over her

pint. 'But you're on those dating sites because they are seriously *fun*.' She reaches across the table to take Makena's phone out of her hand, looking down to the screen.

'Hey,' Makena objects, snatching it back as we all laugh.

Lola met Benj at university, back in the days when online dating was for the desperate and deluded. Back when men and women would cross bars and oceans (well, clubs called Ocean and Oceania anyway) to find each other. I look around the crowded bar now. There are groups of guys gathered around phone screens, gangs of girls giggling down at their own. People on dates, people in groups. People keeping themselves to themselves because walking over to someone else's group feels intrusive, unwelcome and, well, a little desperate and deluded.

'Is he on or off?' Lola asks, smiling at Makena. We all know part of her wants to live vicariously through Makena, through Becky, but they just want what she has. Meanwhile, I'm flying the flag for ambitious career women everywhere. Or trying to, at least.

For a moment Makena's eyes seem to say: *Lola, you can't have your cake and eat it too.* But then the need to talk about him, analyse him, pick apart his profile, wins the fight within her. 'Oh, who the hell knows.' She takes another swig of her wine. 'One second we're seeing each other, sleeping with each other, the next he's silent and I'm left waiting to know what's next . . .' She lets out a groan of frustration so loud that the two girls on the next table look up. They smile in solidarity.

'Reckon he's just in it for the sex?' Lola asks.

'Maybe,' Makena sighs. 'I hope not.'

'But he makes you breakfast the next day, right?'

'Yes.' Makena reclaims her smile.

'And he's introduced you to his friends?'

'Not exactly.' The smile vanishes. 'He invited me for lunch with his grandma.'

'Well family trumps friends any day.'

Makena's face lights up once more, hope restored.

'Becky, any thoughts?' Lola looks for some backup for Team Happy Ever After. Becky looks up from her screen, caught in her own confusion.

'At least you have an on-and-off,' she moans. 'Ever since Eve messed with my profile, I've struggled to get even that.'

'Hey!' I look around at the judgemental jury staring back at me. 'I just edited out the wasters and the fuck-boys.'

'And now there's nothing left.' Makena laughs.

'Maybe all the good ones are taken?' Becky looks to Lola as if *she's* taken them all.

'You only need one.' Lola smiles back.

'No one's my type,' Becky looks down, swiping left and left.

'Maybe that's a good thing.' Makena says what we're all thinking.

'Do you think?' Becky looks around the table for answers.

'Yes,' Makena and I shout in unison.

'Hey!' Lola objects.

'Apart from your brother, obviously,' Makena says. Becky dated Lola's older brother for about year. Which is like a decade in adult years.

'Nah, to be fair, he's a bit of a knob.' Lola laughs. She loves her brother really, but by the time the break-up came, our friendship with her was already getting serious.

'Agreed.' Becky nods. 'I'm so glad we got to keep you when it was over.'

'Me too.' Lola grins. 'But Makena's right. The guys you're dating are all wrong. They're online to find company for the night; you're online to find company for life. You need someone willing to slow down, to wait, to work for you.'

'To let your relationship mature, like a fine wine,' Makena adds as she drains the rest of her glass. 'Anyone for another?' We follow her eyes to the bar, only to find another set of eyes staring right back. 'Omigod, he's looking at you.' Makena traces the stranger's stare back to Becky.

'I think it's fair to say he's looking at *you*,' Becky objects. It's a good assumption when it comes to Makena. 'Oh no, wait.' She looks away as though his eye contact burns. 'He *is* looking at me. Oh shit, is he coming over?'

'Becky, it's the 2020s, not the 1920s,' I point out. 'He'll find you on some dating app later anyway.'

'But I hate that.' Becky bemoans the lack of romance. 'I want a proper meet-cute.' She glances across at him, and I know she's thinking about her parents. She thinks she's failed because she hasn't met someone and married young like they did. Whereas failing to follow in *my* parents' footsteps is precisely what I have in mind. 'I'm going to speak to him.' She squares her shoulders, ready to enter the real-life romance arena.

'No you're not.' Makena looks up from her phone.

'Do it!' Lola hisses across the table.

'I need a backup.' Becky hands me her phone. 'Keep swiping,' she says.

I look down at the screen, searching for a man good enough for my best friend. My best friend who just happens to be chatting another man up at the bar.

Okay. Here's one. I read his details out loud to Makena and Lola. Could this be Becky's backup? 'Mike. He's twenty-seven, five foot eight, works as a teacher—'

'Match!' Makena grins, as if having the same profession is a match made in heaven. Has she *seen* the men we work with? The only half-decent one there is Taren. And she knows better than to go fraternising with the enemy.

'No,' I object. 'Becky needs someone different, someone to balance her out.'

I keep swiping. Matt, twenty-six, actor, self-confessed attention-seeking middle child. He looks cute, all Bieber floppy hair and dimples. But does our drama queen really need a king? I swipe on, looking for someone calmer, sensitive, deep enough to balance her in the best way. 'How about this one?' I glance up from the phone. Lola and Makena are grinning at me, and for a moment I worry I'm having too much fun. If I give them an inch, they'll take a mile and get me making my own profile in no time. They nod me on with eager eyes. I guess this part is pretty fun at least.

'Tom, twenty-eight, personal trainer . . .' That would be good for Becky, get her out of the house, finally get her doing that light exercise. 'Spends his weekends mooching around Tooting Common . . .'

'Wrong side of the river.' Lola shakes her head like it's a deal-breaker.

'Yeah, but on the right line,' I argue back. What London lovers have to think about. 'I think she'll find it romantic. North meets south, line-crossed lovers from the wrong side of the tracks . . .' I know for a fact now that I'm having too much fun. Keep it together, Eve. 'He spends his time drinking coffee and eating cake . . .'

'She'll like that part.' Lola nods.

'Oh, and he's a big reader.' I look down at his broad shoulders. He sounds more like *my* type. But Becky needs something different, something to complement her energy. And this guy? Confident not cocky, strong and sensitive, rooted and well-read; different in all the right ways. 'Ladies and erm . . .' I look from Lola to Makena. 'Ladies, we have a swipe right.'

Chapter Six

Max

Tom: Dude, I'm bored. Why are you working on a
  Saturday?
Max: I'm not.
Tom: Average age of current company?
Max: Seventy-nine?
Tom: I knew it.

I look up from my phone and across the courtyard, the community garden party in full swing. We put them on every quarter, each season lending itself to a different celebration. And God knows the patients here deserve a reason to celebrate, Peggy more than anyone. I know you shouldn't have favourites in this job, but I've worked with Peggy for over a year now. She was one of the first patients I visited, and we just clicked. Her family remind me of my own, and, well, there was the tiny fact that we met just after the chance to visit my grandmother was gone.

Looking at her now, chair pushed up to the plastic picnic table, laughing and surrounded by friends, I can tell she's having a good day. From across the courtyard she smiles and waves. I raise a hand in response before I realise that she's actually smiling past me. Turning around, I see Amy striding confidently over to her, a plate of burgers in hand. It's probably too early in the year for a barbecue, but the sun is shining, and with spring just around the corner, there didn't seem any reason to wait. Seeing Peggy and the other care-home residents reaching for the burgers, laughing and chatting, I'm really glad we didn't.

Tom: Let's go for a drink.

Max: No date tonight?

Tom: No, you've edited out my normal crowd.

Max: I promise it'll be better in the long run. You don't want women like that anyway.

Tom: No, you're right.

Max: I'm always right.

Tom: No you're not. You're spending your Saturday surrounded by a bunch of old folk.

Max: The average age has just come down a bit actually.

Tom: Shit, someone died?

Max: No, you idiot.

Max: Amy's here.

I watch as Amy helps an elderly patient to her feet, guiding her across the courtyard and towards her room for a lie-down. I know this is my chance to make a move.

'Is this seat taken?' I say a little flirtatiously as I gesture to the worn plastic chair.

'I thought you'd never ask.' Peggy smiles up at me. Her deep brown eyes swim with memories, even when she's feeling muddled. After watching the early symptoms of her dementia deteriorate, my heart leaps at her instant recognition of me. I know the stats: that once the symptoms start, they never really go, but Peggy's strength shines through regardless.

As I take a seat beside her, my phone buzzes to life in my pocket. Tom's been surrounded by strong women too, ever since I poked his dating profile into shape, but I can tell from the messages he's been sending me all day that he's not been chatting to many of them. Turns out it's much easier to get a conversation going with a cheeky Netflix and chill than actually having to think of something witty or insightful to say.

Tom: Tell her I say hi.
Max: Tell her yourself. Swing round here before we go for a drink.

I used to miss Tom when he was with Yvonne every weekend. It was one of the reasons I ramped up my visits to the care homes in the first place. But clearly without the distraction of a catch-all approach to dating, he now has more time on his hands.

'You young people and your computers,' Peggy says, a glimmer of mischief in her eyes.

'It's not a computer, Peggy, it's a . . .' I begin, before I realise she's joking.

'How old do you think I am?' Her laugh is dirty and deep. 'Don't answer that.'

'I would like to pretend I don't know.' I reach across the table to grab the lemonade and pour us both a glass. 'But your eighty-fourth was a hoot.'

'Max,' she reaches a heavily veined hand to rest on mine, 'you're twenty-seven years old. Please don't use words like hoot.' She erupts into laughter again and I can't help but do the same.

'It *was*, though.' I squeeze her hand tight. 'Roger was trying to dance with you all night.'

'Roger tries to dance with all the girls,' Peggy says, and even though Roger has a good sixty years on Tom, I can't help but think of my friend. 'He can be a right little whacker.'

I spray my mouthful of lemonade everywhere.

'What did you just say?'

'Whacker, Max, *whacker*,' Peggy scolds me, before adding, 'Bit of a wanker too, to be fair.'

And that's it. I'm gone. Where on earth can I find a woman like Peggy, just perhaps fifty or so years younger?

'What are you troublemakers laughing at?' Amy's voice rings through our spluttering, as Peggy wipes a tear of laughter from her eyes. Amy narrows hers at me: *you'll tire her out if you're not careful, Max*. But I'm pretty sure Peggy will be the last one standing at the party, as usual – well, sitting and chatting at this table, at least.

'There's only one troublemaker around here, Amy.' I smile

as Peggy pretends to look innocent. Amy laughs, brushing a loose strand of long curly hair behind her ear.

'Burger?' She thrusts a fresh plate of them under my nose.

'I shouldn't, dear,' Peggy says mischievously. 'I'm watching my weight.'

'So are we,' Amy says. The staff here are brilliant at knowing what to watch out for, how to keep the patients well watered and well fed. Also how to say it in a way that doesn't make them sound like plants. 'Max?' She elongates my name, eyes trying to tempt me.

'I'd better not,' I sigh. 'I'm going out for food later.'

'Ooh, who with?' Amy looks genuinely interested.

'Just Tom,' I say, and I swear her face lights up. She's seen him in passing once or twice: trying to sneak into the odd fund-raiser, or waiting discreetly in our office reception. Turns out sneak and discreetly are tricky words for a man as tall as him.

'Again?' Amy plays with her hair. Peggy nudges me under the table. *Ow.* She's pretty strong for a woman her age.

'What?' I hiss.

'What are you doing with your weekend, sweetheart?' Peggy smiles up at Amy.

'Thanks for asking, Peggy,' Amy says. It sounds like a dig. What have I done now? 'Just having some drinks. Us single late-twenties girls have to stick together of a weekend.'

'So do we mid-eighties ones.' Peggy nods.

'Speak for yourself, Peggy,' Tabatha shouts from the other side of the picnic table. '*I'm* only seventy-seven.' Everyone who registers the comment laughs; Tabatha is hardly a spring chicken. 'Amy, can you help me to my room?'

'That, Tabatha,' Amy looks at me with a wink, 'is an offer I can't refuse.'

As soon as Amy is gone, Peggy gives me another whack under the table. Turns out she's a bit of a whacker too.

'What is your problem?' I can't help but laugh.

'The early stages of dementia?' Peggy looks deadly serious for a second; I don't take the bait.

'I mean with Amy.'

'She *likes* you.' Peggy says it like it's obvious.

'She doesn't,' I hiss back. 'And even if she did, I don't see her in that way.'

'You have to put yourself out there sometime, Max. Life is short' – easy for her to say; she's eighty-four – 'and love is wonderful.'

I know she misses her husband, Edwin, who passed away eight years ago. Her only son married an Australian woman, and though he Skypes from time to time and the world is getting smaller and all that, Sydney is still over ten thousand miles away. *Your grandma was too far away too. Too far for you to visit.* The thoughts threaten to surface before I push them back down.

'Why don't you get on that Kindling dating site?'

'It's called Tinder, Peggy.'

'That's right.' She nods as if it was on the tip of her tongue. How the hell does Peggy know about Tinder? I'd love to find out what she and the girls get up to when the staff and volunteers aren't around. 'Why don't you try to find love on

Tinder? Love is wonderful,' she repeats, and for a moment I wonder whether she remembers saying it first time around.

'I'm not sure people really find love on Tinder?'

'Well, lust is pretty wonderful too,' and Peggy's dirty laugh is back. 'Back in my day, I used to be quite the looker.'

'I believe it,' I say.

'Flirt with someone your own age.' She gives me a little slap on the wrist.

'This man bothering you again, Margaret?'

I look up to see Tom striding across the courtyard.

'You know it.' Peggy raises her arms towards him, inviting him to bend down to her. 'And you also know you can call me Peggy. Margaret sounds like an old person's name.'

Tom grins. I love him for loving her too. For not trying to compare her to my grandma or equate my fondness of her with grief.

'Mind if I take Max from you?' Tom asks.

'Be my guest.' Peggy waves me away.

'See you in a couple of days, Peggy.' I lean in to kiss her on the cheek. It's the most action I've got all year.

'Oh hey, Tom.' Amy walks back out into the courtyard and grins up at him – all of him – before turning to me. 'Bye, Max, thanks for all your help today.' *Hey, Tom, bye, Max.* Although I'm not in the market for a date, it's always pretty hard to market yourself next to a friend like him.

'It's not really working.' Tom takes a swig of his beer, looking down at his phone.

'You breaking up with me?'

'No, I mean your profile.' He laughs, but he actually looks a little concerned.

'Define not working?'

'Well, I've matched with some stunners,' he explains as I take a sip of my own pint, the foretaste of 'but' laced in his sentence. 'But no one is really talking to me.'

'Have you tried chatting to them?'

'Isn't the girl meant to start the conversation?' Tom asks, as if I'm an expert.

'I think it's just on Bumble where the girl speaks first.'

'No, I mean like as a *rule* . . . like, dating app etiquette?'

I shake my head. 'I think it works both ways.'

'Oh, right. Well, before they would always start the conversation, be really forward.'

'Like propose-on-the-first-date forward?'

'That was only one time!' Tom laughs before realising he's just given me an inch. 'Not that that's what happened. I was tying my shoelace and I promise I . . .' I can't help but laugh. 'Shut up, mate, I'm being serious.'

'I know, I know.' I try to muster some sensitivity, which to be fair is usually quite close to the surface. 'Well maybe these new women want you to work a bit harder.'

'I know,' Tom says. 'But I don't know what to say.'

He swipes across his screen to a picture of a woman in her late twenties with long braided hair and a killer smile. She's stylishly dressed, hands on hips in a Superwoman stance. I read through her profile: Makena, aged twenty-nine. Writer.

Loves drinks with her girlfriends in Camden. Art galleries and exhibitions are her vibe.

'I mean, she's proper fit and she likes all this high-brow stuff and . . . well, I can't just drop in with a "hey", can I?'

'I mean, you could,' I say. Isn't that what normal people do?

'But a girl like that is going to get loads of matches. I need to stand out from the crowd.' Tom is six foot something and as stacked as anything; if he can't stand out from the crowd, there's little hope for the rest of us.

I look at him and it's then that I realise just how much Yvonne's cheating has knocked him. And as sad as it is, I totally get it. If you don't have trust in your relationship, romantic or otherwise, what's the point? It's hard to come back from a let-down like that. My mind shoots to my grandma, how I let *her* down, how I wasn't there for her, before I force my focus back into the room.

'Is this about Yvonne?' I ask, taking another sip of my drink, trying to dilute the directness of my question.

'No, not really.' The silence stretching between us gives him permission to go on. 'Well, maybe,' he sighs. 'A little. Like, before, it was easy to just meet up, hook up and end things. But I could properly have a future with these other women, and that's a bit scary . . .'

'It is.' I nod. I get that. It's hard to put your heart on the line, especially if it's already bruised. 'Okay, so what you need is someone you can go a bit slower with; dip your toe in the water without swimming all the way down the aisle . . .'

'Mate, your metaphors are getting worse.' Tom smiles.

'Let's have a look at these profiles.' I hold out my hand.

'Maybe I'll have more luck.' Even as I say it, I don't believe it, but Tom needs help.

'Okay, and while you do that . . .' he passes me his phone, replacing it with his work phone in record time; the screen version of a safety blanket, 'I'll get us another one.'

I look down at his cracked screen, caused by dropping a weight on it when he saw Yvonne at his gym after the break-up. A shattered screen to go with his shattered heart. It's not like I can even blame her that much. He thought they were exclusive, she thought they weren't – a classic case of mixed messages. Now Tom just needs to find a profile on the same page.

Lucy, aged twenty-six . . . Nope, he won't want to date someone with the same name as his sister. Yvon – no way; all Yvonnes are out. Katie, aged thirty-three, proud single mother . . . I can't imagine how brave you must be to put yourself out there like that: *this is me, this is my life – take it or leave it.* But Tom needs someone at the same life stage right now. Alice, aged twenty-four, actress, enjoys late nights out in Soho, sleeping until midday on Sundays . . . She looks like a model, they'd look great together. But Tom doesn't need late nights out and sleeping until midday right now. He needs someone a little sweeter, kinder, funnier. Someone who'll make dating fun and remind him that a bit of romance doesn't go amiss either.

I swipe on, looking from face to face. Man, some of these girls are pretty, but I'm not going to find the girl of my dreams online. Becky, twenty-eight, nights in watching French movies with Camembert and wine. I scan over her answer to the favourite music question. 'The first time I went to see the Coronas it was in Dublin and I was just thirteen. I sang along with thousands of people, feeling seen but safe in that rowdy crowd. They've been my favourite ever since.' I look at her deep brown eyes and her petite figure and her massive smile. I know I'm not going to find the girl of *my* dreams online, but I'm pretty sure I've just found Tom's.

Chapter Seven

Eve

'Eve.' I look up to see Becky back in her bundle on the sofa, Buster pretending to be a cushion by her side. 'I think I drank too much last night.' Her tired eyes gaze at me.

'You think?' I glance back at my diary; Sunday mornings are for planning ahead. 'I *know* I did.'

Becky groans. 'He bought shots,' she explains, as if it's a valid excuse. 'I'm impressed you managed to run.' She looks down at my workout gear, caught between respect and disdain.

'*I'm* impressed you didn't bring that guy home.' I smile across at her before my face falls, eyes darting to the bedroom.

'I *didn't*.' She laughs. 'Turned out to be like forty-five, far too old for me.'

'Not too old for you to accept his drinks, though.'

'Eve.' Becky pushes herself up. 'Generosity has been

shown to seriously decrease anxiety.' She assumes a serious expression. 'Who am I to take that from him?'

'You're such a giver,' I say, rolling my eyes towards the ceiling; man, it's so mouldy.

'I am.' She nods. 'Thus bringing my own anxiety down in the process.' For a woman as hung-over as she is, she's making quite a valid point.

My mind skims over last night. Becky and Lola downing shots with 'just call me Warren'. Makena, Lola and me swiping through Becky's dating apps. Makena making shapes on the dance floor; Benj appearing to take Lola home when she began making slumping shapes of her own.

'Have any luck with that guy?' I ask over my weekly meal planner and open recipe book, trying not to sound too interested.

'Who?' Becky looks up from her phone, confused.

'Tom, was it?'

For a moment Becky looks scared. She was drunk last night but not too drunk to forget speaking to someone. 'Who the hell is—'

'I matched with him on one of your apps last night,' I explain. 'Seemed pretty promising.'

She scrolls through her matches. 'Oh man, he's gorgeous.' She seems to come to life. 'Personal trainer, loves long walks, reading books and watching films with subtitles . . . Eve, he's you in guy form.'

'He's not me.' He seemed calmer than me, a little more balanced.

'Well, to be fair, I really love *you* . . .' Becky looks at me.

'No, I'm not making you breakfast.'

'No, I'm serious.' She grins. 'If he's a bit like you, maybe we'll actually work.'

'He seems pretty great.'

'Plus he's *fit*.' Her eyes widen at his photos, trying to take him all in. 'But you matched with him last night, and he's not said anything yet.'

'Maybe you should make the first move.'

'You know I don't like doing that,' she objects.

'Becky, you stormed across a bar to drink shots with a middle-aged man called Warren last night. You can message some stranger a hello.'

Max

'Hello?' Tom looks at me over his coffee cup.

'Too generic.' I swipe away his suggestion. 'I think you should go in with a question, something to open the conversation right up.'

'How are you?'

'Good, thanks, dude, you?'

'I'm being serious.'

Tom looks down at Becky's profile with anguish. I showed it to him as soon as he got back from the bar, and I could tell he liked the sound of her. She seems like an old soul, wise and well read, at the same time as being a little ball of energy. 'I don't know what to say to her.'

'What do you usually say?' I ask, bracing myself for his answer.

'I don't. They usually start the conversation with something flirty and I go from there. And anyway, you know what happens when I make the first move. I call them the wrong name or forget I've already made the first move.' He looks to me and shakes his head as I gaze down at Becky's photos. She looks so comfortable in her own skin that I know she's going to need more than a 'hey, sexy' or 'well hello, gorge' or whatever else these guys say to get the conversation flowing.

'Why do people say things on these sites they'd never say in real life?' I ask. 'I wonder what the strangest opening line she's ever received is.' I pause. 'Why don't you start by asking her that?'

'Huh?' I know I've lost Tom completely. He's looking at her photos again.

'Ask her what it is and see whether you can compete. It'll show that you know online dating can be full of weirdos at the same time as proving you're not one.'

'Well, okay . . .' Tom says, entirely unconvinced. 'If you're sure . . .'

Tom: Go on then, what's the strangest opening line you've ever received on here? Let's see if I can match it.

Eve

'Oh shit, Eve.' Becky looks at me wide-eyed, her phone in her hands. 'He's messaged.'

'Let's have a look.' I get up from my usual corner of the sofa and walk across the room to Becky bundled up on hers. I look down at his message and laugh. 'Brilliant.'

'That's not brilliant. I've had some right oddballs message me on here.'

'Yeah, but his question suggests he isn't one of them.' I look at his photo, his insightful answers, and am pretty confident that's true.

'But now I have to come up with a funny answer.' Becky groans, hangover in full flow. 'I don't know if I have any.'

'You're kidding me, right?' She tells me these things daily.

'I don't know what to say,' she whines. 'Can't you do it?'

I roll my eyes but can already feel myself surrendering. 'Give the phone to me.'

Max

'Dude, she's typing.' Tom glances up from his phone. 'And now she's not.' He looks again. 'And now she is.'

'Mate.' I place a hand on his shoulder. 'Just chill.'

'I know, but Yvonne—' Tom begins.

'She's not Yvonne,' I remind him.

79

Becky: Honestly?

Becky is typing . . .

Tom and I both wait with bated breath, eager for her to go on.

Becky: 'Hey there, little titties.'

We erupt into laughter. No! Some guy really thought that was the way to spark a romance? Where the hell was he going to go after that? I laugh again but Tom interrupts.

'Where the hell am I going to go after that?'

'Huh?'

'Does she want me to say they're *not* little?' He scrolls back to her photo and I know for a fact he's mentally zooming in.

'No!' I say. Seriously, I knew he was struggling, but I never thought he'd be this bad.

'Well I don't know.' Tom looks at me. 'Can't you do it?'

I know I should refuse, but my hand is already reaching out to take the phone.

Tom: No!

Tom: On behalf of my sex, allow me to apologise.

'Dude!' Tom grabs the phone back. 'Now you've brought sex into the equation.'

Becky is typing . . .

Eve

I look down at Becky's screen as she types: *Why, what's wrong with your sex? ;)*

'Rebecca, no,' I say sternly, reaching to take the phone away again.

'What?'

'You do know that if you send that, you'll be sending signals with it?'

'Oh shit, did I set my smoke flare off again?' She looks behind the cushions.

'I'm serious. Let's just keep it a bit more PG for now.'

Becky: Meh, you can't be responsible for them all.
Becky: Must be some pretty crazy girls online too, right?
Tom: Yeah, I've probably met half of them.

'Half?' Becky turns to me. '*Half?*' I'm sitting back across the room, on to the next stage of my weekly plan: the workout regime. It strikes me that Tom would probably be able to help me out with this part. 'So he's a man-slag, then?'

'I don't think you can say man-slag any more,' I explain. 'It's more politically correct to say . . .' Becky is pretending to snore. 'He's probably just saying he's had his fair share of bad dates. Why don't you ask him about his worst? Everyone loves a story.'

'Can't you just come over here while I send it?'

'Fine,' I say, standing up to walk across the room again.

Becky: Ha! Any good war stories?
Tom: War stories?
Becky: Love is a battlefield and all that.

'Shit, I sent it. What if he doesn't get the reference?' Becky looks at me anxiously. I'm pretty sure he will. I mean, maybe not everyone will know the song was penned by Knight and Chapman, or that it charted at number 30 on VH1's list of 100 Greatest Songs of the 1980s, but Pat Benatar's hit is iconic. 'It's the one from *13 Going On 30*, right?'

Max

'Oh fuck.'

I look up from my book. I thought I'd got Tom up and running now, but clearly my work here is far from done.

''Sup?'

'I think she thinks a PT is something in the army.' Tom looks sorry for every air cadet meeting he missed as a boy, sorry for not being in the army now, sorry for not being good enough. Damn you, Yvonne.

'Give it here.'

He hands me the phone and I look down, trying not to laugh. It's fine.

Tom: Got to love a bit of Pat.

Tom: Okay, well don't laugh, but I once accidentally
proposed to a date.

'No, no, NO!' Tom scrambles to take the phone from me.
'Don't tell her that.'

'I don't think Becky is the type to start picking out rings,'
I say. I don't know her, but I get the feeling her life is so
full of family and purpose that meeting a man would have
to fit around her rather than the other way around. 'It's a
great story, she'll find it funny . . .'

Tom: We were saying goodbye and I crouched down to
tie my shoelace and she turned round to see me there
on one knee and threw her hands over her face to
hide her smile. It was *bad*.

Eve

As I read Tom's message, I'm laughing and laughing. Becky
is laughing too, but not nearly as much as me: maybe it's her
hangover. This guy is proper funny.

'What do I say now?' She looks at me with her big tired eyes.
'How about this . . .'

Becky: Ha! You charmer.

Becky: So what do you get up to when you're not busy
proposing to people?

I look down at my message and smile. The perfect steer into getting to know one another. I hand the phone back to Becky with a silent 'you're welcome' and walk back across the room, picking Buster up from the floor as I do. It's you and me now, boyo.

Max

'Max, remind me what I do in my free time.' Tom looks at me.

'The gym?'

'No, I mean like . . . the new Tom.'

'It's still you, Tom,' I say. 'Just be yourself.'

'Okay, gym, eat and Netflix.'

'Hmm, okay, maybe don't be yourself too much.' I take the phone from him. There's nothing wrong with how Tom spends his free time, not really. But right now he's still rebuilding from a break-up; we need to paint him as just a little bit more *renovated*.

Tom: When I'm not at work? I usually just take it quite easy. Like to get some fresh air, hang out with friends. Read a fair bit too. You?

Eve

'Okay, you're up.' Becky looks across the room to me and Buster, busy writing a shopping list of ingredients we need for our week's meals. 'He mentioned reading . . .'

'You can answer that.' I look down at the list, my week taking shape before me. All perfectly positioned for maximum efficiency, so I can spend more time working on features that will show I'm worthy of Angela Baxter's place. I *am* worthy of Angela Baxter's place.

'Eve, the last book I read was *Cosmopolitan*.'

'Okay, that's not technically—'

'Just come and help me.' She beckons me over. 'You're clearly having fun with it.'

It's not that clear, is it? I don't want to date, online or offline; I just enjoy helping with hers. But I have to keep my head in the zone, my own zone. With my own trajectory: up.

'I'm working on something,' I reply. *Note to self: you're meant to be working. You need that promotion.* I force my eyes back to my open laptop. See, not too much fun. 'Plus I've already done my exercise today; you should be the one getting up.' I nod to the space between us. I've been in and out of my seat countless times while she's just moved a finger across a screen.

'I'm too hung-over,' she groans. 'I have an idea.'

'Don't hurt yourself.'

'Shut up.' She looks at her phone. 'Download the app. I'll

give you my password and then you can read along, intervene when I'm about to say something stupid.'

'Becky, you don't need—'

'My favourite book is *Cosmo* . . .' She pretends to type, reading the proposed message out loud.

'Okay, downloading . . . logging on . . .' And against my better judgement, I begin to type.

Becky: Sounds lovely. Similar, tbh, but I prefer to merge my exercise and fresh air.

Tom: Very efficient of you.

Becky: I like to think so. So what are you reading at the moment?

Tom: I'm a bit of a polygamist . . .

Tom: . . . when it comes to books.

Becky: Ha! Had me worried for a second.

Tom: But at the moment, I'm really loving Proust's *In Search of Lost Time*.

Becky: Let me know if you find it.

Tom: Dad? Is that you?

Becky: If you don't like dad jokes, I suggest you swipe on now.

Tom: I will forgive your dad jokes in exchange for my dad dancing.

Becky: Done. But seriously, I've been meaning to read that.

Tom: I've only just scratched the surface, but so far so good. If you like writers as French as your films, I'm sure you'll get on with Proust just fine.

Becky: Cool. Reckon he's dating online?

Tom: Man, if he was bemoaning the loss of time in the late nineteenth century, I'm not sure he'd be too impressed with how we spend it in the twenty-first.

Max

I look down at Tom's phone and smile. Is online dating always this easy? The conversation with Becky just kind of flows. She seems really cool.

'I don't understand half of what you've just said.' Tom looks over my shoulder. 'But she seems pretty cool.' We're on the same page, and so it seems are Tom and Becky.

'Now to ask her out.' I look at Tom, who seems so confused by the thought that for a moment I wonder what we're doing here. He does like her, right?

'Already?' he asks.

'Well, if we carry on chatting now, you might not have anything to talk about on your date.'

Tom glances at our messages so far. Both of us know that's a very real concern. But as soon as they meet in person, they'll know whether they really share a spark.

'Won't that seem a bit *forward*?'

'You've both swiped right on a dating app; surely the next step is a date?'

'Okay, invite her round tomorrow night.'

'Here?'

'That okay?'

'For me, sure.' I laugh. 'For Becky? Not so much.'
'Why? What would you suggest?'

Tom: What do you think Proust would think to us
   grabbing a drink together soon?

Eve

'I'm going to suggest dinner instead,' I warn Becky, both of
us now logged on to the app and looking at our phones. She
is very much the passenger in this conversation.
   'Why?'
   'Because if you just go for drinks, you'll end up getting
drunk and going home with him.'
   'And?'
   'And you said you wanted to go slower, have something
that lasts a little longer.'
   'Something like dinner?'
   'Exactly.'

Becky: How about dinner?

Max

'Man, dinner sounds intense.' Tom looks at me in
concern.
   'It's this big meal you eat of an evening . . .'

'You know what I mean.' He laughs but still looks worried. 'Just sounds formal.'

'It'll be great.'

Tom: Perfect.
Tom: I could do tomorrow?
   Becky is typing . . .

'God, she's been typing for ages.' There's panic written across Tom's face, but I'm pretty confident she'll reply positively. In fact this whole encounter has me feeling positive.

Becky: I'm busy tomorrow actually. How about next
   Friday?

Eve

'Next Friday?' Becky frowns. 'That's ages away.'

'You don't want to look too available.'

'Yes, but won't he get bored of waiting?'

'Waiting isn't a bad thing.' We both know I'm talking about more than just dinner. 'You deserve someone willing to wait.'

She used to wait until she knew she liked someone before sleeping with them, but after boys started falling by the wayside, she became too fearful to go slow, getting more and more friendly with the one-night stand. The stupid scarcity mentality that stalks so many women.

'Plus I'll be able to finish work in time to help you get ready.'

'Ooh, I like that idea.' Becky looks down at her phone, at *Tom is typing* . . .

Max

'Next Friday?' Tom's shoulders slump. 'Well that's it, she's not bothered. Game over.'

'It's not game over,' I say, shaking my head. 'She's just busy.'

'But that's almost a week away.' He's incredulous. 'Not really in the spirit of dating apps, is it?'

'How's the spirit of dating apps been working for you, buddy?'

But before I can stop him, he grabs the phone from me and starts to type.

Tom: Can't do any earlier?
Becky: All booked up, I'm afraid.

'Man, she's one of those diary girls,' Tom says. I look at him in confusion. 'Like "book your slot or lose your slot" kind of thing.'

'Oh.' I smile. The more I know about Becky, the more I like her. It sounds like she has her shit together, that she's not just waiting for a man like Tom to slide into her DMs and make her day; it sounds like she can make her own day. 'I think I like a diary girl.'

'Well be my guest.' Tom presents her profile in his open palm.

Could I? Could I just make my own profile and match with Becky and explain this whole situation away? But no, we tweaked Tom's profile to find a girl just like her. And she swiped for a guy like him.

'You know online dating isn't for me.'

Tom: Friday is great. Where would you like to go?

Eve

'Not Ciao Becca. Anywhere but Ciao Becca,' I plead with her.

'I wasn't *gunna*.'

Becky: I don't really mind. Know any nice places?
      You're in Tooting, right?

Max

'Not the Castle. Anywhere but the Castle.' I turn to Tom.

'I wasn't *gunna*.'

'So she's in Camden?'

'Wrong side of the tracks.' He raises his eyebrows.

'Why don't you suggest meeting halfway? I know this cool place by Tower Bridge.'

'Too touristy?'

'No, it's tucked just around the back, in St Katharine Docks.'

Eve

'Be good to meet halfway,' I muse out loud to Becky, looking down at my phone in my hand, shopping list now cast aside, Buster trying to pawprint extra treats on the page. 'I know a place near the river, this amazing pub across loads of levels, lit up with fairy lights . . .'

'Sounds great.' Becky smiles. 'What's it called?'

'The Dickens Inn.'

'Very on brand,' she says approvingly. At least she knows Dickens is a writer. Well, was. *Note to self: remind Becky that Dickens is dead.*

'Let's see what he comes up with first.'

Tom: Let's meet halfway.

Tom: There's this cute place near Tower Bridge, the Dickens Inn. Know it?

Becky looks up at me, mouth hanging open. 'Are you sure you shouldn't be going on this date instead of me?' She laughs. 'That's so funny.'

I laugh too. It *is* kind of funny. A carefully curated coincidence.

'So it's a date?' I ask, looking across to my messy best friend, shining through her slump.

'It's a date!' she squeals, beginning to type.

Becky: It's a date.

Max

'It's a date!' Tom reads Becky's latest message out loud, a smile spread wide across his face.

'It's a date.' I grin back at him, wrapping an arm around his shoulder in solidarity.

Tom: It's a date.

Chapter Eight

Eve

Tom: I know what you're saying, but I still think the book is better.

Becky: Have you *seen* the film *Little Women*?

Tom: Yeah, I went to see it with Tom.

Tom: Not me, obviously.

Tom: A different Tom.

Becky: I was going to say, weird way of saying you went by yourself.

Becky: Anyway, I just think they brought it to life so well. And Saoirse Ronan is my queen.

Tom: I've never seen a better portrayal of Amy.

Becky: Agreed. Florence Pugh was everything.

Tom: Laurie was a little weedy.

Becky: Want to get him into your gym?

Tom: Huh?

Becky: For a personal training session?

Tom: Oh yeah, for sure. We could buff him up and make those *little women* look even smaller.

Becky: You are joking, right? You do know they're not physically small?

Tom: Of course I do. I've read the book, watched all the adaptations and seen the new movie twice.

Becky: Twice?

Tom: Was sobbing too much the first time round to really take it in.

'Eve?' Becky calls me from her bedroom. I swipe away from my conversation with Tom – well *Becky's* conversation – not sure why my hand drifted there in the first place. Helping Becky keep the conversation going with Tom has kept me calm lately, Datespace replacing Headspace and helping me come down from another intense week in the office – intensely *frustrating*. Makena spent her mornings probing Angela, following her into the toilets just to catch her in a breathe-out baby-bump moment. We're still none the wiser.

I look down at the open laptop before me. I know I said I wasn't going to work this evening, but Becky will be busy on her date with Tom, and I want my portfolio to be ready for the moment Angela's maternity leave is announced. *Note to self: keep your eyes on the prize. Do not, I repeat, do not get distracted . . .*

'Eve, can you come here?'

I reluctantly put my laptop down. I'll be back to it soon. *Note to self: do not get . . .* Yes, I know. Picking up my phone, I walk into Becky's bedroom.

'I need your help,' she says. She's a vision in three tops, her knickers and a single shoe. 'Sit down.'

'Where?' I look at the pile of everything she owns in the space where her bed used to be.

'Very funny,' she says in a way that shows she doesn't find it funny at all. She's stressed. I sit down obediently. 'I don't know what to wear,' she moans.

'Not that.' I gesture to her current get-up. 'You'll be arrested.' She takes off one of the tops and flings it towards me.

'You've been out to dinner before,' I say, flinging it back. 'What did you wear then?'

'Yes, but not on a first date.'

'They're not all that different,' I say, as if I've been on countless first dates before.

'Well, with Matthew, I could tell he had tattoos and a beard and wore a beanie, so I knew to wear my ripped jeans and some barely there make-up. And with that guy Timothy, I knew he was proper outdoorsy, so I borrowed Lola's Barbour jacket and UGGs.'

'Did it do the trick?'

'No, he ended up taking me to the cinema. I was *boiling*.'

'Well you won't be boiling in that.' I glance down at her knickers.

'*Eve*.' She says my name like a plea. 'I have no idea what Tom likes.'

'Why don't you just go as yourself?' I suggest.

She looks at me like it's a novel idea.

I recline on her bed and bring up Safari on my phone: if

she needs me to sit here, I can at least read some human-interest stories online, start thinking about what I might write this evening. I want to write something that matters – meaty stories like Gareth's extremist schoolgirl – but I know by the time I get the go-ahead, the story will have come and gone. I need to dig deeper, into personal narratives, unique perspectives, innovative insights that last longer than a night.

'Should I wear a beret?' Becky interrupts the thought.

'A beret?'

'Because of all the French films and cheese and stuff.'

'Becky, you do not need to wear a beret.' I look down at my phone again, pulling up *The Paris Review*. She's now just in her knickers, her bra and the shoe. 'You do have to wear *something*, though.'

'Could you *please* put your phone away?' she moans. 'This wasn't the plan . . .'

'The outfit?' Or lack thereof.

'No, tonight, getting ready.' She's scrabbling about in her wardrobe. I'm surprised there's anything left inside. 'I wanted us to be, like, laughing and joking about what I'd wear and everything . . .'

'Like in *Sex and the City*?'

'Exactly like in *Sex and the City*!' She smiles. 'That bit in the movie where they're sorting out Carrie's closet with the "take" and "toss" cards . . .'

'Oh dear God.' I roll my eyes, phone still clutched in my hands.

'I'll toss *you* if you don't put that phone away,' she threatens.

'Hold on a second.' I swipe across my screen, and the sound of RUN DMC's 'Walk This Way' starts to blast from my phone. I turn the volume up.

'Now that,' Becky twirls in her underwear, 'is more like it!'

She throws a black dress my way and I reluctantly put it on. I look into her floor-length mirror and we both laugh. It just about fits width-wise, but due to our height difference, you can now see my pants as clearly as Becky's.

'Now who's getting arrested?' She creases with laughter, flinging another outfit towards me. I remove the black dress, replacing it with an orange number that I wear off one shoulder. It looks like a top. Grabbing another dress from her bed pile, I tie it around my waist. I look ridiculous. Becky throws her head back, laughing even harder and shaking her hips in time to the music. Grabbing my hands, she swings me around as we sing at the tops of our voices. Then we hear it: an almighty *rip*. I open my mouth to apologise, but Becky is already on the floor, heaving with laughter that I'm sure would kill her if it wasn't so full of life.

'Ladies and gentlemen.' Becky looks from me to Buster, now stalking his way across the piles of lace and denim on her bed. 'I present to you our finalists.' She has spread the chosen outfits on the floor. The first: black jeans, her long-sleeved black top, cropped to show an inch of flesh. A denim jacket and pink scarf for lightening the look as she walks into the bar. The second: dark blue mom jeans, an oversized white shirt with just a hint of black bra underneath, a leather jacket of mine to layer over the top.

'I vote this one.' I point to the second outfit. 'It kind of gives the impression that you've come straight from work – your really *stylish* work . . .'

'You do know I teach primary school kids?' Becky laughs. 'You might look like that when you leave the office, but I leave work looking like a science project. Remember that time I came home with yellow feathers sticking to me like Big Bird?'

'Becky, I don't think you've ever looked like Big Bird.' I glance down at her shoe options, nodding as she picks the boots with the highest heel. At least she'll be *Bigger* Bird in those.

'I think the black one.' Becky gestures to the first outfit. 'Makes me look Parisian.'

'He might not ask you to go to Paris on your *first* date.' I try to manage her expectations. I've been helping her chat to Tom all week; he seems really cultured and romantic.

'I know *that*,' she objects, like I'm the crazy one. If it wasn't for me, she'd be wearing a beret.

'Yeah, I know, but if your expectations for getting ready were movie-montage perfect, I don't know what you're hoping for later.'

She knows I have a point, but before she can say anything, my phone buzzes. Buster jumps off the bed onto the bedside table, pressing his paws into Becky's open eyeshadow pallette before walking across her all-black outfit.

'Shit.' She scoops him up at arm's length.

'Looks like Buster's siding with me,' I tell her.

Tom: Is it okay that I'm a little nervous about tonight?

'Who is it?' Becky looks at the phone in my hands.

'It's Tom. Do you want me to log out of your profile?'

'Absolutely not.' She shakes her head. 'I need your help.'

'Do you want me to reply?'

She nods, and I begin to type.

Becky: Yeah, I get it. First dates can be nerve-racking.

Tom: There's so much that could go wrong.

Becky: But there's so much that could go right.

Tom: Plus I'm a bit scared you're going to jump down
   my throat about the digital media thing.

Becky: I won't, I promise.

'Why would we jump down his throat about that?' Becky
looks up from the app on her own phone; she's now wearing
the blue jeans and white shirt.

'It was just something we were chatting about yesterday,'
I explain. 'You were there.'

'I know, but . . .' she looks sheepish, '*Love Island* was on.'

Becky isn't just the kind of girl to watch a trashy reality
TV show like *Love Island*; she's the kind to stream reruns of
old series on Netflix – unless a new series has started and
I've missed the boat.

'Can you just give me the highlights?'

'Sure.' I remember the conversation well. 'Tom was suggesting that print carries more prestige.'

Becky nods. 'I've heard you say that before; that's what we think, right?' She's playing fast and loose with the word 'we'.

'*We* do,' I agree. 'But we also think paywalls are a good thing.'

'Paywalls?'

'When you're reading an article online and then it makes you subscribe to see more.'

'Oh, I *hate* that.' Becky sits on the edge of the bed to put her boots on. She sees me shaking my head and mirrors my motions. 'We *don't* hate that?'

'We don't,' I agree. 'We think it's recognition for the people producing the content.'

'Got it.' She nods. 'And what's this thing about little women? Were you talking about me?'

'No.' I laugh. 'We were talking about the novel *Little Women* by Louisa May Alcott, which came out in 1868.'

'Eve, that's too long ago! You know I don't know anything about history.'

'It was also a movie in 2019,' I add.

'Oh thank God.' She smiles, back on safe ground. Well, *safer*, at least.

'It's about a young woman called Jo—'

'A *little* woman,' Becky corrects with pride, trying to force herself back into the loop.

'Not physically,' I tell her. 'But she's a teacher—'

'Like me?' Becky interrupts again.

'A little. And a writer—'

'Like you?'

'A little.'

'Okay. A little like me, and a little like you. Got it.' She looks down at my messages to Tom again. 'Maybe I'll be a bit more like you though, just for the first date.'

I slam the door behind Becky, the bang sending Buster scarpering across the kitchen even though I've just put his food out. That's not like him. I walk into the living room and sit on the sofa, opening my laptop but suddenly drained of inspiration. That's not like me either. Getting Becky ready for her date this evening was fun. By the time she left, she was practically humming with nerves and excitement. I felt pretty giddy too. And now that she's on her way to her evening with Tom, I'm not sure I want to carry on with my own. *Note to self: you want this, you've always wanted this.*

I look at my fired-up screen: *come on, Eve, just start writing; the rest will come.* That's what I told Becky. Well, not writing, but talking: just start with this line, the rest will follow: 'How do you think the film adaption of *Far From the Madding Crowd* compares to the book?' But now that I'm so far from the madding crowd that I could finally get some work done, I feel a little lonely. Lola will be with Benj, Makena with Ajay.

The cursor blinks on my blank white page, but the words won't come. Maybe I used them all up on Tom. Buster struts across the living room towards me, having snuck back to the kitchen to polish off his food in record time. He sniffs in my work bag, looking for more. And I'm after more too.

If I can just get enough pitches and pieces together to prove I'm worthy of more work, more *meaningful* work . . .

I bend to pick Buster up, and my post scatters out of my handbag and onto the floor: *another* letter from the water company screams from the top. Okay, if the article inspiration isn't coming, maybe I can get do some life admin. Put my evening to good use while my best friend is putting it on Tom. But not too much. I told her to go slow, make him work for her. Not give everything away for free.

I open the bill. Wow, Thames Water aren't giving it away for free either. The next letter is a thank-you card from a recently married friend to 'Becky and Eve'; we've been living together so long that people now just address us as a couple. Maybe that will start to change if things go well for Becky tonight. I open the next letter in the stack: my mobile bill. Man, I use too much data. Then the next: junk mail from some PR firm. And then my gaze falls on a small envelope nestled within the pile.

This one isn't branded. It's on creamy white paper, black handwriting dancing across the front. My jaw drops like the stone in my stomach. It can't be. Can it? There's no way. Absolutely no way. But even though the envelope is shaking in my trembling hand, I know for a fact that I'd recognise that handwriting anywhere.

Chapter Nine

Max

Walking into the office, I try to look calm. But today has just been one of those days. I should have known that popping to the care home in East Croydon on my lunch break was biting off more than I could chew. Which is ironic given that I haven't had a chance to eat all day. What was I thinking? No one pops to East Croydon.

'Hey, Max.' Heather smiles up from her desk as I walk by. 'Thanks for looking over that press release.'

'Any time,' I say, before I can stop myself. Her smile grows wider. I want to be the kind of guy who has all the time in the world to stop and help other people, but today I feel pulled in a dozen directions.

'Max-aaay.' Paddy swivels around in his chair as I approach. Just breathe, Max, breathe. 'How was she?' he asks, and I'm not sure whether he means Amy or Peggy. Sadly, I've not had time to see either.

'Couldn't fit in a second visit today.' I try not to sound too disappointed. I hope Peggy wasn't too disappointed either.

'The fact you even fit in one is amazing,' Paddy smiles as I bury my head behind my monitor, trying to stifle a yawn. This week has knackered me, my new role now in full force. Staying up late to help Tom message Becky probably didn't help either. He started off well, but then she started talking books and Tom tagged me in quicker than you could say 'training session at 6 a.m., I'm going to bed, dude'.

I know I could have told him I needed to go to bed too, but Becky was in full swing and the two of them hadn't really chatted all day. I didn't want her thinking Tom had gone cold before they'd even had a chance to meet. They seemed good for each other.

'That's it.' Paddy gets to his feet. 'It's officially the weekend.' For him maybe, but I still have so many emails to catch up on. Plus I haven't even scratched the surface when it comes to developing new fund-raising projects for our department. 'Please tell me you're not hanging out with Peggy tonight.'

'I could do a lot worse,' I joke, though it's true.

'Yeah, but it's Friday night,' Paddy objects. He has a point.

'Don't worry, I'm meeting Tom for a drink,' I say, and for a moment I wonder whether Paddy wants an invite. But Tom's asked to meet me so I can prep him for his date this evening. 'I'm helping him out with something,' I explain.

'You do know you're allowed to spend time *not* helping other people?'

'A day wasted on others is not wasted on one's self.' I lift the quote right from the pages of *A Tale of Two Cities* and can't help but smile at the thought of all mine and Becky's Dickens references last night.

Well, *Tom* and Becky's references anyway.

Crossing Tooting High Street, I can see Tom in his usual spot through the window. His behaviour, on the other hand – more specifically what is *in* his hand – is far from commonplace. He's reading a book. As I walk into the pub, he glances up from it, looking a little sheepish. He's reading my copy of David Nicholls' *One Day*. It's a brilliant love story, but Tom wouldn't know about that; he's still on the dedication page at the front, his phone clutched in his other hand.

'Hey, man.' He stands to greet me.

'Can I get you a drink?' I turn around to see one of the waitresses from the bar standing beside me. Her name is Lauren and she works here every Friday.

'Hey, Lauren. I don't mind coming over to order.' My eyes shoot past her pretty face towards the swarms of people gathering around the bar, her rosy cheeks testament to how rammed it is in here tonight.

'No, it's fine. I'm sure you've had a busy day.' She smiles as I take a seat. 'Dementia charity, right?'

There's nothing wrong with *her* memory. It must be months since we chatted about what I do for work.

'That's right.' I smile.

'He's actually just got a really big promotion,' Tom boasts beside me as I try to kick him underneath the table.

'In that case, you definitely don't need to get up to order. Pint of pale ale?' I nod, and she heads back to the bar.

'Whoa, you're in there, mate.' Tom smiles over his own pint. I assume he had to go to the bar for his.

'With Lauren?' I push a hand through my hair. 'No, there's no way.'

'Dude.' Tom sighs. 'I may not know all the writers and directors Becky bangs on about.' He gestures to the phone in his hand. She doesn't *bang on* about anything. Her messages are fast becoming the highlight of my day. 'But I know a flirt when I see one. You're really bad on picking up on cues.'

I know he's talking about Lauren, but my mind jolts to my grandmother, the grief of losing her never far from the surface: I was bad on picking up on those cues too. But no, I can't think about that right now. Tonight is about Tom and Becky.

'How are you feeling about the date?' I ask, happy to deflect attention away from me. There's no point me even trying to find the girl of my dreams when I'm so far from the man of mine. No woman deserves to deal with the baggage I've lugged around with me this past year. No one needs my grief in their life when I'm barely even dealing with it myself.

'All right,' Tom says, but I can read between his lies. 'Okay, I'm terrified,' he admits.

'What are you scared of?'

'I'm not sure. It's just all a bit new, isn't it?' He sighs. 'Dinner and everything.'

'Yeah.' I try to empathise, but the last woman I had dinner

107

with was Peggy. 'It's a step up from Netflix and chill, I guess.'
Or rather watching half a film then going all the way.

'But that's what I'm good at.' Tom looks into his pint.

'Is this about Yvonne?' I ask, daring to go there.

'It's not, actually,' he says, looking surprised at the thought.
To be fair, I'm a little surprised too. 'I did see her today,
though.' That bit is less surprising. Yvonne may not be one
of Tom's clients any more, but she still trains at the same
gym. Tom is usually able to plan his sessions to avoid hers,
but sometimes seeing her is inevitable.

'Did you guys speak?' It annoys him when they don't. It
annoys him when they do.

'Nope.' He shrugs. 'Just saw her across the gym.' For
once, I buy his nonchalance. He might actually be starting
to move on properly this time. 'To be honest, I was just
thinking about tonight all day. Dude, I'm going to screw
this up.' He sounds panicked.

'You will with that attitude,' I tell him. I look up to see
Lauren with my freshly poured pint, and smile my thanks.
Tom smiles too: *make a move, dude*. But the only move I'm
planning to make tonight is to steal my book back from
him and reread it.

'Seriously, I think she's expecting a lot from this evening.'
He takes a sip from his pint.

'What gives you that impression? She seems pretty laid-
back to me.' I recall how easily our chat – *their* chat – flowed
last night.

'Well that's what *I* thought too, until . . .' Tom turns his
screen towards me.

Becky: I, for one, have *great expectations* for this evening.

'I've literally just booked dinner, that's it.' He looks from his phone to me, panic still scrawled across his face. 'Have I missed something?'

'Yes.' I laugh. '*Great Expectations* is the title of a Charles Dickens novel. She's making a joke about tonight – you're going to the Dickens Inn, remember?' I hold out my hand and Tom obediently passes his phone across.

Tom: Provided you don't send me round the *twist*.

'Bit harsh, dude.' Tom looks up from his screen, now returned to his hands.

'*Twist* as in *Oliver Twist*; it's another Dickens reference.' I smile at an increasingly worried Tom.

'Oh I'm so screwed.' He rests his head in his hands. 'I don't know anything about that, or any of this.' He scrolls through our chat and points to the relevant exchange, and suddenly the fact that he's making a last-ditch attempt to read my book today makes sense.

Becky: Oh *One Day* is the best!
Becky: I've always kind of wanted to do the same thing
   as the author does in the book.
Tom: Write?
Becky: Kind of. You know the way he writes about the
   characters on the same day but just different years?
   Well, I've always wanted to do something similar,

mark out a significant day with a significant other and
keep a record of everything that happened on that
date for decades.

Tom: That sounds like a great idea.

Tom: Not for the characters though. We all know how
that ended.

'No we don't, dude, we don't *all know* how it ended.' Tom
looks at me pleadingly.

'I don't want to tell you,' I say, excited for him to read the
book and its dramatic ending himself. 'It'll spoil it.'

'It's either that or Becky brings it up and I look like I've
forgotten – or didn't read it in the first place – and spoil our
date instead.'

'Let's just say it doesn't end well for the main characters,
either of them,' I say.

'Okay, I'll steer clear of the details.' He pushes the closed
book across the table towards me. 'But she did say she was
looking forward to chatting about literal fiction more.'

'Literal fiction?'

He doesn't look up from scrolling through our messages,
tracing his finger along the screen until he stumbles upon the
sentence he's looking for. 'Oh, *literary* fiction,' he corrects,
turning his phone towards me so I can see for myself.

Becky: I find the differentiation between literary and
commercial fiction pretty arbitrary, tbh.

Becky: I mean, I know literary fiction is meant to be
more character-driven, and commercial more about

110

plot and all that, but tell me Rebecca Bloomwood isn't a protagonist and a half?

Tom: I want to guess she's the main character in that romcom *Confessions of a Shopaholic*.

Becky: If you did . . .

Becky: You'd be right.

Tom: Confession: I've never read it.

Becky: *Them*. There's more than one.

Tom: Really? I didn't know that.

Becky: Yeah, well you wouldn't. As soon as a woman writes something commercial, it's branded as 'chick lit' and covered in glitter and most men will never go near it.

Becky: Do you know what the male equivalent of women's commercial fiction is?

Tom: Tell me.

Becky: Commercial fiction. It's just commercial fiction.

Tom: Man, I can't wait to hear your thoughts on that in person!

Becky: There's plenty to go around, ha!

Becky: I'm actually writing an article about it for the newspaper I work for.

Tom: Really? I thought you were a primary school teacher?

Becky is typing . . .

Becky: Sorry, I meant *write* for.

Becky: Sometimes I like to write the odd article on the side. Break up all the teaching.

Tom: Can't wait to hear more about it.

111

Becky is typing . . .

Becky: Probs best you don't get me started, tbh. I want
to hear all about you.

'She wants to hear all about *you*.' Tom looks at me, the
colour draining from his cheeks.

I stare at his cracked screen. That's just some Yvonne-
induced insecurity talking. It's Tom's photos Becky has seen.
Tom's answers on his profile – for the most part.

'That's not true.' I shake my head, taking another sip of
my beer. 'It's all you, bro. It's just my best-friend duty to
help you on your way.'

'You sure?' He drains the dregs of his drink. 'Time for
another?'

'I'm sure.' I nod, looking down at the time on my own
message-free phone. 'And absolutely not. If it's my duty
to help you on your way, I need to help you the hell out
of here.'

'Oh shit.' Tom clocks the time. 'I need to be going. Man,
I'm nervous. It's a long time since I read a book, especially
one with a romantic plot.'

'The woman gets hit by a bus in the end.' I hold up David
Nicholls. 'So it's not all about the romance.'

'Oh good.' Tom pretends to be relieved. I'm sure the main
characters didn't feel that way when their love story came to
such a brutal end. 'Do I look okay?' He stands to show me
his thin-knit green jumper, layered over black jeans. 'I wish
you'd been in to help me get ready.'

'Why? Were you planning on giving me a fashion show?'

'You know it.' He laughs. 'Proper movie montage like.' I choke on my final chug of beer at the thought.

'You look great,' I say. 'Now go show Becky a good time.' He raises his eyebrows. 'Not *that* good a time,' I amend. He reaches into his pocket to pull out his debit card, but I wave it away. 'Don't worry, I've got this.'

Tom's eyes dart to the bar. 'I bet you anything it's *Lauren* who's got this.'

'It's on the house.' Lauren looks up at me as I finally make my way to the bar to settle up.

Tom might not know his literary fiction from his literal fiction, but he's pretty damn switched on in other areas. And that's why I know he and Becky are going to have a brilliant time tonight. Tom might not be that cultured, but he's smart and funny and kind – and provided he doesn't put his foot in it about any of our messages, or worse, mention Yvonne, I know he's going to smash their date.

'No, seriously,' I say as customers glare at me from both sides. Why am I holding up the queue? And more to the point, why am I refusing a free drink? 'I want to pay for it.' I put my book under my arm to reach for my card, tapping it on the reader.

'Any plans for tonight?' Lauren asks.

'Just chilling with David Nicholls.' I nod to the book.

'Well, if you get bored . . .'

'Bored of this novel? You've got to be kidding me.' I laugh.

It's only as I'm leaving the bar that I realise she was trying to flirt. Why do I find it so easy to be cool as Tom, and yet struggle around women when I'm just being me?

Walking into the cool evening air, I brush off the thought. At least I have the flat to myself this evening. Weaving my way up Tooting High Street, my mind drifts to thoughts of Becky and Tom. They'll be arriving for their date soon. The thought makes my stomach sink a little. But why? This is a good thing. Tom has been at a loss since his break-up, and here is the promise of something new. I'm happy for him. But then it has been quite nice having him around the house a bit more lately.

Couples walking hand in hand and groups of friends pass me on either side as I wind my way down the side streets of south London. I guess even in a city of nine million people, it's easy to feel lonely. Counting down the houses to our flat, I can't help but think of Peggy. She must be pretty lonely too. I feel bad for not being able to visit her today.

As I reach into my back pocket for my keys, my phone buzzes to life beside them. I look down at the caller, and it's as if my thoughts have magicked her into the moment: it's the care home, *Peggy's* care home.

But why would they be calling at this time on a Friday night? They promised they'd only call out of hours if something happened to . . .

No, *not Peggy*.

Chapter Ten

Eve

I sit on the edge of the sofa, cradling the letter in my hands. Trembling, I turn it over and over, his handwriting causing a lump to rise in my throat every time I see it. Eve, Eve, Eve. I read my own name again and again. My mum had wanted to call me Anna, caught at loggerheads with my dad over it: the way they'd always been, the way they would be countless times again. Then they'd played for it. A game of blackjack to decide whether I'd be an Anna or an Eve. Turns out my whole life was just a game to him.

Looking down at the envelope, my heart hammers in my chest, each breath becoming harder and harder to take. I don't need this right now. I could just throw it away, pretend I never received it, pretend I have a normal family. Isn't that what I'm doing already, acting happy families with the Amatos? But no, they *are* my family, the ones who have always been there for me, are *still* there for me. Would that be the case if I was no longer Becky's plus-one?

Before I realise it, Buster is by my side, curling his ginger body into a little bean. I can do this. I can hear from my dad without hearing every other thing he should have said.

With shaking hands, I tear open the corner of the envelope, then a bit more, before it rips right open and there's no turning back. I pull out the pages within it, the same handwriting scratched along every inch of the paper. For a moment, I want to scan to the bottom, to find out the ending before deciding whether it's worth starting it in the first place. The same way I used to with every book I began, scared it wouldn't end happily. Before I grew up, before I finally developed some self-control. But my eyes don't need to flick to the end this time. *My darling Evie.* Three little words. Said over and over when I only ever wanted to hear three others: *I love you.* Though if I was waiting for those, I'd be waiting a lifetime. Just like I've spent the last ten years waiting for . . . *Dad.*

Tears gather on my lashes as I whisper the name out loud. As I get to my feet, Buster darts across the room towards Becky's door. My heavy legs follow him, leaving the letter behind, but it's only when I see her empty room that I remember she's not here. Perching on the edge of her bed, I let the tears fall. Why is he contacting me now? Why not on my birthday, or the birthday before that, or the birthday before that?

I reach to my phone, searching for distraction. For a moment my fingers move to message Tom, longing to lose myself in talking to him. But why the hell would I message Tom? My stomach churns at the thought. I matched with him for Becky. For my *best friend*. A best friend who happens to be starting the happily-ever-after she deserves. I stopped chasing mine after my dad left.

But maybe it's not what I think: too little said far too late. Stashing my phone, I force myself from Becky's empty room back into the living room. Breathe, Eve, just breathe. You can do this. *Note to . . .* Oh, I don't know. Just remember to read between his lies.

Sitting on the edge of the sofa, I reach for the discarded letter, unfolding it to read his opening sentence again. *My darling Evie. I'm sorry it's taken me so long to write. I have no excuse . . .* That isn't true – my dad is the king of excuses – but against my better judgement, I plough on. *I know I've not been there for you, for so many milestones, but I promise I've missed you through it all. After your mum left, I tried my best, but the grief became unbearable until I could only think of one thing to stop the pain . . .*

Mascara tears stain the sentences I've just read. *One thing to stop the pain.* I used to believe that. Used to buy his bullshit that liquor was a lifeline. But I'm older now, wiser, wise to his ways. I know it isn't true; that there are talking therapies, GP services, addiction phone lines, community courses, rehab.

I'm sober now, and I know you have every right not to believe that, but it's true. And I have no idea whether you want to hear from me after all this time, whether this letter will even get to you, but I saw your name in the newspaper, and Evie, I'm so proud . . .

Disbelieving, I read the words again. *Evie, I'm so proud.* Deep within me I know my eight-year-old self is savouring every syllable, but my late-twenties self knows better. There are only so many missed dance recitals, missed birthdays, missed moments you can take before you realise that maybe not having that person in your life at all would be less painful than being disappointed again and again and again. If you don't expect them to be there, then your expectations are always met. And since I stopped having a relationship with him, I've started to set and exceed my own expectations: I got myself through sixth form, university, got myself down to London. All by myself.

Sobbing into the silence, I hear a meow by my feet and see Buster looking up guiltily from my handbag.

'This isn't your fault, boy,' I whisper, lifting him into my lap. He snuggles into my side as I breathe deeply, looking around at the life I've created for myself here. I found this flat by myself, found friends, found a family, found work, found hope – an ambition and a drive that I could be and do so much more. I gave my dad so many chances, but now is my chance to make my mark. Not as the child of a broken home or the daughter of an alcoholic. Just as me, Eve.

With Buster on my lap, I find the strength to finish reading. *I didn't want to just barge myself into your life, but I did wonder whether you'd consider letting me be a part of it again. Maybe I don't deserve to be a father to you any more, but maybe you'd allow me to be your friend.*

Friend? I don't need another friend. I need a father. I need a dad. Well, I did once.

118

With trembling hands, I fold the letter in half and half again, sliding it back into its envelope. Breathe, Eve, just breathe. As I wipe stray tears from my face, my heart rate quickens in my chest. Why the hell would he get in touch after all this time? My chest pounds, my legs shake, my palms sweat. *Note to self: run.*

Gently lifting Buster from my side, I get to my feet. My mind is muddled, caught between wanting to run towards my dad and run away from this moment. Only the sound of my trainers on the pavement and the feel of my heart in my chest and the fresh air on my face can clear this mess.

Rushing to my bedroom, I pull some leggings from my wardrobe and a sports bra from my drawer. It feels like ages since I was dressing up, laughing and singing with Becky before she walked away for her date with Tom. Lacing up my trainers, I feel the urge getting stronger. I need to stomp this out. To stomp my dad and his letter and his wayward words out of my mind.

Darting back into the living room, practically running before I've even managed to leave the flat, I see the offending letter still sitting on the sofa. If Becky finds this, she'll have a thousand things to say. She always has, especially when it comes to my dad. I'll tell her about it soon, once I've had time to work things out for myself. I know she'll back whatever decision I make. But I also know there's a part of her that likes the sound of him, that longs for tales of our misadventures and the memories we made together before everything fell apart. But how could she have a soft spot for someone she's never met?

I grab the envelope, rushing through to the kitchen, stretching up to a cupboard so high that I know Becky won't be able to reach it. Tired Tupperware and half-eaten chocolate bars fill the dark space. Standing on tiptoes, I place the envelope behind the chocolate; a secret behind bars.

Running into the darkness, I can finally breathe. I fix my eyes forward and run. I run and run and run, feeling the impact of my feet on cold, hard concrete. I don't look back, leaving our flat and this evening and the letter behind.

Dad wrote to you. He actually wrote to you. He's sober. He's back . . .

Blood pumping, heart surging, legs racing, I try to untangle my thoughts as the streets of north London blur by. So, he says he's sober. That he wants to be my friend, be in my life. Maybe he could be. We used to be best friends. And there have been moments, days even, when I've wished I could talk to him, share an article, a story, a song.

I force my legs to run faster, my body to tilt forward, pushing my panic to the pavement as I turn the corner towards Primrose Hill. Maybe I have missed him some days. But then there were other days, better days, where I felt in control. Where I felt level-headed and clear-minded and like I had a handle on my life in a way he never did. *Note to self: you don't need him any more. Maybe you never did.*

The thoughts come thick and fast, but with every pace I force them to the floor, running faster, leaving them behind, beginning to reclaim the control I've worked so hard for.

Just think of something else, Eve, something better. I fix my eyes forward; I just have to keep moving.

I run a mile, and then another, then another, until I stop counting, time suspended. *In Search of Lost Time*. The book title races through my mind and I can't help but think of Tom, a sickness washing over me as I do. Why the fuck am I thinking about him again? *Note to self: you were messaging him as Becky, it's only fun as Becky*. To be myself, to let someone see every part of me, is something else entirely. My dad taught me that. *To love is to be vulnerable*. That's what he sobbed the night my mum left. I push the thought down, stamping it to the floor.

Pushing my body forward, I lean into the moment. All this emotion, all this feeling: it's nothing but fuel for creativity. Every writer who has ever made their mark has written from a broken heart. Into the silence, I let the ideas rise, my tired legs begging me to stop.

Maybe I could write about this? About the impact of relationships in forming your identity. About how addiction can make someone forget what really matters. But no, it's too raw. It's too soon. Maybe I could capture something of this feeling in someone else's story. I wonder what human-interest stories Tom has heard at the gym, when people are there trying to process their pain. I could just message him. *No*. He's with Becky. But for a second, pretending to be her feels simpler than being me.

Breathing in, breathing out, I lose myself in the moment, feeling the pain in my heart force its way into my legs. It feels better there; at least this pain is productive. Pressing forward, my mind is finally stilled. Arms tensing, calves cramping, I keep going, running on and on. Turning the corner out of the park, I savour the silence, tracing my way back to our flat, back to my home . . .

'Becky?' I breathe, surprised to see her petite figure tottering along in front of me. How long have I been running? 'Becky?'

'Eve!' She turns around, beaming. 'You're out late.' She looks from my sweat-wet face to my workout clothes.

'And you're back early,' I pant, looking down to my phone, still tracking my run. How the hell have I been running for two hours? I study my stats, aching but satisfied. 'And alone.' Even after our chats about taking it slow, making him wait for something more than a one-night stand, I'm still surprised.

'Left him wanting more,' she says proudly, before adding, 'I *hope*.'

'I'm sure you did!' I give her a little squeeze.

'Get off,' she laughs, though she holds my glistening forearm tightly. 'I'm meant to *not* be getting hot and sweaty tonight.'

'So . . .' I elongate the word, falling into step beside her to walk the last stretch home. 'Tell me everything.' I want to hear all about it. Probably so I don't have to think about my dad.

'Oh, I will,' she says, her eyes wide. 'But first, did *you* have a nice evening? I thought you were planning to write?'

I want to tell her about the letter. That I didn't write because someone else wrote to me. I'll tell her eventually, as soon as I've decided what the hell I'm going to do about it.

'Writer's block.' I shrug. It isn't technically a lie. 'Thought I'd run it out.'

'You're an inspiration to us all.' She squeezes my sweaty hand in hers.

I laugh, letting the praise soothe me. 'Okay. Tell me about your date.'

'It was good.' She grins. 'He's fitter than his pictures.'

'How is that even possible?'

'I know, right?' She laughs. 'He was shyer than I expected, though, and I struggled with some of his book chat. He definitely had an agenda for the topics he wanted to talk about.'

'Paywalls?'

'Had to channel my inner Eve for that one.' She winks.

'Sounds like you remembered your lines, though.'

'I accidentally let slip that I've been watching *Love Island* reruns, though.'

'Oh?' I say. If I know Tom, which I feel like I do, he won't like that.

'But I saved the situation by describing it as a social experiment exploring gender stereotypes.'

'I've never been prouder.' I can't help but laugh. 'So, second date?'

'Well that's the thing.' Her face falls a little. 'I don't know. I want to, but . . .'

'But what?'

'He didn't actually ask for one.' She shakes her head.

'Do they usually?'

'Yeah, over breakfast.' She raises her eyebrows. To be honest, I've witnessed a fair bit of that. 'But we didn't talk about it, and we didn't kiss, and he didn't come home with me.'

'No?' I pretend to look for a six-foot-something male smuggled in her leather jacket.

'No!' she echoes. 'So what should I do, should I text him?'

I'm focused on Tom, feeling further and further from my dad's letter. The strategy of dating. A safe distance from getting too invested, from getting hurt. I think back over Becky and Tom's messages, so many of which I wrote myself. From the books he reads and the films he watches, he seems romantic, longing for the thrill of the chase. The kind of guy who loves a strong woman but values the opportunity to show some strength himself.

'Yes . . .' I say.

'Right.' Becky reaches for her phone.

'. . . but not yet.'

'Oh?' she asks, confusion written across her face.

'Yeah, for now I think we should let him sweat.'

Her eyes linger on my Lycra as she stuffs her phone back in her pocket. 'I swear you won't be content until we all do.'

Chapter Eleven

Max

'It's Amy.' Her voice on the other end of the line isn't warm and bubby like usual, but cold and flat. Panic surges through me and a numbness fixes me to the spot. *Please not Peggy, please not Peggy.* 'I'm calling about Peggy. She's . . .' *Oh shit.* I close the door of the flat behind me, longing to shut out the world. A silence stretches on as I throw my book onto the sofa, perching myself on its edge. *Please don't say dead, please don't say dead.* '. . . taken a turn for the worse.' Relief washes over me, then a new kind of panic sets in.

'What kind of turn?'

'She's had some problems with her breathing, developed a fever . . .' Amy's voice chokes up. I know she loves Peggy as much as I do. 'So we took her into hospital. It's pneumonia.'

Pneumonia? No. How is that possible? She was fine just days ago. Would she still have been fine if I had been able to visit? I know enough about pneumonia to know that's not the case, and yet I can't help but feel that had I been there I might have been able to help. If only just to take her to hospital.

'She's stable now,' Amy goes on. I can barely hear her over my thoughts: I should have been there. I should have been there.

'Oh thank God,' I breathe. 'I should have been to see her. I'm sorry, it was just so hectic. I should have put her first. I should have—'

'You were just doing your job,' Amy says, as if subtly reminding me that visiting the care homes and befriending the patients is above and beyond my remit. But she doesn't know about my grandma. How she wanted me to visit her one last time and I was too wrapped up in my own life to realise that it would be my last chance. I remember reading something about grief being the thing with feathers, but it sure as hell doesn't fly far enough away. 'She's stable now,' Amy repeats, but now I feel anything but, my legs chattering all the way down to my feet.

'Okay, thank you,' I say, my voice a little shaky too. 'I'll go and visit her now.'

'Max.' Amy sighs down the line. 'Visiting hours are over until tomorrow.'

I look down at my phone, a notification from Tom flashing across the screen: *Made it, mate, she's gorgeous.* He sent it almost an hour ago; they'll be well into their date by now. I thought I'd be in my book. I never saw this coming. But I should have, I categorically *should* have.

'Are you okay?' Amy asks. 'Do you want some company?'

'No, no, it's all right.' I look around our living room. It feels too big without Tom here. 'I think I just want to be alone.'

'Okay.' The silence stretches for too long. 'But Max? You do know you being there wouldn't have changed anything?'

I hang up the call, shards of our conversation suspended in the air. *She's stable now. You being there wouldn't have changed anything* . . . Maybe not for Peggy, but for me it would have, for me it would have meant everything. I can't help the guilt from rising all over again.

The calls from my mum feel like just yesterday. The one where she told me my grandmother was ill. The one where she told me Grandma was moving back to Mumbai to be closer to her siblings. The next where she asked me to go and visit her . . .

Mum, I've told you, I can't this summer – work is too busy and I'm going away with friends, I can't afford it . . .

So many excuses. Then the call that changed everything. *Max, I'm really sorry. It's Grandma, she passed in the night.* Passed in the night. Like she'd passed a parcel or passed a test. But no, she had *passed*. My smart, vibrant, funny grandma – the woman responsible for so much of who I am – was now in the *past*. Along with my chance to say goodbye. I won't let that happen again.

At least I do something that matters now, Grandma's death making me reassess everything: my priorities, my work at the bank. Now I have a job I love, where I can spend time with people like Peggy. To actually be there this time.

I think I just want to be alone. I replay my final words to Amy.

I'm pushing everyone away, keeping them at arm's length. But I'm just too much of a mess right now to let anyone in. Maybe that's the real reason I won't go online. Not because I won't find a great girl there, but because I'm just not that great a guy. How can I even contemplate letting someone in when I've let so many people down?

I'll make it up to Peggy tomorrow. Be there whenever she wants me to be.

But who will be there for you? The thought comes from nowhere.

And then another: *I want to message Becky.*

God, Max. Keep it together. I push the thought away, deep down with my grief. But now, with Tom out of the house and thoughts of Peggy and Grandma taking up space in my mind, I'm not just alone. I feel lonely. I feel really fucking lonely.

'Oh shit.' Tom's whisper is as loud as his normal voice. 'I didn't mean to wake you.'

'And I didn't mean to fall asleep.' I clear my throat to speak my first words in hours.

'Big night?' Tom comes to sit on the end of the sofa I'm lying across, picking up my discarded novel.

I look at him, not knowing whether to say anything, knowing that if I speak the words they'll begin to mean more than they should; signalling the beginning of the end for Peggy. Tom's brow crinkles in concern as he notices my bloodshot eyes.

'Just tired, I guess,' I say.

'Max?' Tom says my name seriously, probing me to say more.

'How was your date?'

'*Max?*' he repeats. His eyes narrow, as if to say: *you're not changing the subject, mate.*

'Peggy's in hospital.' I try to keep my voice under control.

'Oh shit, dude.' Tom's frame stiffens. 'What's happened?'

'Amy says she's got pneumonia.'

'Oh shit,' Tom says again, worry etched on his face. 'And? Is she okay now?'

'She's stable.' I repeat Amy's words, still on a loop in my mind.

'Well that's good.' Tom sighs, bending down to take off his shoes before moving across to the kitchen, opening the fridge and pulling out two cans of beer. He offers one to me and I accept, only then realising that I haven't really moved since I arrived home, since I got the call from Amy. 'But how are *you*?'

'I'm . . . yeah . . . I'm okay.'

'Max.' Tom says my name again, eyebrows raised. 'You can be honest with me.'

'Okay, yeah, I'm pretty shit, to be honest. It's just brought back lots of stuff . . .' My sentence trails into nothingness.

'Grandma stuff?' Tom asks. I used to talk to Tom about my grief before I started sounding like a broken record. I should be starting to mend by now.

'Yeah.' I shrug, not really knowing what to say next.

'I guess that's probably to be expected.' Tom isn't sure what to say either. 'Is there anything I can do to help?'

'Yes.' I smile at him. 'Tell me about your date with Becky.'

Tom's eyes linger on me for a moment and I know he's wondering whether to press me further, whether he should probe at the places that right now hurt like hell.

'What do you want to know?' He surrenders, grin growing wider.

'I don't really know.'

'That's not like you.' He looks at me with his head on one side.

He's right. I'm usually the one with the questions, but I just feel tired, thrashed around by the week. The phone call this evening was the final blow.

'Quick statistics and then more tomorrow?' he asks, clocking my puffy eyes.

'Deal.' I want to hear all about Becky, but right now I'm struggling to stay awake. 'Conversation?'

'A strong seven. She's so cute and funny – not as quick-witted as some of her messages, but kind of endearing.'

'So lots to talk about?'

'Yeah, managed to navigate all the book stuff, I think.' He grabs my novel and gives it a little wave. 'She's proper into that kind of thing,' he adds. 'You'll love her.'

I laugh, but for some reason it's a little forced.

'Attraction?' Tom asks, and answers his own question. 'At the start of the date, another seven; she's not my usual type,' he explains. Yes, I know. His usual type is Yvonne. Before her, it was easy-going girls who were just a bit too easy. 'But getting to know her boosted it to an eight and a half.'

'AL?' I have to ask about the Awkwardness Level, but he wouldn't be smiling like that if it was high.

'I'd say a two; there were some moments at the beginning. And then I fumbled on some French movie chat and I think she was, like, trying to dumb it down for me a bit, but apart from that, I'd say it was a solid first date. And, well, the sex?' My eyebrows climb upwards. Tom smiles. 'The only person I'm sleeping next to tonight is you.'

'You would be so lucky.' I force another laugh. 'So date number two?' I ask, surprised that we've got to the end of our statistics without a single mention of Yvonne. It's the first time that's happened since before they met.

'Yeah, I er . . . sort of need your help with that, bro.' He looks a little sheepish. 'I bottled it when we were saying goodbye. I was going to go in for the kiss, but then I remembered that Becky isn't like Ruby or Dami or the other girls I've dated lately . . .'

'I think her name was Dani . . .'

'That's not the point,' Tom says, but the look in his eyes tells me he feels bad for dating so many girls that he's started forgetting them. 'I just don't know the rules of *romance*.' He looks at me like I do, like I'm some sort of dating Yoda.

I glance at my novel, lying next to me on the sofa; at the stack of others building up in the corner of the room. I guess I know the theory.

'Need to sound like a knight in shining armour like you.' Tom laughs.

'Just be yourself,' I say for the thousandth time, trying to ignore his comment.

131

'Okay, I'll ask her to come over tomorrow to watch a movie.'

'Just be yourself but slower,' I amend. 'Let's sleep on it and message tomorrow.'

As Tom leaves the room, my thoughts return to Peggy. She's stable now, I remind myself, glad of Tom's distraction. Tomorrow is for stabilising things with him and Becky.

Chapter Twelve

Max

Light cascades into my room, dancing along the patchwork quilt my grandma stitched to life. I stretch my limbs to the four corners of the bed, and then I remember: *Peggy*.

As I move around my room, pulling on a hoodie, threading my legs into a pair of crumpled jeans, I imagine her small frame nestled in the corner of a too-big hospital bed. She's a fighter, I try to tell myself. And I am too. A fighter for families losing their loved ones long before they've taken their final breaths. I need to visit her before it's too late. I promised I would be there.

I promised Tom I'd be there for him too, to help him bag a second date with Becky. But then it's first thing on a Saturday morning; surely Tom will be training with a client by now?

Moving towards the living room door, I'm surprised to find it closed. I'm even more surprised to hear grunts and groans coming from behind it. I remember Tom's words from the night before: *Okay, I'll ask her to come over tomorrow.* I don't know much about online dating, but surely Netflix and chill only happens in the morning when it's the morning after the night before? Pushing open the door, I find Tom's topless body stretched horizontal across the floor, moving up and down with every pant and press.

'Have I just woken up in some teenage girl's brain?' I laugh, watching him work out.

'I did wonder that, dude,' he replies, not missing a beat. 'Turned the TV on to find some chick flick half watched on Netflix.' *Confessions of a Shopaholic.* Just one of the ways I tried to solve my insomnia last night. A mid-evening nap and a busy mind are not the easiest companions to snuggle up with at night.

'Thought you'd be training a client by now.' I try to change the subject as he halts mid press-up, managing to hold himself in a perfectly horizontal plank as he looks up.

'Kept my morning free just in case things got hot and sweaty with Becky,' he says, and for some reason the thought jars with me. Becky is more than one-night-stand material. 'Plus, the most crucial client is yourself, Max,' he adds earnestly before releasing his core to the carpet and sitting cross-legged on the floor.

'That something they tell you to say at the gym?' I laugh, moving towards the kitchen to put the kettle on. Tom reaches for his kettlebells. The gym he works at is this ultra-hip place with a wannabe-hip clientele who are mad about their mantras.

'It was until Peggy visited us, now she's everyone's most crucial client,' he replies. A few months back, he arranged for our patients to use the equipment for free, so there are now some new hips mingling with the hipsters. 'How is she?'

'I've not heard anything since Amy rang,' I call back over the sound of the kettle. Under normal circumstances, I know Tom would latch on to any mention of Amy, probing to see whether there was anything going on, but right now our minds are set on only one woman.

'I'm sure she'll be okay,' he says.

'Yeah, I'm going to go and see her this morning.'

'Can you help me message Bex first?'

Okay, so our minds are set on *two* women.

'I'm not sure she likes being called Bex,' I say as Tom makes his way into our little kitchenette, an impossibly small space that makes him look even bigger.

'How do you know that?'

'Well, she's got Becky on her profile, refers to herself as Becky in her stories . . .'

'Yeah, good point.' Tom sighs. 'See, this is why I need you to help me again.'

'Okay, okay.' I put a hand up in surrender. 'I'll go and see Peggy in an hour or so.' Even as I say it, worries rush around my mind, but I remind myself once again that she's stable. And that Tom is asking me to message a girl who may just be as bookish as me. 'What did you have in mind?' I ask.

Tom turns his phone around to face me.

Tom: Round two?

'You are joking, right?' I perch my coffee on the side and take the phone from him.

'I thought it was funny.' Tom looks genuinely out of his depth. I haven't seen him this way since she-who-shall-not-be-named.

'She's not a boxing opponent.' I shake my head.

'Well what would you suggest?' he asks, his eyes begging me to work my magic.

'Nothing to do with rings,' I quip.

'Who mentioned rings?' Tom looks shocked, like he's accidentally proposed again.

'I was making a boxing joke . . . Oh, it doesn't matter. How about this?'

Tom: Hey, thanks so much for a great evening. I hope you got home okay? X

Eve

'I got a text!'

I jump out of my skin, steadying myself by planting my hands against the tiles. With shampoo suds in my eyes, I move my hands like a mime.

'You're not in *Love Island*, Becky,' I shout over the sound of my shower. I don't need to see her to know she's sitting on the closed toilet lid, phone cradled in her hands. 'And nor am I. Can't a girl get a little privacy around here?'

'No, we're family.' She laughs. 'This is what family does.'

I can't help but think of my dad, of his letter, hidden out of sight. 'And no, we're not on the Love Island.' She says it like it's an actual holiday destination and not just a reality TV show. 'But you still got the reference.'

'Unfortunately,' I shout into the steam. 'Can you not wait until I'm finished to solicit my assistance . . .' My sentence trails off along with the shower. Damn it, the water pressure in this flat is so patchy. Just like the mould climbing up the walls, smattered across the ceiling. Man, we need to talk to Matilda. I can't win this fight alone. Nor can I finish this shower. Only one thing helps make the pressure come back . . .

'I'm on it,' Becky shouts from her spot on the toilet. She begins to pump the flush up and down, and before long, the shower pressure starts to pick up again. I wonder why that works. A big part of me hopes we never find out. Ignorance is bliss. Isn't it always? *Note to self: maybe you can just pretend you never got that letter?*

'Thanks for that.' I grab a towel from the rail and wrap it around me before stepping out of the shower. I swear Becky loves to be naked, but I have zero intention of baring all.

'You're welcome.' She smiles, a glimmer in her eye. 'Now you owe me.'

'Okay, okay,' I say, making my way towards the sink to brush my teeth. 'What did he say?' I gurgle through a mouthful of foamy mint.

'That he had a good time and hopes I got home okay.'

'But he didn't ask to see you again?' Even as I say it, I wish I hadn't.

'No, he didn't.' Becky's face fills with horror. 'He doesn't like me, does he? If he did, he would have asked by now. Maybe I just wasn't "Eve" enough for him?'

My mind scrambles to hold on to her last sentence. Does Tom want Becky to be more Eve? But no, he likes Becky; all the photos he's seen are hers. I just littered her profile with a bit of literature. Plus, what if he does? The thought makes me feel a bit sick. Becky likes him; the 'mates before dates' rule is now fully engaged.

'Of course he likes you,' I mumble, before spitting out my toothpaste and repeating the words. 'Of course he likes you; he's just starting a conversation, surveying the scene . . .'

'Like a detective?' Becky lights up. She's been watching those crime shows again.

'Yeah, like a detective,' I nod as she goes to type.

'Great, what should we say?' I don't know why she keeps saying 'we'.

'Let's make him wait a little longer,' I say, looking down at my crumpled workout gear on the floor. Make him sweat. I scoop it up, hoping Becky is too distracted by Tom to see it. I ran for over two hours last night; today should be a rest day. She knows I run too much, rest too little when I'm getting restless. But I'm just not ready to tell her about the letter yet.

She looks at me, content to follow my lead. Trusting me. Even though Tom's message isn't the only one left unanswered.

Max

'Maybe she's been mugged.' Tom looks at his screen, as empty as his coffee mug.

'She hasn't been *mugged*.' I shake my head, holding out a hand to refill his drink. I scoot past him to reach into the fridge, pulling out eggs, bacon and a rogue half an avocado that's been in there for far too long. Tom nods, squeezing into the space between us to grab a pan from one of the drawers and put it on the hob, our silent conversation lacing into our spoken one. *You do the eggs, I'll do the bacon.* 'And I thought I was the worrier?' I laugh.

'But she's read the message and she's not replied,' Tom moans. It's good to see him actually bothered for once. And carrying him through this is helping me feel lighter.

He looks at me and I nod vigorously at the smoke coming from the bacon, our wordless conversation still going strong: *would you put the extractor fan on? I'll get the plates.* Tom gets my messages even if he doesn't get Becky's, reaching across me to the switch.

'She'll just be making you sweat,' I say, looking at his glistening torso. 'And it's working.' I flip the bacon over, its glorious scent filling the room.

'Okay, maybe not *mugged*.' He bats away the thought. 'But maybe she tripped in those heels and hit her head and landed in a bush.'

'You're being ridiculous. Someone would have found her by now.'

'I don't know, dude, she's pretty small.'

'She's not in a bush.' I place two rashers of bacon on each of the rolls Tom has prepared.

'All right, maybe she's not in a bush. Maybe she crossed paths with another man who had just been on a date as well. Their eyes met and he asked, "Good date?" and she said, "It was all right," and he said, "Well I can show you a better one . . ."'

'And you think I'm the romantic,' I say as Tom slides a fried egg onto each of our rolls. 'That's a nice meet-cute.' I add a scoop of avo to each before closing them up.

'A meat what?' Tom looks worried.

'A meet-cu—' I stop as his phone buzzes.

Becky: Yeah I really enjoyed it too. And home safe, thanks for asking. X

Eve

'I still think we should have gone for "Becky can't come to the phone right now, she's been eaten by a massive bear".' Becky laughs as she hands me a bacon and egg sandwich. I wouldn't usually eat this, but it's the weekend, and I'm pretty sure I've burned about ten thousand calories in the last twenty-four hours. Half from running, half from my racing mind. 'Your message has just closed the conversation right down.'

'And getting eaten by a bear wouldn't?' I bite down hungrily on my bacon, happy to have Becky back in the flat.

And Lola on her way over. It's hard to think about my dad when the family I've built for myself is around.

'But what if he doesn't reply? If that's the conversation over?'

'Becky, if he gets put off by one message, he's not the man for you.' I stretch my legs along the sofa, my feet almost hanging off the end of it. I look from my socks to the wall, the mould spots I scrubbed off just yesterday now back with a vengeance. My nemesis. Out, damned spot! I wonder whether Tom is a Shakespeare guy. For a moment, dread fills my stomach. And not just because of the mischievous mould. What if he doesn't reply?

'We really need to talk to Matilda about the mould,' I say. 'And the shower. And the door. And the—'

'I messaged; she hasn't replied.' Becky's face says: *story of my life*.

'Tom's going to reply, Becky,' I say. I'm sure of it. As sure as him liking Shakespeare. 'It's not over until it's over.'

Max

'Well that's it, game over.' Tom looks up from Becky's reply.

'It's not game over,' I say. For a man who did a hundred press-ups before breakfast, he sure is quick to throw in the towel.

'Maybe I wasn't bookish enough,' he sighs. 'I know I said it went well, but I don't know, maybe I didn't remember everything you said. Maybe I should apologise for—'

'Don't apolo—' but I know he's already sending her a message.

Tom: Sorry if I wasn't entirely myself last night.
Becky: Why, who were you instead?
Tom: Just a shyer, fumbly version of me, I guess.

'Hey!' I grab the phone back from him.

'I know, I know . . . do not apologise for who I am.' Tom repeats the line I've told him so many times post-Yvonne.

'No, don't apologise for who *I* am.' I try to laugh away his latest message: am I a shyer, fumbly version of Tom?

'I wasn't, but seriously, dude, I was a bumbling idiot half the night. No wonder she doesn't want a second date. Help a brother out.' He passes the phone my way, and not-so-reluctantly I begin to type.

Tom: Do you usually have that effect on guys?
Tom: I think you make me shy, ha.

Eve

'Oh shit, I was too much.' Becky throws a hand to her forehead. 'I knew I was too much.' She's snuggling into my side now, Buster on the other. She would have been bubbly, fun. But she wouldn't have been too much. 'I did my walrus impression,' she confesses.

'Not with the straws?'

'With the straws!' she cries.

'No!' Her impression is hilarious. But it's not first-date material. I thought she knew that. 'Repeat after me: only one woman can pull that off, only one woman can . . .'

'Rachel Green, Rachel Green,' she chants back to me. 'Fix it?' She thrusts her phone at me.

'Sure, where's the time-machine setting?' I pretend to search the phone in my hands.

'I'm serious,' Becky moans, her big brown eyes pleading.

I know I shouldn't be this involved, that if Tom and Becky are going to stand a chance, she's going to have to type herself, to be herself. But they just need to get to know each other better. And if we don't get this second date, they might not have the chance. Okay, here goes.

Becky: They usually just buy me dinner, buy me
    flowers . . .
Tom: Sweet. Any cars?
Becky: Just the Ferrari – oh, and one Porsche, but it
    gets a bit boring after a while.
Tom: Yeah, sounds pretty dull.
Tom: I promise the only Porsche you'll be getting from
    me is the Shakespeare variety.
Becky: Aha! I knew you were a Shakespeare man!
Becky: But I'm pretty sure it's Portia?
Tom: And she passes the test with flying colours.
Becky: Didn't know we had an observer in the house.
Tom: *Observer*? More of a *Guardian* man myself.
Becky: Ha! That's not what I meant.

Becky: But me too.

Becky: Well, apart from the man part.

Tom: Thank God.

Tom: I mean I'm open-minded and everything, but I've only got room for one man in my life.

Becky: Shakespeare?

Tom: Okay, maybe two.

Tom: Willie Shakespeare and my housemate Max. He's pretty great.

Max

'*Dude!*' Tom grabs the phone back from me and I can't help but laugh. This is too much fun. For a second I think of Peggy, the guilt over my grandma, the fact that I should be at the hospital by now. But I'm feeling calmer, lighter. Everything feels better in the morning, each new day bringing a new perspective. 'Keep to the script!'

'Mate, I'm *writing* the script,' I tell him.

'Yes, but we want Becky to like *me*, not my *pretty great* housemate.' Tom narrows his eyes. He's not actually that insecure, is he? Becky would never go for a guy like me. 'Just help me ask her out.' He passes the phone back to me.

'Okay, okay.' I smile, our living room filling with light. 'I can write to a brief . . .'

Becky: Bet my housemate's better.

Tom: You're on.

Tom: How are we going to settle it?

Becky: We could make them race?

Tom: Max says can he borrow your Porsche?

'What's she saying?' Tom looks over my shoulder at the screen.

'That her friend's better than yours.'

'Only one way to know for sure.' He grins. 'Double date?'

'I don't want to double date.' I don't want to date full stop. Well, not really.

'Please, dude.' Tom's eyes beg me. 'I could really do with the backup. Just until we get up and running.'

'I'm not sure that's a good—'

'*Please?*' he asks again, and even though I know he should go it alone, I really want to help him. Plus helping Tom is helping me feel less alone in the process.

'Fine.' I roll my eyes and begin to type, trying to ignore the butterflies in my stomach.

Tom: There's only one way to settle this.

Tom: Dinner. BYOBF.

Becky: BYOBF?

Tom: Bring your own best friend.

Eve

I read Tom's messages, not sure why they're giving me butterflies. Probably just the buzz of Becky's romance beginning. *Note to self: this is nothing to do with you.*

'Oh please, that will be so much fun,' Becky begs beside me.

'I'm busy this weekend, and all this week . . .' I need to focus on work.

'It can wait.' Becky grins, as if she's learning from the best. I'm out of my depth.

'You sure?'

'Only if you help me keep things ticking along with Tom until then.'

'You can do that by yourself,' I say, secretly loving the feeling of being needed.

'I know, but it's so much easier with you.'

Chapter Thirteen

Eve

The blue banner of my maps app catches my attention from behind the article I'm reading: *you have reached your destination*. I push the glass door into the restaurant with one hand, the other still holding the screen safely in view. The music and chatter hits me as soon as I walk in, the dim fairy-light-spotted stairs up to the dining area demanding I surrender my scrolling. I'll have to finish reading the rest of the article later.

Ascending the bookcase-lined stairs, I read spine after spine as I go: *Pride and Prejudice, The Great Gatsby, The Catcher in the Rye* . . . My eyes feast all the way until a waiter passes me holding two plates piled with food.

'We've got a table booked for four,' I say to the stunning waitress in front of me. She's dressed in skin-tight black, attire almost as stylish as the space behind her.

'What name is it under?'

'Tom . . .' My eyes scan the tables, searching for sight of him.

'Last name?' She looks at me and I know I should remember. I know his favourite book, his favourite drink, his favourite meal. But I can't for the life of me remember his last name. Tonight is going to be weird. Too weird. My anxiety accelerates at the thought.

'It's booked for four at seven,' I say, a little panicked. 'I know he asked for the table in the window.' I messaged him about it last night. Well, as Becky.

'Could it be under a Max Charan?'

Max, yes. Max is the friend.

'That's it, yes.' I smile, trying not to look so worried.

Tonight will be fine. Tonight will have to be fine.

I follow the waitress across the floor towards the window. Pulling out a velvet-covered chair, I gaze over a traffic-twinkling Farringdon Street. I'm surrounded by dusty old books. And house plants, illuminated by fairy lights twisting through their branches. Famous quotes are scribbled on all sides. The ethereal atmosphere starts to slow my heart rate. Maybe tonight will actually be okay. Maybe meeting Tom is exactly what I need to make sense of the space he's occupying in my mind. *Note to self: you're only thinking about him to force out thoughts of your dad.* Well, maybe that's right. I still haven't told Becky about his letter. And if I tell her now, she'll wonder what took me so long.

What's taking *her* so long? I look around the restaurant, then down at my phone. No messages from Becky, but a hundred between her and Tom on the app. *Note to self: you promised you wouldn't read them without her here.* Just ignore them, Eve.

As I'm about to lock my screen, a new email flashes across it. It's from the cystic fibrosis foundation. I emailed them to ask if they could connect me with this bereaved family who I thought might be ready to talk about their experience to bring the issue to light. And to publicise the incredible fund-raising efforts they're making to fight it. I read the message under my breath: *We love what you're doing, Eve, but the family have informed us they don't want to speak to the media.* I sigh. All the best human-interest stories seem to find their way onto personal blogs rather than into the national papers, where they could reach a wider audience. But these stories are still out there, I just need to find one – one family turning heartbreak into something magical, something that matters. Then I need to convince the management team that these stories matter too.

'Oh man, I'm so late,' Becky says, make-up smudged under tired eyes, her hair a bird's nest. 'I forgot I had detention.'

'What did you do now?' I laugh.

'Well Homework Club, but it's essentially the same thing,' Becky says, ignoring my joke completely.

'They've not arrived yet,' I say, beckoning her to sit down, to breathe, just breathe.

'I know.' She clutches her tote closer to her chest. 'Tom's been messaging me the whole way here. He's just said something about a new study on running and mental health that Nike have just brought out. Can you say something about your experience?' She holds her phone out to me.

149

'Becky, you've been on a run before.' I really shouldn't be playing the role of Tom's online lover any more. Especially now that I'm about to meet him in the flesh.

'The only place I need to run is the bathroom to sort this mess out.' She pushes the phone across the table, smudged eyes filling with fear. '*Please?*'

'Fine, fine,' I say.

'Or you could just log on to my profile on your phone?'

'No, no, it's okay. Just go.'

I don't know why I'm reluctant to log on to the app on my phone. Why all of a sudden I feel like I need the boundary. Why I feel like for the first time in a long time I may be tempted to cross it.

Max

'Crossing the road, dude,' I say, ushering a phone-holding Tom away from the oncoming traffic. I quite literally don't know how he survives without me. 'And now a lamp post.' I grab his shoulder to steer him right. Just like I steered him right towards Becky. She's about to become a reality to me, rather than just a nice idea for my friend. My heart starts to race as we get closer and closer to the glass walls of the Fable.

'Bro, can you help me with something?' Tom asks, still staring at his screen.

'I've saved your life about three times in the last three minutes,' I point out, and it's only then that he bothers to look up.

'Becky's just mentioned something about a sport initiative I've never heard of.'

'I thought sport was your specialist subject?' I say. Mine would be nineteenth-century literature. Either that or *Great British Bake Off* trivia that no self-respecting twenty-seven-year-old man would ever need to know.

'I think this falls more into the charity category.' Tom looks out of his depth. 'Something about a girls' football scheme. Didn't have her down as a football fan.'

'I don't think she is,' I muse, mind filtering through my Becky trivia; I'm surprised to find there's quite a lot of it stored in there. 'She just keeps abreast of current affairs.'

'Who said anything about her breasts?' Tom looks startled.

'No, *abreast*,' I correct, though I can tell his mind is elsewhere, racking his brain for what he knows about charity schemes. 'We're nearly at the restaurant; can't it wait?'

'And risk having to fumble through this face to face? Please, dude?' he pleads.

'Fine, fine,' I say, taking the phone from him.

Tom: Level Playing Field? Yeah, it's a great scheme. Did you hear they got funding?

Becky: Yeah, read it this morning. It's amazing. Business bods using the pitch paying for schoolgirls from disadvantaged backgrounds to play for free? It's bloody genius.

Tom: Yeah. Wish I'd thought of it.

Becky: And the name? Brilliant.

Tom: Yeah, it works on so many levels.

151

Tom: Pun not intended.

Becky: Provided you're not playing the field. Becky doesn't introduce her bestie to just anyone.

Tom: Did you just refer to yourself in the third person?

Becky: Maybe. So what?

Tom: Ha! Just one player in my sights at the moment.

Becky: Well I can't see you right now. And Eve hates people being late. ETA?

Tom: Just walking in now.

I look up from Tom's phone to follow him into the fray. The Fable is as lively as ever, a low hum of activity matching its sultry hues. Climbing the stairs to the main restaurant, I look up at the large purple sign suspended from the ceiling – *Once in a while in the middle of an ordinary life, life gives you a fairy tale* – before we're ushered towards my favourite table in the window.

A single figure sits there smiling into her phone, and I know it's not Becky. Light blonde hair falls poker straight, framing a fair-skinned face warmed by rose-kissed cheeks. Even sitting down she looks tall, one milky-white leg folded over the other, but she wears her height well. Just like the red fabric falling loose down her arms, floaty hemline folding flirtatiously around her thighs. She must be six foot, but in the flickering fairy light she could still pass for a pixie. As we walk closer, she lifts her chin, her green eyes scanning the sheer size of Tom before settling on me.

Eve

I look up from messaging Tom to see him in the flesh. All of him. And there's a lot. Six foot three or four. Muscles for days. He's exactly like his photos, but bigger. And those blue eyes? No photo could ever capture them. He fixes them on me, and I panic. This is Becky's date. *Becky's date*, I repeat to myself, forcing the beat of my heart to steady. Forcing my eyes to the friend.

Max is smaller than Tom, but he's still tall, probably as tall as me. He's good-looking too: a messy mop of dark hair, stubble lining his sharp jaw. Deep brown eyes and a strong nose and lightly tanned skin. He's looking at me too. But of course he is; I'm sitting at Tom and Becky's table, typing to Tom on Becky's phone. I reach to turn it face down as they approach. Stop staring, Eve. Just smile. Or stand. Just do something.

'You must be Eve?' Tom opens his arms a little and I stand to kiss him on the cheek. He goes in for a second, catching me completely unawares, my greeting croaking in my throat. He's here. The man I've been messaging night after night. I move to welcome Max, nailing the two-kiss routine second time around. 'I've been stood up?' Tom looks to the empty space around our small circular table as they both sit down.

'I'm here, I'm here,' Becky arrives behind him, leaning down to embrace him. Max shoots up beside her to shake her hand, formal and awkward. But Becky ignores the handshake and throws her tiny arms around him. Max's outstretched hand is trapped between them.

'What took you so long?' I mutter as soon as she's beside me. But I can already tell. Her face is freshly made-up. Hair slicked back in a high pony. Perfume spritzed in all the right places.

Tom overhears my question. 'It's my fault,' he says apologetically. 'I've been distracting her with messages. We both saw that this social enterprise we've been following finally received funding today. We were just too excited about it to wait – plus we didn't want to bore you with it.' He looks at me earnestly. He has no idea the only person he'd be boring with that is Becky.

I look at her now, a deer in the headlights: *What? What initiative?* She leans her elbows on the table, subtly reaching for her phone.

'Level Playing Field?' I say before she has a chance to incriminate herself. 'Yeah, Becky was telling me all about it too.' I will her to focus on the next words to fall from my mouth. 'An initiative to empower schoolgirls to play football in their own community – it's brilliant! Plus we *love* the name.'

'Right, what are we having?' Max says, changing the topic abruptly. Maybe he's hungry, I think. Skipped lunch at work. What is it he does again?

'My head says duck salad,' Becky speaks into her menu, 'but my heart says sticky ribs.' Her eyes widen, guilty as sin. Mine dart from Tom to my menu, trying not to look guilty myself. Panic starts to rise before I sip it back into place with my drink.

'Well, you did run this morning,' Tom assures her with a smile as big as the rest of him. I choke on my water and all eyes look at me.

'Went down the wrong way,' I mumble.

'Anyone want to share small plates?' Max searches for takers. Classic millennial. Struggling to commit to just one thing.

'What do you fancy?' Tom asks me.

Sickness churns in my stomach and I have a horrible feeling it's more than just hunger. I *can't* fancy Tom. It's just our messages. I search the menu, struggling to read the words. I usually know exactly what I want, but right now? Oh God, I really don't know.

Max

As I reach to the charcuterie board in the middle of the table, Becky's hand touches mine, both of us going for the last slice of salami. For the briefest of moments our eyes meet, and I wonder whether she has any idea that these are the hands that have messaged her so often. It's strange seeing her in the flesh. She seems pretty nervous too. Not nearly as natural and quick-witted as her messages, but then I for one know just how easy it is to come across better on the page, when you have more time to think, the freedom to say exactly what you feel. Well, not how *I* feel but how Tom feels. She's here for Tom. And I'm here for Tom too; yet another thing we have in common. I surrender the salami and her beautiful smile spreads even wider.

155

'How great is this place?' I look at the quotes on the walls and the books beside us. There was a reason I picked it: I knew Becky would be on her best form when surrounded by books.

'I love it here,' Eve agrees, as if the restaurant has been on her radar for some time.

'It's amazing,' Becky hums back at me, eyes wide. 'Like a proper fairy tale.'

'But not like a *proper* fairy tale,' I laugh. 'They were never this *nice*.' Becky looks at me as though I've just killed Christmas. 'Society seems to have sanitised the stories along the way.' Even though I'm sure I've talked to her about this before as Tom, she looks completely lost. 'Not many of them were set in an enchanted forest like this one,' I add.

'*Shrek* is set in an enchanted forest,' she says, and I laugh hard over my lager. She, on the other hand, is deadpan. Clearly Tom has shared his love of that stupid movie with her, and now she's pulling his leg. I knew her humour was dry, but she's not even cracking a smile.

'But back in the day, fairy tales used to be pretty *grim*,' Eve says, and I know she's referencing the Brothers Grimm; that she and I are on the same page.

'Like Hansel and Gretel kidnapped by a cannibalistic witch,' I agree.

'Though she lived in a house made out of gingerbread,' Becky points out.

'Still not sweet enough to satisfy her hunger for children.'

Eve laughs. 'How about the Pied Piper of Hamelin?' she says, while Becky and Tom look confused.

'Eurgh, yeah, leading children away like rats with his pipe. *All* pretty grim, to be honest. But then loads of the children's classics are.'

'Yeah, Lewis Carroll always freaked me out as a child,' Eve says, her eyes now on mine. I can only imagine the chats she and Becky have about this kind of stuff around theirs.

'Lewis Carroll?' Becky interjects, keen to chip in. 'You're entirely bonkers . . .' She begins to quote from *Alice in Wonderland*, then stutters to a halt like she's forgotten what comes next.

'But I'll tell you a secret,' I prompt, feeding her the next line.

'All the best people are.' She beams at me as she finishes the quote, and for a second, I see a glimpse of the Becky I've been talking to this whole time. Well, that Tom has been talking to.

'*Alice*?' I can't help but laugh, keen to discuss the book further.

'Becky.' She looks a little taken aback. It was much easier to keep up with her offbeat humour onscreen.

'Good one, Becky!' Eve gives her a playful nudge. 'We all know you were quoting *Alice in Wonderland*.'

'I was?' Becky looks confused; White Rabbit caught in the headlights. 'I was!'

157

Eve

'What was all that about?' I turn to Becky as soon as Max and Tom are out of earshot, checking out the draught beers at the bar.

'What?' Becky looks nonplussed.

'Alice?' I say, trying not to laugh. Why was she quoting books she doesn't know?

'Oh, I read the quote on the mirror in the toilet earlier. You and Max were chatting all that fairy-tale malarkey, and Tom thinks I'm good at that stuff so I thought I'd say it, and then . . . then I totally blanked and forgot how it ended, and I had no idea what book it came from.'

My mouth hangs open, ready to say something, anything that will make her feel like being herself is okay. But then aren't I the one who helped her be more like the person Tom would want to be with? Before I can think of anything decent to say, our mains materialise, and so do our men. Well, not *our* men, *the* men. I watch as Tom takes his seat next to Becky and smiles at her. He's a lot shyer than I imagined him. He reaches out and picks up a nearby book, turning it over in his big hands.

'Oh I love this one,' he says. He sounds a little wooden, as if he's reading a script. But then maybe Becky has that effect on him. Wasn't that what he said in one of his messages after their first date: *I think you make me shy.*

I clock the book: George Orwell's *1984*. Man, I love that one too. I love how Tom looks holding it.

No, Eve, no. I force myself to look down at my food. What the hell am I thinking? I'm not sure I'm thinking at all. I'm just so tired post-work, post-letter, in need of that promotion, in need of something else. *Note to self: do not fixate on the one thing you cannot have.*

'It's such a commentary for where we are now, Big Brother's constant surveillance,' Tom is saying.

I push my food around my plate, feeling a little sick. Part of me loves that Tom is perfect. He's with my best friend after all. Another part of me can't help but feel he's pretty perfect for me.

'Oh man, talk about *drama*.' Becky looks up from her sticky ribs. I try to catch her eye, to warn her. When she ignores me, I kick her under the table. Big Brother is not a TV show. It's an idea. In a book. Surely she knows that?

'Ow.' Max nurses his leg.

'I'm so sorry,' I mouth across to him, but he's already smiling, shaking my apology away.

'I know, the depiction of sex throughout . . .' Tom says, self-conscious with Becky's eyes on him.

'Series Three? I know, but it was after the watershed . . .'

'*Animal Farm*!' I shout over Becky to no one in particular. All three of them look at me like I'm mad.

'Now *that's* a good book.' Max saves me. Oh thank God. I glance at Tom; he looks confused. To be fair, it took me a long time to digest that book too. 'All animals are equal, but some animals are more equal than others,' Max says.

Opposite me, Tom cuts into his chorizo. A chunk flies across the table, leaving a mark on my dress.

'I'm *so* sorry, Eve.' He looks mortified for a moment.

'It's okay,' I laugh. 'It's good to know the pigs are still on top.'

Max

I brush a stray tear from my eye, my body still heaving. I'm trying to pull myself together, but Eve's *Animal Farm* joke may have just killed me.

'At least someone got it,' she says, eyes darting to Tom in something like confusion.

I look at Becky in the same way, sure that George Orwell must have been on her must-read list. The two of them get up to powder their noses or do whatever girls in loos do, leaving me and Tom to wait for the bill. I know better than to think feminist Becky will let us pay.

'Dude, stop making me look bad,' Tom says as soon as they're a safe distance away.

'Oh, I . . . I wasn't trying to,' I reply, stunned.

'Well you are.'

'I was just trying to help.' Like you asked me to. Like you've asked me to for weeks.

'I know . . . it's just . . .' Tom looks upset, and my stomach plummets to the floor.

I was just trying to help the conversation along. Well, and maybe get Becky talking about some of the topics she buzzes about in her texts. Dammit, Max, stop thinking about Becky. She's not yours to think about. I look at Tom, my housemate, my best friend, and I feel bloody awful. I don't like Becky. I do *not* like Becky.

Eve

'I think Tom likes you.' Becky looks at me in the mirror as she brushes her ponytail.

'Do you think?' I smile back at her reflection. 'That's good.'

'No, I think he *really* likes you.' Her smile is gone. 'Like he would rather be here with you. I mean, it's you who fed me all my cultured lines. I feel like I'm drowning out there.'

'You are *not* drowning.' I look at my best friend, all worried and insecure, and feel sicker than I have all meal. She really likes Tom. And Tom really likes her. It's obvious. 'And remember what Coco Chanel said: real beauty begins when you just decide to be yourself.'

'See! I don't know quotes and stuff like that, I don't know any—'

'Becky, it's written on the mirror behind you.' I force a laugh, but I know she isn't finding it funny. 'Plus he *clearly* really likes you.' I turn to face her. 'And why wouldn't he? You look stunning and you're smart and he's not been able to take his eyes off you all meal.' It's totally my problem that I've not been able to take my eyes off *him*. I'm just trying to work him out. Filter real feelings from the fake.

'Do you think so?' Becky's eyes plead with me.

'I *know* so.' I put my hands on her shoulders and give her

a little squeeze. 'Now go get your man!' I try to inject some excitement into my voice, but for some reason my eyes are welling with tears. Stop it, Eve. Stop it. It's just seeing the results of our communication here in the flesh, knowing they're not going to need me now.

'Eve, what's the matter?' Becky looks at me with concern.

'It's just everything with work, going for this promotion . . .'

'I know, it's a lot.' She puts a hand on my arm.

'Nothing a big sleep won't cure,' I say, hoping to God that's true.

'About that . . . Would it be okay with you if I stay at Tom's tonight?'

'You don't have to ask my permission,' I say, though I can taste the irony as I speak. She's been asking my permission for weeks: to send the right messages, the right signals, at the right moments. Like I'm any good at it myself.

'I know, it's just I've really been trying to take it slow this time.' She says it as if there are no secrets between us.

Which makes me feel even worse. Because let's face it, I have a couple of my own. There's my dad's letter. The fact that I'm stressing about my family. That I'm stressing about hers. Then there are these weird mixed feelings I have for Tom. The ones I can't make sense of. *Note to self: you are a good friend.*

Another note to self: you're a fucking liar.

No I'm not. I'm just tired. Overtired. Overworked. Over-emotional.

'Exciting,' I say, feeling like it's anything but. 'You ready to go now?'

162

'Yeah, but if you want to stay for a bit longer, I'm sure Max would love that.' Becky beams. 'You guys seem to be getting on well?' Her eyebrows rise to the ceiling. As if she's seen something I haven't. Thankfully, she hasn't seen it all.

'What are you insinuating?' I ask, happy to deflect the attention from Tom.

'I think he likes you,' she says, even though just moments ago she was telling me Tom did.

Max

It doesn't take long after the girls return from the bathroom and we've argued back and forth about the bill for the atmosphere to change. On one side of the table, Becky and Tom fold further into one another, her hand now laced in his, his other hand stroking the top of her leg under the table. I don't want to watch but I can't look away, the shifting ambience shifting my mood. So Becky's coming back with Tom, what does it matter? If I had a penny for every date Tom had brought back to ours, I'd probably be able to afford my own place. But right now, with my loneliness forcing its way into the forefront of my mind, I'm not entirely sure my own place is what I'd spend my millions on.

'Time to call it a night?' Tom smiles in mine and Eve's direction. He's clearly not addressing Becky; *their* night is just beginning. And sadly, so is mine. A long evening with the duvet over my head, pillow wrapped around my ears, trying not to think about whatever is happening in the next room.

Oh God, the thought makes me feel sick. And yet the fact that it does is even more excruciating. I don't like Becky, I can't like Becky. She isn't mine to like.

'Shall we all share an Uber, drop you off on the way?' Becky turns to Eve, looking a little sorry though for what I'm not quite sure. Maybe the fact that Eve and I are about to endure the most awkward journey of our lives, just two plus-ones feeling less and less invited.

'I think I want to walk,' Eve says, and I swear I see something like sadness flit across her face before she replaces it with a smile. Is she okay?

'You can't walk by yourself.' Becky shakes her ponytail; it's so lush and bouncy. Oh Max, stop it. You don't like Becky, you just like her words. Words I need to keep well away from. My mind shoots to our sticky bathroom door, the memory of Ruby in the shower turning to Becky in my mind's eye.

'I could walk with you,' I say, any excuse to avoid that cab ride before taking the really long way home. Any excuse to avoid sounds and sights I don't need to witness.

'No, no, you really don't have to . . .' Eve begins.

'That would be great, Max,' Becky beams as Eve prickles beside her. No one wants to be left with the booby prize.

As if too tired to argue, Eve nods and we all make our way downstairs, the 'love gives us a fairy tale' sign mocking me as Becky and Tom walk hand in hand in front. Outside the restaurant, Tom claps me on the back.

'See you at home, dude,' he says before lowering his voice. 'Thanks for walking Eve.'

'You're the best.' Becky throws her little arms around me and the scent of her honey shampoo fills my mind, bringing it alive with hope and colour until she lets me go.

'Camden, right?' I turn to Eve, and unlike with Becky, I don't need to look down. But Becky's with Tom now; I have to stop thinking about her. Time for fresh air and fresh thoughts and fresh conversation with Eve. 'Great evening, wasn't it?'

'Yeah,' she says, forcing a smile. She'd no doubt rather be alone, but I don't want to be with Becky and Tom right now. 'Got much planned for the rest of the weekend?'

'I'm working on a series of articles for a work project,' she explains.

'It's journalism, right?'

'Right.' This time her smile seems a little less strained.

'What sort of thing do you write about?' I ask, genuinely interested.

'Honestly?'

I nod. Honesty is always the best policy, so why do I feel like I'm lying to Tom? Perhaps even lying to myself.

'My main job is writing for the newspaper's Thursday supplement,' she says. 'But I'm far more interested in covering human-interest stories, strong narratives that prompt change.' She says the last bit with poise, like she's rehearsed it countless times before.

'Balancing the passion projects with getting the job done; I understand that.' I breathe into the evening air. Did I just refer to Peggy and the other service users as a *project*?

'What is it you do again?' Eve turns to me, long legs striding at pace. At this rate we'll be in Camden in no time.

'Director of fund-raising for a dementia charity,' I say, even though I rarely tell anyone my new title.

As we walk, I tell her the basics, only then realising that we didn't really cover them over dinner, too busy keeping up with Tom and Becky.

'So what you're saying is you're a pretty big deal?' Eve grins.

I didn't say that, did I?

'A pretty big deal in a pretty small place,' I agree with a laugh.

'Better than being a little fish in a big pond,' she sighs; it's obvious she knows what that feels like.

'So tell me about a piece you're working on now. One you actually care about,' I say before she can reel off more clickbait headlines she's written for the supplement.

'Well, I've been looking for health-related stories, ones that raise awareness. Families living with cystic fibrosis, fighting cancer, alcoholism; the stories the newspaper thinks we've heard again and again without realising that everybody's story is unique.'

'Sounds like you're developing a column,' I muse out loud, happy to be distracted.

Eve looks at me, smile wide and genuine, and for just a moment I feel like she's happy to have me here, crashing her thousand-mile-an-hour walk. 'I'm developing a column,' she repeats, then laughs as if a penny has just dropped. Surely she didn't need me to point that out?

'What's the next story about?' I ask.

'Do you really want to know?'

166

'Of course I want to know,' I say like she's bonkers; but then *all the best people are . . .*

Eve

To start with, I didn't want Max to join me on my walk. I wanted to be alone to clear my head, to clear it of Tom and whatever he and Becky are doing now. To question why the thought bothered me in the first place. But now here he is, genuinely listening to my article ideas in a way few people ever have.

'Becky usually has a one-article attention span,' I tell him. Unlike Tom, enticing and intimidating, Max feels like a safe space. 'And my friend Makena can maybe take one and a half before she brings the conversation back to whatever tacky task we have to do that day.' His eyes are fixed on me the whole time. I swear he'll walk into a lamp post or something if he's not careful. 'Makena's my work wife,' I add.

'Work wife?'

'Like my best friend at work, the person I spend the most time with other than Becky,' I say, not meaning to sound so sad. It's just that if Becky's going to start stopping around at Tom's, Makena might beat her to the top spot. 'Don't you have one?'

'A work wife?' Max laughs. 'Well, there's Heather, but she's got her own husband and they're both in their sixties, and then there's Paddy . . .' he laughs again, harder this time, 'but to be honest, I'd rather keep looking. Still, at least he's passionate about what we do. His grandma has dementia,' he explains.

I wonder if Max has some connection to the disease too. I'm pretty sure Tom told me – well, told Becky – that the two of them met working for a bank. So what prompted the change?

'Do you have a personal tie to the charity? A reason to be there?' I ask into the air as our final destination draws closer and closer.

'I . . .' He stutters for a second that seems to stretch between us. 'Hey! Are you just trying to dig for another story?' He laughs away my question.

No, I wasn't really thinking about that. *Millennial man inspired to leave banker salary and dedicate life to those living with dementia.* I guess it would fit with the pieces I've been trying to pitch; the new *column* I'm trying to pitch. Before I can ask again, though, we arrive at the flat.

'This you?' Max gazes up at our town house. It looks nicer from the outside.

'Well, round the back,' I say, eyes darting down the dark side of the house.

'I'm afraid I promised I'd walk you to the door,' he says, as if dreading Becky's wrath.

When we reach the back of the house, Buster springs up the basement stairs like a guard dog.

'Cute cat,' Max says.

Buster purrs, which is categorically not like him, and I pick him up, holding his furry body like a barrier between us. Though I don't feel like Max is going to kiss me or anything. Not one bit. 'And thanks for the chat.'

'Any time.' Max shrugs. 'No doubt speak to you soon.'

I turn my key in the lock and give Max one last smile. Then as soon as he's out of sight, I kick the door, hard, and it flies open. If he was to see this, he'd think I was breaking in. Like I was lying about living here. But I wasn't lying about that – just about so many other things.

Kicking off my shoes, I look into the darkness. I'm completely alone. Well, apart from Buster. Maybe I should get used to that now. I switch on the kitchen light and lean against the worktop, my heartbeat starting to accelerate. I want to run, to run this feeling out. But then there's every chance I'd run right past Max. It was nice of him to walk me home. But now he'll be heading back to his and Tom's.

Before I realise it, tears are prickling in my eyes, spilling down my cheeks. My chest heaves, my heart feels heavy. Heavy with doubt, with confusion, with fear. I cry harder, thinking of Max: his kindness, his encouragement. He looked at me like I had it all together, but really I'm just a fraud. My thoughts shoot to Tom, wondering how our little messages amounted to so much. And then I think of Becky. Why does all this feel like betrayal?

Come on, Eve, hold it together. I reach for my phone. Headspace? I don't feel like more silence right now. Datespace? Redundant, my role in Becky's romance now complete. I could get my own profile, but I don't have time. I need to focus, focus on getting this new role, stepping up, stepping into the only thing that matters. Telling the stories that matter.

As I push myself away from the worktop, my foot catches

on something. I look down to see a pile of letters held together by an elastic band, a Post-it note stuck to the top one. No one ever sends us post here. I pick it up and read the note: *These came to the office after you left. Was passing by. M x*

So, Makena can find our door now? I flick through the letters. Bills. Junk. Bank statement. Wedding invite.

Then that handwriting again. That stupid fucking handwriting. I don't need this now. Don't need *him*. I don't need my dad.

Chapter Fourteen

Max

'I'm here to see Margaret Gable.' I smile down at the man on reception, even though everything in me wants to scream. I hate hospitals – how they look, how they smell. But I love what they do. Taking care of people when they need it most.

'Are you a family member?' the receptionist asks. It's a perfectly simple question, one I've been asked every time I've been to visit Peggy since she was admitted, so I'm not sure why the answer feels so complicated. No, I'm not technically a member of Peggy's family. But right now, I'm all the family she has.

'I'm one of the volunteers at her care home,' I explain.

The man picks up the phone. After a minute or so, he puts his hand over the receiver. 'You're with Amy, right?'

'No, I'm not with . . .' I start, before his eyes widen as if to tell me it would be easier if I was. 'Yes, I'm with Amy,'

I sigh. And now that Tom is officially with Becky, maybe it would be easier for everyone if I actually was. .

'Peggy.' I reach a hand to rest gently on hers as she opens her eyes. I hate seeing her in here, seeing someone so full of life edging closer to the end of it. She's better than the first time I visited her, just after Amy's call almost three weeks ago. But she's still a shadow of herself. Maybe it's a good thing I didn't see my grandma like this. Easier to remember the opinionated, optimistic woman I knew. But only easier for me. It would have been harder for her. Still, I'm here now, writing memories all over again.

'Who . . . who are . . .' she stutters. Her frame is thinner, her movements fragile. 'Who are you?'

'It's Max.' I look into her tired eyes, hoping to calm her confusion.

'Who?' She looks around her for a reference point, scared and bewildered.

'Max from the care home,' I say, heart hammering hard against my chest.

'Max,' she whispers, her breath weak, before a little smile circles her lips. No, she can't be . . . 'I'm just pulling your leg, I recognise you really.' Her laughter erupts into the ward around us, the coughing fit that follows reminding us both how unwell she is.

'Peggy!' I put a hand to my heart, for the first time in a long time glad to be in a hospital; I'm pretty sure she almost gave me a heart attack. 'Don't do that to me.'

'Gets you every time,' she laughs, her sense of humour still strong despite her physical frailty. 'What are you doing here?'

'Visiting my favourite patient, of course.'

'Exactly,' Peggy confirms, as if I'm the one who needs reorienting here. 'What are you doing visiting a seventy-something-year-old woman on your weekend again?'

'Peggy, you're eighty-four . . .'

'Won't let me forget about anything, will you?' Her raspy laugh fills the ward around us again.

'Because I want to.' I reach to hold her hand once more, squeezing it a little tighter. Because I didn't visit Grandma. Because Tom is busy visiting Becky.

'But it's not your job to.' Peggy shakes her head. 'What's this new role again?'

'Director of fund-raising,' I tell her, remembering how my job impressed Eve. Peggy smiles, seemingly impressed too. Am I the only one who thinks I'm a fraud? 'To be honest, I'm not sure I'm making a good job of it—'

'And I'm the one who's supposed to be losing the plot?' Peggy interrupts. 'Max, I can't stop the staff at the care home from singing your praises. And believe me, I've tried,' she smiles, rolling her eyes in fake disdain.

'Yeah, I think I'm all right at the day-to-day stuff, pretty good at managing Paddy—'

'Which sounds like no mean feat,' Peggy points out, but I know she likes the sound of him; she likes the sound of anyone who reminds me that it's important to laugh.

'It's the new projects thing that I'm struggling with. I need to come up with some big fund-raising event. Developing new ideas doesn't always come that easy to me.' I remember how easily new ideas sparked with Becky, even with Eve. Why can't I do it by myself?

'And they won't,' Peggy says, 'if you're always in here with me. You should be out there making memories.' I hate myself for thinking of Becky. 'Just make sure you're not spending so much time with the dying that you forget to actually live.'

'You're not dying.' I squeeze her hand a little tighter, heart prickling at the thought.

'I'm nearly a hundred . . .'

'You're *eighty-four*.' I shake my head.

'Exactly, get some friends your own age.'

'You've met Tom,' I say, deciding not to tell her about Becky. She'll ask too many questions, see right through me. 'Plus, I'm happy keeping you company.'

'I don't need company,' Peggy objects, and for a moment she reminds me of Eve, rejecting my offer to walk her home before she realised she actually didn't mind.

'Everyone needs company,' I say. 'Don't you get lonely?'

'Don't you?' Peggy's eyes sear into my soul and for a moment I feel exposed.

Of course I've felt lonely. When I was a little boy and my grandma used to scoop me up and tell me everything would be okay. When I was a man and she wasn't there to do it any more. I was gutted when I found out she was leaving the UK, but I never for a second thought she'd be leaving this life so soon.

'Sometimes,' I say, surprised to feel a lump in my throat.

'Me too,' Peggy admits, and I feel awful. She's watching

her friends pass away, of course she feels lonely, but what's my excuse?

'It's just sometimes everyone in this city seems to have it all together,' I sigh. Just look at Tom and Becky, and Eve.

Peggy smiles, her kind eyes on me. 'Everyone struggles beneath the surface.'

'Do you think?' I say, attempting to keep the quiver from my voice. The last time I opened up like this was with my grandma. She always knew how to traverse the depths of me, probe in places few would ever go. I was my parents' only son, I needed to show them I was strong, that I'd always be okay, but my grandma had always been my safe place.

'I know.' Peggy squeezes my hand. 'And I know what you're going through.'

'What?'

'Grief.'

The weight of the word hits me as soon as she's said it.

'You do know it's okay to miss her?' Peggy asks, and for a moment I think of Becky. 'Your grandma,' she says. 'I know she means the world to you.'

'She did.' I nod.

We've not talked about her much, not really. But I guess that's why I like being around Peggy; even without saying anything, I know she understands. I had the same bond with my grandma. The kind where you say little but communicate so much. Grandma loved me not because of what I *could* be, but because of who I was.

'She *does*,' Peggy corrects. 'Edwin still means the world to me too.'

'Of course he does,' I say, trying to deflect the attention away from me. Peggy raises an eyebrow like she knows what I'm doing. 'You're so strong, Peggy. I can't even . . .'

'Do you know the hardest thing about living with dementia?' she asks, if only to quell the lump in my throat. She knows when to push, and this isn't it. I can't deal with her illness and my grandma all at the same time. 'A lot of it is just so hidden. It's not always the dramatic parts.' She holds her free hand out to the hospital beds around her. 'It's the quiet times, the moments in the care home where it's just me and my thoughts, trying to make sense of them, wondering what will happen next.' Tears spring to her eyes as I try to gulp back my own; she needs me to be strong. 'I don't want anyone to try to fix it, not really. I just want to know other people feel the same way. Sometimes I imagine it, Max.' Her eyes glimmer with hope. 'I imagine every person living with dementia, and all their friends and families, coming out of their houses and lining the streets of London, together and proud, like "here we are, we struggle, and we're not ashamed". I'd have loved to have seen something like that.'

I look at her, her hand still in mine. She said *loved*, past tense, as if all her dreams are now somehow behind her. But I can do this, the charity can do this. A sponsored walk, shutting down the streets of London and then bringing them alive with people, helping them feel a little less alone.

'I think it's a great idea,' I say, and Peggy smiles, closing her eyes as if she can see it inside her head. 'But it'll make an even better reality.'

*　　*　　*

'This,' I look up from my reading to see a piece of paper held in front of me, 'is brilliant.' The page drops to reveal Heather's face beaming back at me. It's been less than a week since Peggy and I first came up with the idea, but already it's starting to cement in my mind. 'I think you should go for it.'

'So what are we going for?' Paddy asks as soon as Heather is out of earshot. I turn to him, and he looks so eager I swear he might explode.

'I've been thinking about a new fund-raising event.'

'About bloody time,' he laughs, perching on the edge of his chair.

'I can't help it if you're a handful,' I quip, but we both know that the real reason I've been distracted lately is Becky – no, wait: *Peggy*. 'When I chat to our service users, one thing comes up again and again,' I explain. 'Beyond dementia itself, everyone just feels so lonely, like they're the only ones going through it. Even for family and friends, it's as though prolonged illness is a thing you can talk about with people once or twice, but then that's that.' A little like grief. 'So people just stop talking about it, and carry around this loneliness and . . . Do you know what I mean?' I know I'm not explaining it very well, but Paddy seems to be nodding along.

'Totally,' he says. 'Loneliness is pretty universal.' He shrugs. Does he feel it too? We've never really talked about stuff like that. 'So what's the idea?'

'A sponsored walk around central London, where people can join for a little bit or for a lot. Some people might just read about it in the media.' I break off to jot down that we'll need a way to make the housebound feel included, and we'll need to talk about press coverage as well, get some news-papers on board. 'Either way they'll be able to see how many people have been struggling with this behind closed doors and it'll finally be in the open.'

I pause, trying to gauge his response. I know I'm doing it for Peggy, so that she can see this one last dream of hers become a reality, but surely if it's a good idea for Peggy, it'll be a good idea for others like her.

'Max,' Paddy says, and I'm almost stunned to hear him say my name properly. 'It's sick.' I know him well enough to know this is Pads for great. 'How can I help?'

'Oh man, we've got loads to do,' I sigh. We'll have to bring the whole team in on this. 'We need route confirmation to secure a temporary traffic regulation order . . .'

'On it,' Paddy scribbles it down before firing up his screen to start the search.

'We'll need a temporary events notice, a safety advisory group liaison with emergency services, first aid cover . . .' Oh crap, there's so much that could go wrong. 'But there's also so much that could go right,' I say out loud.

'Huh?'

'Oh, it's just . . . something Becky says,' I explain, even though I have no idea why Becky's messages keep shooting into my mind. I really needed to cool off on pretending to be Tom. It's confusing enough navigating my own emotions. And we have too much to do. For Grandma – no, wait: for *Peggy*.

'You really like her, right?' Paddy raises an eyebrow.

'For Tom.' I force a smile. 'The walk?' I remind us both of the task in hand.

'How should it end?' Paddy asks.

'I'm not sure. Maybe just try and find a few alternative routes . . .'

'No, I mean *how* should it end? Like, you're inviting all these lonely people out onto the streets to show them they're not alone, and then what? They just go home?'

'I'm not sure.' I don't mean to look so worried. It's just that now that I've said it out loud, I feel like I'm actually going to have to pull this off. Though to be fair, that ship kind of sailed around the time I promised Peggy I would do it. 'Any ideas?'

'Well personally,' Paddy says, putting a hand to his chest, 'if I was lonely and isolated and got the courage to force myself outside, I'd want to go somewhere where I could chat to people, have a drink, maybe a dance, make me feel connected.' I know he's thinking out loud, but he's making a lot of sense. 'To be honest, I'd probably just want someone to invite me to a big fucking party.' He laughs.

'Well in that case,' I laugh with him, 'let's throw a really big fucking party.'

'Who is *that*?' I look up to follow Paddy's gaze across the office and over to a figure I've seen countless times before but rarely here in our headquarters.

'That's Amy,' I turn back to Paddy, whose jaw is pretty much on the floor. I forget that he only joined the charity towards the end of last year; that although he's heard Amy's voice down the phone plenty of times, he's never seen her in the flesh.

'*That's* Amy?'

'Put your tongue back in your mouth, dude,' I say.

'Why the hell haven't you asked her out yet?' Paddy slaps me on the shoulder.

'I've told you before . . .' I begin my usual excuses: I don't think she's interested, she's not really my type. And if she knew how pathetic and lonely I was, I wouldn't be her type either. Leading ladies are drawn to leading men, just like Becky with Tom. 'And anyway, I'm pretty sure she fancies Tom.'

'You think everyone fancies Tom,' Paddy says accusingly. 'And I know I've heard your explanation before, but if I'd known she looked like *that* . . .'

I look across to Amy's slight figure, her long curly hair cascading down her back, trying to see her with fresh eyes. She's brilliant, sure. But I've always imagined the woman I'll end up with won't be a caring blonde but a small and feisty, opinionated and funny, seriously smart brunette – and I'll be a slightly more together version of me.

'She's fit, man.'

'She's also coming this way,' I hiss. 'So shut up and pretend to look busy.'

'Hard at work?' She arrives beside my desk. I look up, and out of the corner of my eye, I can tell Paddy is doing the same. 'No women twice your age to chat up?' she teases.

'Try *three* times my age. How is she?'

'Yeah, she's doing a bit better now.' Amy smiles before clocking Paddy. 'Hi, I'm Amy.'

'Patrick.' He smiles back. I've never heard him refer to himself as Patrick before.

'Nice to meet you,' she says. His mouth is still hanging open. *Keep it together, Paddy.* 'Anyway, I'm meant to be in this meeting.' She turns away.

'Good luck,' I say as she sashays over to the other side of the office.

'Good luck finding a woman hotter than *that*,' Paddy says as soon as she's disappeared.

'I've told you she's not my type,' I retort, bringing my attention back to the task in hand. Who in this office would know about safety advisory group liaisons?

'I think we might need to clone this Becky girl.' Paddy shakes his head.

'Why?' I choke on my coffee.

'Your type is pretty narrow.' He laughs, his eyes thankfully not on me but on the route he's mapping on his monitor. 'And it seems to me she's the only one that fits the bill.'

Chapter Fifteen

Eve

Becky: Last night was really fun. New favourite movie for sure.

Tom: Becky, you didn't have the foggiest what was going on.

Becky: What, unlike you?

Tom: I'd say I got a good ninety per cent.

Becky: Of the pizza?

Tom: Hey! You had your fair share.

Becky: Still maintain we should have got them to cut it in half for us.

Tom: We're not animals, Rebecca.

Becky: No, but I'm doing a good impression of a sloth right now.

Tom: Thought you were going to smash a 10K before work?

Becky: Just warming up.

'Yeah, warming up your croissant,' I say, reading Becky's screen over her shoulder. She jumps out of her skin, phone still clutched in her hands.

'I could have done a 10K,' she objects, glancing up from her chat. 'Hey, you look nice.' She eyes my flower-dotted maxi dress. I fully intend to reclaim my leather jacket from her and throw on some biker books to match now it finally feels like winter is over.

'Thanks.' I smile at her. I only get to make an effort for work. Becky gets to get ready for Tom now. *Note to self: do not be jealous of your best friend.* 'How was it?' I ask, looking at my watch. I needed to leave for work about three minutes ago.

'How long have I got?' She laughs, rolling her eyes at my timekeeping.

'That depends. Haven't you got a class to teach?'

'Oh *crap*.' As she jumps to her feet, a ginger flash darts across the room. 'I got distracted.'

I know. She's been distracted a lot over the month she's been seeing Tom, but then again, so have I. With every message I send him on her behalf, I think about my dad's messages, his letters, just a little bit less.

'Need any help this morning?' I ask, not sure why three minutes late is turning into three minutes more when it comes to messaging Tom. No doubt I'm drawn to feeling useful, needed.

'There was this one bit.' She scrolls back through the chat. 'Something about the film we watched last night, and before you ask me the title, it was long and it was in French . . .'

It was one Tom had suggested a couple of evenings ago,

when he and Max were in the pub together. Just when I thought he'd stopped surprising me. Not only had he found an outdoor screening, but it was being shown in its original subtitled black and white. I knew Becky was going to hate it.

'He said he liked the subtle use of the fourth wall, how they broke it beautifully . . .' Confusion laces through her dark brows. 'But we were outside, Eve, *outside*.' She fixes her gaze on me. 'There were no walls anywhere.'

'Oh Becky.' I can't help but laugh. 'It's a performance convention . . .'

'In English, please?'

'It's where the actors address the audience directly, breaking down the wall between them,' I explain. Becky nods along, but I know she's not taking it in.

'Okay, well next time I can look a *little* less confused.' She smiles. For a moment, I feel as warm as the weather.

'How did you handle it this time?' I think about Becky looking around her at all the non-existent walls. About Tom watching her like: *what did I say?*

'Oh, I just kissed him,' she says, brown eyes shining. 'Works every time.'

I don't even bother to look up at the News Building as I tap my security card at the gates in reception and make my way into the body of the beast. Emerging from the lift and onto our floor, I try to tell myself today will be different. Again.

Note to self: that's what you've been telling yourself for years.

And yet the rumours about Angela's pregnancy are now

in full swing. I need them to be true. The newspaper's editorial team is as static and impenetrable as a brick wall. If I was waiting for a space to step up, I would be waiting for one of them to retire or die – or go off on maternity leave.

'Hey, Ken.' I greet Makena absent-mindedly as I flick through the new post on my desk at speed. Bills. Junk mail. No sign of the handwriting I've tried and failed not to think about ever since I first saw it.

'Do not call me Ken.' She fixes her eyes on me, dramatic; daring me to do it again. 'It makes me sound like a middle-class white man.'

'Speaking of which,' I mutter as we both clock Taren walking our way.

'Ladies,' he says as he strides past in the direction of the commercial director's office. Again. At least our commercial director Celia is a woman, even if she thinks and talks like a man. It's how you have to act if you want to get ahead here.

'It wouldn't surprise me if they were related,' I say as soon as he's out of earshot.

'Or shagging.' Makena's eyes follow mine all the way to the closed office door.

'Maybe both?'

'Eve!' She laughs. She may have arrived in the office before me again, but she's still in no rush to get started. 'I think even our management team would draw the line at incense.'

'*Incest*,' I correct. 'Incense is that stuff you burn that smells nice.'

'Do you know what, that might make a good article idea,' she muses out loud. 'Incense,' she says again before I can ask her which one. Pieces on incense over reporting on incest; kind of has our roles down to a T. 'What are you working on right now?'

'Family changed forever after cystic fibrosis diagnosis now fights for a better future.'

'That sounds brilliant,' Makena says diplomatically. 'But I meant what are you working on right now in *work*.'

'Oh, the top ten bags to hit the high street this season.' I sigh.

'Man, I'd love to do that piece *properly*.' She smiles at the thought. 'I can just imagine it, sitting front row at a runway show, reading the style stars first-hand rather than regurgitating content from our competitors.' She rolls her eyes, her daydream over.

'One day you will.' I smile, holding out hope for her.

'And one day you'll write tell-all exposés on incest in the office,' she replies.

It's not that I necessarily want to write about gritty topics. I just want to write about something that *matters*. But Makena has heard this so many times that I decide to save her another regurgitation.

Bringing up my emails, I start to go through my inbox. Next to me Makena laughs loudly at whatever Ajay has just messaged her. His on-off behaviour is finally firmly on. Just like Becky and Tom.

'How's Ajay?'

She looks up from her phone as if she's surprised, as if her girlie giggles and loud laughter wasn't carefully curated to invite this inquisition.

'He's amazing,' she beams, and I swear I see all thirty-two of her pearly whites.

'I'd love to meet him sometime,' I say. If only to prove to myself that I'm just in need of company. That I'd enjoy my time with Ajay as much as my time messaging Tom.

'That would be great!' Her excitement reverberates between us.

'How about tonight?'

'Oh.' Her face falls, and she looks a little awkward. 'Tonight's no good, actually . . .'

I'm not sure why the mood has suddenly shifted. What is she hiding? Probably nothing compared to me. Panic begins to build in my bloodstream at the thought. *Note to self: you can't control everything.* Not in Makena's life maybe, but I could be in control of my own career.

'We're actually going for dinner with Lola and Benj,' she explains, and for a moment she looks a bit guilty.

'Sounds fun,' I say, as I mentally start to build some busyness into my evening. I could go for a run. But then I ran this morning. I could work on some article ideas, keep building my portfolio. But I'll be pretty tired by then. Still, I need distraction. Something to keep my mind off Tom. No, off my dad. This weird feeling is just about my dad.

Eve: What are you up to tonight? Fancy hanging out?

Becky: I'm with Tom tonight, sorry.

Becky: He's training until later, though, so could do dinner?

Eve: Sure. Where shall we go?

I look down at my phone, happy to have plans even if I can't help another prickle of panic from threatening to rise. Am I being squeezed out? I fought so hard to create a space for myself. A space in a family, a space in this office. And now my dad is trying to occupy the space in my mind.

'Check your inbox, check your *inbox*,' Makena hisses across at me.

'What the . . .' I look up from my phone, startled, embarrassed to be caught not working. This isn't like me. I'm getting distracted, more distracted than I've felt in years.

'It's official!' Makena beams.

'He's asked you to be his girlfriend?'

'Why would that be in your inbox?'

'Good point,' I say, scanning my emails. One titled 'Announcement' leaps out at me.

We are delighted to announce that Angela Baxter, one of our lead features editors, is expecting her first baby . . . Oh shit, it's actually happening. Angela is now noticeably pregnant, but I wouldn't put it past her to book a half-day to give birth and be back in the office by the following morning. *We will be looking to recruit her replacement for a year-long maternity cover . . .* A year! Adrenalin shoots around my body, forcing out my anxiety. This is my chance. *We will be advertising this role shortly, but we welcome internal applications. Please join me in congratulating Angela at drinks after work today . . .*

'He does know pregnant women can't drink, right?' Makena laughs across at me.

'Probably not.'

'At least he's congratulating her.' She laughs again, enjoying the excitement. 'I heard him describing maternity leave as flaky the other day.'

'Well I'm not planning on flaking any time soon,' I say. I'm a single woman living in a house share; my family planning amounts to whose turn it is to feed the cat.

'You're going to *rock* this,' Makena says. Everything in me wants to pull up my CV and send over my column idea with it, the column Max pointed out.

'Makena?' We both look up to see Taren behind us.

'Taren.' Makena seems to narrow her eyes at him. He's always been competition, but now his status as the enemy is official.

'Celia wants to see you in her office.' He looks down at her; he looks down at all of us. Makena nods at him, then turns to whisper to me.

'If I'm not back in ten minutes, alert the media.'

'They *are* the media.' I lower my voice too, adopting a dramatic tone.

'No, seriously.' Makena's laugh rings around the room. I love her for never hiding her true feelings, for never stifling her sass. 'After what I said in the last pitch meeting, it's highly likely that Celia will be stashing my body in one of this season's top ten bags.'

I stride confidently into Ciao Becca. The announcement about Angela's maternity leave was the fuel I needed to fire up all four of my cylinders and start focusing on what matters again. On telling the stories that matter.

189

'Eve!' Leonardo dances across the restaurant towards me, hips moving in time to some early-noughties Justin Timberlake. Sofia must be out.

'We thought you'd *died*.' Becky jumps to her feet to throw herself at me.

'Why?' I laugh as I'm ushered towards our table in the corner.

'You're late,' Becky says. 'You're never late.'

'I was working,' I tell her.

'Work better than you thought it would be?' she asks as Leonardo pours me a glass of red. I didn't even tell her this morning that I was anxious. She can still read my face like a book; probably the only book she'll read all year, despite what Tom thinks.

I smile and take a sip of my drink – a small one. As soon as I'm done here, it's back to work. Depending on when the job advert goes up, my days of feeling *supplementary* could soon be over.

'No! They made the announcement?' Becky squeals, throwing her arms around me. 'This is your time, Eve. I just *know* it.' I grin back at her. I'm not usually one for counting my chickens, but I kind of feel that way too.

'Angela's officially up the fluff?' Leo says, piling our plates with pasta.

'Dad, it's up the *duff*.' Becky rolls her eyes. 'And yes.'

'And our Eve has got the job?' He looks at me hopefully.

'No . . .'

'Not yet.' Becky forks up her first mouthful. 'But it's only a matter of time.'

190

'Oh crap.' Leo looks at the door as Sofia walks into the restaurant. 'Girls, I'm telling you, that's the last time I play this drivel for you . . . This is a traditional Italian restaurant. The free pasta is one thing, but you don't own the place . . .'

'You tell 'em.' Sofia gives her husband a massive kiss on the lips before turning to throw her arms around me, holding me for what feels like several minutes before turning to offer Becky the same over-the-top embrace.

I used to find their family dynamics weird, before I became a part of them. I wonder whether Tom will feel the same, whether he'll throw our rhythm offbeat. Leo dances Sofia across the room, changing the music back to the traditional tracks.

'Oh *please*.' Becky rolls her eyes at her parents, Sofia giggling flirtatiously.

'You're not much better.'

'If Tom and I ever get like that,' she nods to Leo now spinning Sofia in circles, 'you have permission to kill me.'

'Couldn't afford the rent without you,' I point out.

Then it hits me. If Becky ever moved out, I literally couldn't afford the place without her. I'd have to move further out of London. Further away from Ciao Becca and Leonardo and Sofia and everything I've built.

Note to self: stop worrying about things that haven't happened yet.

'Anyway, your parents are great.' I try to push the thought away. 'Is Tom close to his family?' I say before I can stop myself.

'Yeah, he is.' She smiles. 'Proper close to his dad.'

Even as she says it, I feel gutted that I didn't know that

about Tom. Jealous, even. When he and Becky first started dating, I swear I knew him better than her. Now they're doing fine without me.

'Are you sure you don't want to get in touch with him?' Becky asks.

Shit. Who? Tom? Message him as just me? Wouldn't that be weird?

'Your dad,' she prompts.

Oh, right. My dad. I look at her, not sure why she's saying this now. I still haven't told her about the letter.

'I do miss the good bits sometimes,' I sigh, throat tightening. I don't need this.

'Why don't you just think about it? Put the thought back on the table.' She looks down at her pasta, trying to underplay the seriousness of the suggestion. If only she knew that thoughts of my dad are already the centrepiece.

'It's hard to take the good without the bad,' I say, looking across the room at her parents, still hand in hand. 'You wouldn't understand.'

'Perhaps I would if you let me,' she sighs, before realising she's threatening my chipper mood. And I'm chipper for a reason: Angela's going on maternity leave, my chance has come and now isn't the time to let myself get distracted. 'Sorry, I know it's not that simple. It's just you're so *good* at relationships.' She looks down at her phone, and for a moment I feel exposed, like she's caught me thinking about Tom. 'Why don't you get yourself online?'

'It's just not the right time,' I remind her. 'Dating is so distracting.' So why do I love getting distracted by Tom?

'Tell me about it.' She sighs in surrender.

'I mean it's bad enough online dating as you.' I think fondly of our nights snuggled up on the sofa, messaging Tom together; of other nights when it's just me on her app, sharing my own story.

'Well hopefully your assistance is no longer required.' She shows me her screen but there are no messages on it, just the time. 'Got to go, actually.' She smiles at the thought, but my mind has stalled on her words: *your assistance is no longer required.* 'No, no, feel free to stay,' she says as I reach for my jacket. 'You know my parents won't mind if you work from here.'

I do know that. What I don't know is why Becky referring to them as *my parents* is reminding me they're not really mine. Maybe it's because she's on her way to be with Tom, my role in their relationship becoming redundant. Or that my role in this family doesn't work without her here.

'It's okay.' I smile through the painful thoughts. 'I really need to work on my application.' *Note to self: at least you know that role is meant for you.*

Chapter Sixteen

Max

People pass me on all sides as I weave my way down Tooting High Street and back to the flat. I've read in Eve's latest supplement that coupling-up season is over, but I swear spring is the season where winter romances move up another gear. Or maybe it's that the sunshine is inviting everyone outside. But not everyone. Peggy and the others at her care home are still inside, and now that my visit to see her safely back from the hospital is over, I'm heading home too.

Hooking a right to turn off the high street, I lose myself down a quiet lane, taking solace in the fact that I made Peggy's day even if I have no idea how to spend the rest of mine. The way her face lit up when I told her the route for our walk had been approved was everything, her dreams of uniting dementia patients and their families moving in the right direction. I just have to keep my promise to her, the way I never did with my grandma.

Pushing down the thought, I open our front door, slowing a little as I do, wondering what will welcome me: an eerily empty lounge that is feeling less and less like a *living* room with every day Tom isn't here. Or worse, a room so full of life – of Becky's laughter and light – that it makes me feel even darker. I've gone from being in the house alone to leaving the house because I can't keep my eyes off her, but either way you cut it, I'm feeling pretty lonely.

At least I've never been more convinced that I want to spend my time helping those who feel the same way. If only I'd been able to hang out with Peggy longer, but Amy and the gang were putting on a pamper day for the women at the home. Turns out Peggy has a better social life than me. I can taste the irony. I can also smell the bacon.

Shit, Tom and Becky must be home. My stomach turns at the thought. There's only so long I can be around Becky before facing the cold, hard truth: I really miss pretending to be Tom, if only to be able to speak to her.

'Hey, buddy,' Tom says over the sound of the sizzling pan in his hands. I look around our kitchenette in search of Becky. It's obvious she's not here.

'Becky round?' I say, watching him shred bacon on top of two chicken salads.

'No, this is for you.' He smiles across at me. 'Thought you'd need to eat something after visiting Peggy.' Nice to know I'm so predictable. 'Not seen you much this week.'

'Work's pretty busy.' I shrug. And I've been avoiding you and Becky like the plague.

'Peggy's walk official yet?' Tom asks.

195

'It's all going in the right direction.' I accept the plate Tom offers me before we make our way to the living room. It feels good to have him back; maybe we can spend the day together. That way I won't have to spend another Saturday alone with my thoughts. Some of which are so bloody stupid I have no idea what to do with them. Mostly thoughts about Becky: articles she'll like, new albums from her favourite bands.

'Let's do something today.' Tom reads my mind, though thankfully not all of it.

'I'd be up for that.' I smile, feeling warmed by the thought. Finally, a bit of headspace. 'What did you have in mind?'

'It's such a nice day.' His eyes dart outside to the blue sky, my mood lifting a little at the thought of getting back out there. 'Park?' I nod, before Tom grins again. 'I know, why don't we invite Becky and Eve?'

My heart picks up pace at the thought. I don't want to spend the day hanging out with Becky, mostly because I'm scared I'll enjoy it too much. But it's not like I can say no now that I've just told Tom I'm up for it.

'Great idea.' I force a smile. Hang out with the girl my best friend is dating who I have more in common with than any woman I've met for years? *Great idea.*

'Owns seven cats, on her way to buy one more.' Eve laughs as my eyes trace a woman seemingly wearing not one but two anoraks on a gorgeous spring day. Eve may just be my people-watching match.

'International spy who works as an obstetrician in the week but dresses a little like an international spy at the weekend in hopes of perfecting a killer double bluff,' I reply, both of us giggling as our suspect's sunglasses fall further down his nose and we watch his eyes dart across Green Park.

Out of the corner of my eye I can see Tom brushing a loose strand of Becky's long brown hair behind her ear before reaching to the grass beneath him to pull out a dandelion and offer it to her. She blows, whispering a wish. I wish I didn't have to see that. I wish I could still speak to Becky properly. Even though we've all been together for a couple of hours, she still doesn't seem herself around me, not like when I was messaging her as Tom. In person, she seems warmer but ditsier, not nearly as passionate about so many things we chatted about. But then Tom has changed too, suddenly uncovering his romantic side.

Maybe it's just the feeling of being in love that changes people. I've read about it a thousand times, but here I am seeing it in the flesh. I know part of me still wishes I was privy to that side of Becky, the side that will talk about Shakespeare until the sun goes down. I look at her now and her eyes meet mine. She smiles before turning away, and for one ridiculous moment I wonder whether she feels it too, whether she knows it's *my* chat, not Tom's, that she fell for in the first place.

'Next place?' Becky jumps up. Does she really have to be so sweet? Although she also seems to have the attention span of a child today. How she managed to stay still long enough to watch the extended edition of *The Lord of the Rings* films back to back is beyond me.

'How about the National Portrait Gallery?' I suggest.

'Yes!' Eve is already on her feet.

'No, no, no.' Becky shakes her head. I thought she'd love that? Tom looks at her, a little confused: he thought she'd love that too. 'I mean, *usually* I'd love that.' Becky's eyes dart to Eve. 'But it's so sunny today. Let's go to Oxford Street.'

Oh God, please, no. Oxford Street on a Saturday? I can't imagine anything worse.

'I can't imagine anything worse.' Eve steals the thought from my mind. 'Plus, being in and out of the shops is hardly in the sunshine.'

'Yes, but I need some things for summer,' Becky pleads. I'm not sure I can stand to watch her spin around in sundresses. 'Thirty minutes tops.' She fixes her eyes on Eve and then turns to me. *'Please?'*

And to that face, how the hell can I say no?

Becky is dragging Eve away from the Waterstones window display and in the direction of Zara or H&M Home or wherever it is she wants to go next. It's almost as if she's doing it for Tom's sake, to make a point of being drawn to style as well as substance. But isn't substance exactly what I've been helping him with?

'How are things going with Becky?' I ask him. She's pushing Eve past another bookshop, an invisible force field inviting her in. Just be yourself, Becky, please. Yourself is brilliant.

'Yeah, really good, thanks.' Tom beams back at me, his skin a little darker in the sun. 'Feel like we're starting to settle into seeing each other, feeling more at ease around each other.'

Really? I'd not heard Becky mention the kind of things she talks about in her messages all day.

'That's really good, dude,' I say, looking at the two girls now in fits of giggles in front of me. Becky's feisty enough to take on Eve, even though she's a good foot shorter than her. I guess we'll have to save the bookshops for another day, which is no bad thing given that Becky and I would be drawn to all the same sections.

'There is just one thing.' Tom lowers his voice a little and my heart starts to race. What? What has he noticed? 'It's just, we've not slept together yet . . .'

'What?' I can't help my mouth from dropping open.

'Oh crap, it's bad, isn't it?' Tom's face falls.

'It's not bad . . .' It's just surprising. Ever since Yvonne, Tom has been the king of the one-night stand. And now that Becky is staying over at ours more and more, and they've been seeing one another for about six weeks, I just assumed . . .

'Like, I remember you saying to take it slow, at the start, when you helped with the . . .' He glances at Becky and Eve walking in front of us, clearly nervous about being exposed. 'When you helped with the messages. And she told me she wanted to take it slowly too, that she was trying to only sleep with people she could see a future with.'

'That's pretty cool,' I say. I was fairly sure sex was the only thing people went online-dating for, but clearly she's different. She wants it to mean something, just like all the stories she's immersed herself in. All the stories I've read too.

'Yeah, that's what I thought, but now I'm not sure whether we've made it mean too much, like put the pressure on so much that to sleep together now will mean we're getting married or something.' Tom's looking at me like I'm the expert again. I keep my eyes on Becky, remembering all the messages we've shared back and forth. She deserves something special. 'Obviously we've done other stuff, everything *but* . . .' he goes on, and I really wish he hadn't. Now I can't stop imagining it, and to be honest, the thought makes me feel sick.

'I'm sure you'll know when it's the right time.' I smile weakly.

'Yeah.' Tom tries to laugh off his concern. 'You know when you know and all that.'

All *I* know is that I like Becky more than I should.

'Anyone want a coffee?' I say, looking up from the cobbles of Carnaby Street to see Becky bouncing into yet another clothes shop. 'We've been walking for hours.'

'Better get used to it, bro.' Tom laughs, glancing over his shoulder to smile back at me, his hand in Becky's – mostly just to hold her, but also to hold her back. I know he's had enough of shopping too, but isn't love supposed to give you strength for these kinds of things?

'Huh?'

'You're trying to pull off a sponsored walk, aren't you?'

Oh yeah. Peggy's Walk. Seeing her this morning feels like so many miles, so many clothes shops ago. I have no idea how Becky finds the time to feed this habit alongside all her others: running most mornings, cooking most evenings and reading regularly.

'Show . . . me . . . the . . . *coffee*.' Eve's sentence stutters with ellipses. She looks knackered. She'd no doubt rather be researching human-interest stories, far more interesting than this.

'Why don't you guys grab a coffee and we'll just dash to one last shop?' Becky says. She said *one last shop* four shops ago. Plus part of me is hoping that once we settle down for a stop, she might start feeling like she can be herself again.

'Are you sure you don't want us to come with you?' Eve's eyes dart to Tom, along with those of almost every other woman winding their way down the street.

'No, it's cool.' Becky smiles. 'Go get buzzed.' She fixes her big brown eyes on me and I swear she's buzzing enough for everyone. All that intrigue and insight inside one tiny body; my heart jolts at the thought.

'Coffee?' Eve glances at me, and I know I need to turn my head away from Becky.

'So what's this walk thing?' Eve asks over her flat white. At our table outside, we're soaking up the last of today's sun, and with Becky and Tom a safe distance away, I can finally breathe. It's only now, seeing Eve stifle a yawn, that I wonder whether she's been feeling the same, like being around Becky and Tom whilst she's got so much else on her mind is harder than she's making it look.

Before I can stop them, my eyes dart to a small woman in a fluffy pink coat, her fishnet tights visible beneath it. 'Nursery teacher by day, club dancer by night.'

'For a second there I thought you were talking about Becky.' Eve laughs, reaching to tie her long blonde hair in a messy bun on her head. She looks effortlessly cool in a light summer coat, white T-shirt and jeans.

'She teaches primary school, though, right?'

'Someone's been listening.' She smiles. Little does she know I've done more than just listen. 'Anyway, the sponsored walk?'

'Oh yeah, it's a fund-raising initiative I'm trying to get off the ground,' I explain.

'Sounds like you're doing more than just get it off the ground,' Eve says, nodding me along, and before I know it, I'm telling her everything. How I moved from banking to the charity sector, about meeting Peggy, getting to know her and the way she lives. And how she suggested something that would make her feel connected, like she wasn't so alone.

'That's amazing, Max,' she says, eyes fixed on mine.

I wonder whether she feels lonely too. Although I can't imagine a woman as together as Eve ever feeling like she doesn't have the world at her feet. She turns away to watch the people walking by, and I know for a fact she's making up backstories for each of them in her head. It's what I do too.

'I was going to ask you, the night you walked me home . . .' she begins. I have no idea where she's going with this, but I don't feel on edge with Eve. 'What made you move from banking to the charity sector – not how, but *why*?' She says it like a true journalist.

'The salary,' I say, deadpan. She stares at me before realising I'm joking and throwing her head back in laughter. 'Honestly? It's a long story.'

'We've got time,' she says.

'Do we? I thought Becky said they were just dashing to one last shop?'

Eve sighs, stifling a smile. 'I've known Becky for years. Trust me, she's never dashed anywhere in her life.'

'Well okay then,' I say, even though that doesn't sound like the busy Becky I've spent my evenings talking to. But then maybe my messages, Tom's messages, make her feel like she can truly be herself. 'It all started when my grandma got sick,' I begin, and sitting here with Eve, surrounded by strangers in Soho, I start to share my truth.

'Surely you know that's not your fault, though?' Eve says, taking a sip from coffee number two.

Becky and Tom are still nowhere to be seen, but we've stopped clock-watching. Why have I just told her all of this? About my promise to my grandma, to my family. About how letting them down so badly brought me down too.

'Try telling my family that.' I can't stop now that Eve's gentle probing has got me in full flow. 'I was the only one of them who didn't make it to see her in time.'

'But are you sure they're angry at you for that – that you're not just angry at yourself?'

'I was her favourite.' I spill the sentence, feeling my throat tighten with tension.

'Maybe you just need to have some grace for them,' she says, but she's never met my parents. 'We need to be careful of how we deal with those about us, when every death carries to some small circle of survivors, thoughts of so much omitted, and so little done . . .' She speaks softly and I savour every syllable. She's quoting Dickens.

'And so many more which might have been repaired!' I finish. '*Oliver Twist*?'

'I don't think anyone's nailed writing about grief better than Dickens.' She smiles.

'Except maybe C. S. Lewis?' I say, and her eyes widen as if to say: don't even get me started on Lewis. 'In any case, I for one am not nailing it. I think about her every day.'

'Do you think about *her* or about the guilt?'

No one's ever asked me that.

'Aren't they the same?'

'I don't think so,' Eve says, and I know that if we don't change the subject soon, I'm going to cry, and she really doesn't deserve to see a grown man cry, especially after a day spent on Oxford Street. 'So anyway, therein lies the true story behind Peggy's Walk.' I laugh, forcing the space between us to feel lighter. How did things get so heavy in the first place? 'Feel free to publish,' I add. 'But in case you think I'm not joking, absolutely *don't*.'

'Your secret's safe with me,' she says, and I believe her. 'How does it end?'

'The story?' I ask. Badly? Depressingly? With the protagonist fancying his best friend's new girlfriend? 'I'm still trying to work that part out.'

'No, I mean the walk,' Eve says.

Oh. I guess Paddy has sorted the answer to that one.

'With a really big fucking party,' I say. 'I'm just not sure where yet.'

'How about here?' Eve's eyes trace their way down Carnaby Street, past lovers and friends and tourists with skin of every colour dressed in every colour under the sun. Soho? Isn't this a place where you can come as you are, just be yourself? I look at Eve, the sunlight illuminating her smile, wide and warm.

'I think that's a brilliant idea,' I say. Why didn't I think of it? 'Anyway, you've heard all about me.' Too much about me. But just saying stuff out loud has made me feel lighter. 'Now it's your turn . . .'

Chapter Seventeen

Eve

I look at Max leaning back in his chair, the last of the sunshine kissing his features. *Now it's your turn.* My heart starts to beat faster in my chest, caffeine surging through my veins.

'Well . . .' I start, not meaning to stall. 'What do you want to know?'

'What made you want to go into journalism?' He smiles.

It's a question I've heard a thousand times before. But from Max it feels like it carries more weight. Like: what *really* made you want to go into it?

'Well . . .' I begin again. For a moment his gaze on mine feels a bit intense. But then I realise he's just listening, like *really* listening. Why does that feel so rare nowadays? 'I guess I loved how journalists search for the truth,' I explain, not used to being the interviewee. 'The stories I read in newspapers growing up never seemed sugar-coated or sickly sweet; they felt balanced and a bit more . . . real.'

'Before fake news?' His laugh is as warm as the evening. 'For sure.'

In reality, there were other reasons I loved those stories. For starters, reading real-life accounts of the bad stuff as well as the good made me realise that I wasn't the only child whose home life was pretty fucked up. And then, when a person with a life full of lemons used them to make lemonade, it showed me that the story of your past didn't have to dictate your future. It could galvanise it instead.

'If anything, fake news just makes me more passionate about sharing the truth,' I say, my stomach sinking. It's not like I've been telling Becky the truth. 'I go on social media every day and see story after story about these picture-perfect lives; at least journalism, *real* journalism, can be a bit more honest.'

'I guess you can be anyone you want online,' Max muses, clearly worried by the thought.

'Yeah, but I promise you there are real journalists out there who still want to write the truth.'

And I just want to be one of them. Which is pretty ironic given all the lies I have hidden at home, hidden in my heart. For a moment I think I see Tom, like I have the power to conjure him into being. Max turns his head to follow my distracted gaze. A little smile circles his mouth and I know he's about to create another people-watching story.

'Quit the high-school football team to become Grimsby's first male cheerleader.' He fixes his eyes on the tall, broad torso of a man who isn't Tom after all.

'Good one,' I laugh, pretending I was people-watching all along. Like I was making up fake stories about strangers whilst slamming fake stories about strangers. Like I wasn't trying to fake it in front of a thousand strangers myself.

Note to self: you do have your shit together at work, at home, with family, with friends . . .

'I wonder where Becky and Tom have got to?' I say. Sharing time over. Max's face falls for a moment and I force my eyes from him to my phone. It's only then that I notice that Becky sent me a text fifteen minutes ago. 'Oh, she says she found the perfect pair of shoes in Office but they didn't have her size so they've headed over to the one in Covent Garden. She says she's sorry about a thousand times.' I leave out the bit about giving me and Max more time together. She's such a meddler. But then what does that make me?

'The only person I feel sorry for is Tom.' Max laughs. 'The perfect pair of shoes?'

'Like freaking Cinderella.' I shake my head, remembering Max's fairy-tale chat from our night at the Fable. At least I managed to get Becky through that pretty unscathed. I imagine Tom putting that perfect pair on her feet now, Becky squealing, finally finding her prince.

Note to self: you do want your best friend to have a happy ending. Yes, but do I always have to make do with *happily enough*?

'Anyway, where were we?' Max says, figuring we have a bit more time before the prince and princess gallop back again. 'Oh yeah, fake news and true stories . . .'

Fake friends and true feelings? No, Eve, no. You are not a fake friend — even if you haven't told Becky about your mixed-up feelings after your mixed-up messages. Even if you haven't told her about your dad's letters.

'When did you realise that journalism was what you wanted to do?'

'When I was eight,' I say, too quickly. I regret it instantly. Max seems like the kind to see too much and let go of too little.

'Why?' He leans forward on his elbows.

I know the rehearsed answer: because that's when we had to write like reporters in creative writing class. I also know the real one, and for some reason I can taste the truth on the tip of my tongue. I look at the people strolling, slouching and skipping down the streets of Soho. Out of their days and into their nights. Some dressed in nothing but designer. Others dancing in head-to-toe glitter. This is a place where everyone can be themselves, their full selves. So why am I still trying to hide half of me?

'Because that's the age I stopped believing in fairy tales,' I admit to Max, to myself.

He leans back in his chair. There's still no sign of the *perfect pair* returning, but for now it feels like there's nowhere Max would rather be. His quiet confidence makes me feel comfortable, his softness creating space.

'It was on my eighth birthday that I found out my mum was having an affair.' I wait for him to interrupt: *on your bloody birthday?!* That's always Becky's line. But Max just listens. 'My mum got drunk and my dad took her to one

209

side to try to make her drink some water. I just remember her pushing him off and saying that he was so boring and no wonder she was sleeping with someone else.' The words fall from my mouth and I have no idea why I'm telling him this. 'I thought sleeping with someone was like having a sleepover. So I didn't really get it when my dad stormed out; sleepovers were meant to be fun, right?'

Even now, I feel so sorry for that naïve little girl. I fix my eyes on Max, expecting him to look sorry for her too. But his expression isn't one of sympathy, pious and detached; it's one of intrigue. And, well, I've always been a storyteller, and this captive audience is making me want to continue with the second act. Except this isn't an act, is it? This is my truth. The one I locked inside myself many years ago.

'After that, my mum left to be with this other guy, She wrote to me a grand total of two times.' *Like the two letters hidden in your kitchen cupboard.* 'But we were okay, just the two of us. Well, for a while. I remember my ninth birthday. I thought my dad was brilliant.' I can't help but laugh. 'He was loud and erratic and invited every single person in my class to this insane party.' Max doesn't look impressed. I guess he can imagine what's coming next. 'By my thirteenth birthday, he was even wilder. I swear once I hit puberty he just didn't know how to relate to me as his daughter any more so he figured he'd just try to be my friend.' I sigh. 'I suppose I should have known then that he had a drinking problem, around the time he let a bunch of teenage girls do tequila shots in the back garden.'

'Bet you were the talk of the town.' Max's smile is soft

but not patronising like the smiles I've shared these stories with before.

'Yeah, I was the most popular girl in school,' I say. 'Until it didn't feel that cool any more. I guess I needed a father, not a friend.'

'You guess?'

'Well I *know* now,' I correct. 'By my eighteenth birthday he just wasn't there any more, and do you know what? It was so much easier.'

'How so?' Max presses forward, not an inch of him longing to be anywhere but here. By this point Becky is usually too upset for me to carry on. Or too excited by the possibility of a reunion, a movie-magic happy-ever-after. It isn't her fault, though. We don't go down this road often; I put the roadblocks in place myself.

'I got a fresh start, no baggage.' I smile. 'I managed to get myself off to university, where I could reinvent myself.' For a moment Max's face screams: *I know about reinvention.* I wonder who he used to be before he became the man sitting in front of me now. 'I was able to take that little bit of passion and fan it into flames . . .'

'And now you're a phoenix.' His hand reaches to mine on the top of the table for a moment. What's weird is that it actually feels normal.

'Huh?' I laugh, only then realising that two tears are trickling down my cheeks.

'Doesn't matter.' Max shakes his head, draining the dregs of his coffee.

'Yes it does,' I insist, brushing away the tears.

'It's cheesy.' He laughs, cheeks pinkening a little.

'I don't mind a bit of cheese – sometimes. Don't tell Becky, though.'

'I promise not to, if you promise not to cringe,' he says, and I nod him my word. 'You were surrounded by flames but you rose above them, then you fanned your own flames to rise by yourself,' he says, perhaps the only thing since I started sharing that has made him look uncomfortable. 'So in my eyes, Eve,' he smiles softly, 'you're a fucking phoenix.'

'You're right,' I say, and his brow furrows in confusion: *I am?* 'That *is* pretty cheesy.'

'Hey!' He pushes my hand playfully, then glances down the lively street in search of Tom. They should be back any second. 'Do you ever hear from him now?' He returns his gaze to me.

'Tom?' I ask, my own eyes still on the street.

'Your dad.' Max sounds confused: *what's Tom got to do with this?*

I look at him now. My dad's letters weigh heavy on my heart, but sharing my story with Max has made me feel a bit lighter.

'No, I don't,' I say. As soon as I utter the lie, for some reason it doesn't feel right between us. 'Well, I didn't,' I admit. 'But a month or so ago he sent me a letter.' I wait for wide eyes, a dropped jaw, a sign that Max is enjoying the drama of my life, so juicy to others but so raw for me. But he just looks on, soft and safe, welcoming me further in. 'I guess he searched my name on the internet or something and found my writing on our website, and then wrote a letter to my office.'

I can't unsay it now. Even though Becky doesn't know. And part of me wishes I was telling Tom. I just know he'd have some good advice.

'What did it say?'

'That he misses me and wonders whether we might be able to be in touch.'

'And?'

'And nothing. I didn't reply.' My heart is hammering in my chest, warning me to shut this down. Where was that warning when I was messaging Tom? *Note to self: maybe don't trust your heart. Trust reason. Trust logic.*

'I get it,' Max says, smiling in surrender. Not forcing me to do or say or be anything.

'But then he sent me another letter. He said he knew I probably wasn't interested, but part of him worried that I hadn't got his first letter, or worse, that I didn't think he meant what he said. He said that wasn't a chance he was willing to take any more.' I guess that part is sweet, at least. Max's expression tells me he thinks it's sweet too. But he doesn't know my dad, not really. Although right now, he knows a lot more than anyone else. 'So he's given me his number, says if I want to call first, just to sound him out at a distance, he'd be up for that. However I want to play it . . . but I'm not a game, Max.'

'You're not.' He smiles in agreement. 'But nor is life. And you only get one.'

'So what are you saying?' I don't mean to snap. It's just,

what does he know? But I know that ship has sailed. He already knows too much.

'That if you want to call him or see him, it doesn't mean you're going to go back to square one.'

But *do* I want to see him? Do I actually want to connect with him, phone to phone – or face to face – after all this time? And what if he doesn't show, just stands me up like all those birthdays and dinners and graduations in the past? But I guess part of me wonders. Part of me still hopes . . .

'You're different now, you're stronger.'

I'm a fucking phoenix.

'And life is really short,' Max goes on, and I know he's thinking about Peggy. 'So if you want to do something, trust yourself and don't overthink it.'

'Don't overthink what?' I hear Becky's voice behind me, lovebirds now materialised, shopping bags in both of their hands. I assume all the bags belong to Becky. My eyes dart to Max and we have a silent conversation.

Please don't tell anyone what I've told you.

Your secrets are safe with me.

'Eve's application for this role,' Max says. 'I know she's waiting until they officially put the advert out, but I keep telling her she should send her CV and her column idea now, get ahead of the game.'

I know he's covering for me, but why didn't I think of that? Taren will wait in the wings, pretending to play by the rules, but I have to be smarter, more strategic. To get into the places where men can simply stroll.

'That's a great idea.' Becky beams back at him and Max

smiles all the more. Becky has a way of making everyone feel like they're her favourite. 'I'm so sorry we're late, by the way. It's my fault . . .'

'Seconded.' Tom smiles at me. Gazing up at him from my seat, he looks even bigger. And I hate my heart for hammering at the thought. 'I swear I've completed your walk already, dude.'

'Well you've landed in the right place.' Max grins. 'We're going to try and see whether we can host the finishing-line party here.'

'That's a great idea!' Tom echoes Becky's excitement from before. You'd be forgiven for thinking they were perfect for each other, but I know a thousand tweaks have gone into this.

'It was Eve who thought of it.' Max looks at me as he gets to his feet, more than happy to share the credit. I just hope he isn't the kind to share secrets.

Buster purrs by my side, enjoying the warmth of my open laptop, whirling with ideas. What I've written is just a scratch on the thousands of thoughts thrashing around my mind. Becky has gone back to Tom's for dinner. I was invited, of course, her efforts to push me in Max's direction not lost on me. And I guess I kind of enjoyed being with him today, but now I need to be alone.

Looking around the silent room, my feelings for Tom threaten to surface. We spent most of the day together, but I still miss chatting to him. The moments where Becky looked to me, in need of a line, are still some of my favourites. But they can't be. The two of them are an item now.

Note to self: you do not fancy Tom, you do not fancy Tom.

And then there's the tiny fact that I told Max about my dad's letters before I've even told my best friend.

I turn my attention to my CV, open before me. Experience after experience I've made for myself, without my dad. His letters are still stashed in their hiding place, but for some reason they feel less threatening now. Clicking from my CV to my column presentation, my mind moves to my coffee with Max, our conversation. I know I should have been telling Becky, but being with Max felt good. Not in the tingles-down-my-arm way that just a flash of Tom's smile can kick-start, but different, much deeper. Like gulping fresh air into the very core of myself, or returning to a warm house after a long, cold walk. The thought of it makes me feel peaceful in a way few things have of late. I've shared the truth with an almost-stranger and it has made me feel lighter. And now I'm about to do that a thousand times over, if the newspaper will just give me a chance.

I gaze down at my screen, rereading my email to Richard for the hundredth time. It was Max's idea to send it right to the top, just like it was his idea not to wait another moment. *If you want to do something, trust yourself and don't overthink it.* I replay his words from today. And then click send.

There's no going back now. But I don't want to go back. I've wanted to tell stories, *real* stories, ever since I was eight years old. And this is my chance. I want it, like

216

I want Tom. No, I don't. I can't. I force my eyes back to the screen, rereading Richard's email receipt over and over. I don't want Tom. I want this role. And then Max's face forces its way into my mind, asking, 'But what do you want from your dad?'

Chapter Eighteen

Max

Tom: Morning, beautiful.

Becky: Is it?

Tom: I meant you.

Becky: Ah, thanks. Sorry, still waking up.

Tom: Would have thought you'd have been out for your run by now.

Becky: You been at the gym?

Tom: Yeah, two clients this morning but kept the rest of the day free. Still want me to come to yours for lunch?

Becky: Yes please.

Tom: We'll have to run together soon, though.

Becky: Soon.

Becky: But first, lunch.

'Need any help, mate?' I look across at Tom, stretching along the length of the sofa.

'Nah, it's okay.' He smiles down at his screen. 'Becky just avoiding exercise.'

'That doesn't sound like her,' I say. I hate myself for remembering.

'She's seemed a bit less motivated lately.' He sighs. 'Busy with work, I think.'

'Need me to throw in some conversation starters?' I say, a little too hopeful.

'Thanks, dude, but I think I've got this.'

I *know* he's got this. He's had it for almost two months now, my role in the romance now redundant. I force my eyes back to my book, but somehow even rereading *Far From the Madding Crowd* for the millionth time is not enough to stop me feeling completely alone. Tom's either been out or occupied with Becky. But not frantic and flirtatious in the way he was with Yvonne. Sweeter, slower, like in amidst all the weirdos and one-night stands online dating has to offer, we've finally curated something real. Mission accomplished. They don't need my help any more. I turn the page, hoping I can turn away my sadness. This is ridiculous. Becky never liked me and I never liked her.

'Fancy Becky?' Tom asks from across the room.

What? No, I don't. *I don't.*

'Fancy *joining* me and Becky?' Oh, right, that makes more sense, but the guilt on my face must have said it all. 'What did you think I said?' Tom laughs, eyes now back on Becky's messages. What are they talking about?

'Will Eve be there?' I ask, knowing I can only stomach being around Becky and Tom if Eve is there to distract me.

219

Speaking to her is a little like talking to Becky, back when we used to message into the night. It isn't the same, but chatting to Eve, with all her ideas and ambition, makes me feel a bit more connected again.

'Let me check.' Tom beams from ear to ear, excited by the thought.

It would be so convenient if I was with someone too, if I could stop being the shadow in his relationship. I know my grief has impacted him too. Baggage has a way of throwing you off balance with everyone. It's the reason I stopped telling him about it. It was good to speak to Eve, though.

'Sorry, dude, Becky says she's writing today.'

'Becky's writing?'

'I was talking about Eve, you doughnut.' Tom laughs.

'Sorry, still waking up.'

'You sound like Becky.' He laughs again, but it's anything but funny. '*Eve* is writing today,' he confirms, and I can't help but feel a bit disappointed. I guess I won't be seeing Becky this afternoon.

'Things looking good for her promotion?' Maybe part of me wants to see Eve too.

'I don't know, let me ask.' Tom glances at me, a little smile circling around his mouth. I know he wants me to fancy Eve, but then he wanted me to fancy Amy and Lauren and anyone else who has ever shown an interest in me.

I watch him message Becky, ignoring my envy. Keep it together, dude. You do not fancy Becky.

'Okay, so Becky says . . .' Tom begins, and I hate the fact that these are now the magic words. 'Eve's feeling pretty

220

hopeful. The advert came out a week or so ago and since then there's been lots of talk internally about diversity and inclusion. Oh, and she says that some guy called Taren is a white middle-class class-A dick.'

I can't help but laugh. I can hear Eve's voice in every sentence Tom reads out loud.

'So not a done deal, but she's going to spend today writing and researching and whatnot so she's prepared when they call her in for an interview.'

Tom looks up from the message like: *does that answer all your questions, dude?* No, it doesn't. I have a thousand more questions for Becky. And I guess I have a few for Eve, too – just a couple about Peggy's Walk that have come up over the past week and that I'm pretty sure Eve's smarts will be able to slice through.

'So do you want to join me and Becky?' Tom asks, pretty half-hearted. We both know it would be easier if I didn't.

'No, that's okay.' I sigh. 'I need to do some work too really.'

'Don't work too hard.' Tom smiles. 'You're beginning to sound like Eve.'

From the depths of my bedroom, I hear the front door open and close, Tom making his way towards Becky: *living room's free, dude.*

I look down at the sheets of paper scattered across my bed, at the spreadsheet on my laptop. Just concentrate on Peggy's Walk. Do not get distracted. But it's already too late; my mind has followed Tom out of the door and towards the object of his affections. Well, *person* of his affections. Becky's no object: she's smart and fiery with brilliant taste and is more like me than any woman I've ever met. Well, in our messages. In person feels different, and why wouldn't it? Tom is there in all those moments and she thinks she likes him. She *does* like him. Like I said, she has brilliant taste. She also had really good taste in friends. Eve is great too. But why am I thinking about Eve? Just concentrate, dude.

I gaze down at the documents demanding my attention. Just think of Peggy, *think of Peggy.* This walk is all about people like her. People living on the inside just wanting to be seen. But we can't invite elderly, lonely people out on a walk without enough people to look after them: we need more volunteers. And we need to do something for the ones unable to come outside: find some way they can see what's going on and feel less lonely too.

I look at my message-less phone screen, blank but for the Wi-Fi sign. That's it — we could stream parts of the walk online so that people who can't walk with us can *watch* with us, can feel a part of us. And we'll need to secure some press coverage too. Something to publicise Peggy's Walk far and wide to everyone cooped up inside. I scribble the idea at the bottom of my notebook, already overflowing with thoughts. Right now, I have far more questions than answers. Am I really cut out for this? But I promised Peggy I'd make it happen.

I return my attention to my spreadsheet, trying to force the negative thoughts away. Right now, I feel like I'm sinking, but when I was chatting to Becky, I felt lighter, so many evenings spent laughing at her words. Now I spend countless nights sitting in the same spot feeling isolated by my thoughts again. Completely alone.

Just like Grandma when she died.

I shake my head; she wasn't alone. She was with her family, surrounded by brothers and sisters in a way I never have been. This is my grief again, telling me lies. Maybe my thoughts about Becky aren't true either. Maybe it's just loneliness getting the better of me. I need to stop wallowing. I know not everything is about me now, know what is important. My work: helping people, being there, keeping my promises. I just need to get up, get out, be there for someone, do what I say I am going to do.

No more Becky; she's with Tom now.

And I need to be with Peggy.

'How's my favourite girl today?' I ask Peggy across one of the flower-dressed tables filling the care home's main reception room. She looks tired, a little spaced out, but something about my being here seems to make her come alive.

'Max, I'm one hundred and seven. I should not be your favourite *girl*.'

'Peggy, you're eighty-four.' I laugh, shaking my head. Her sporadic age joke is so well worn that it can't help but feel like home. It's as if being here with her is making me feel like I can breathe again, even if Becky is still lingering in my mind.

'But if I am still managing to be your favourite girl, I must be doing something right. Either that or you're doing something wrong.' Her eyes narrow across the room, and I follow her gaze all the way to Amy. I swear every time I visit, Amy is on shift. No wonder everyone thinks there's something going on between us.

'The only thing I'm doing wrong is . . .' I think of Becky and Tom, and then of the walk, of the lack of volunteers to make the ratios work. I can't tell Peggy, can't have her thinking I'm letting her down. 'Not bringing you more chocolate.' I look down at the empty wrappers between us, my eyes catching on Peggy's liver-spotted hands.

'Max, I've already got dementia, I don't need diabetes too. How are *you*?' She says it with eyebrows raised, and for the briefest of moments she reminds me of Eve. Eve, who is spending her Saturday following her passion, not getting distracted by who her best friend is dating. I need to take a leaf out of her book.

'I'm okay, thanks. Your walk is keeping me nice and busy.'

'It's not my walk,' Peggy says, her voice croaky. 'It's your walk and everyone else's too.' I know that, I really do, but somehow doing it for Peggy makes me feel like I might actually see this through. 'How's it coming along?'

'Great, thanks.' I force my mind to concentrate on all the good bits. 'Route secured and we're well on the way to getting all our other permissions granted. It just takes a bit of time. And we need to work on the volunteers a bit . . .'

'I'm sure Amy would be happy to help.' Peggy grins, eyes

widening at the thought. I don't have the heart to tell her I need a lot more than just Amy.

'Stop trying to meddle.' Even as I say it, I taste the irony.

'I'm not.' Her eyes twinkle and she pushes a strand of grey hair from her heavily lined face. If she needs to get her kicks by playing matchmaker, who am I to deny her that? 'Look, Max, if anyone can pull this walk off, it's you. It sounds brilliant, but I don't need you to—'

'Peggy, I've promised you a walk and a walk you shall get. Just think of what it will mean to all those people who feel so alone.' I smile, taking her fragile hand in mine.

'I know, I know.' She sighs, her smile soft and sad. 'But promise me you won't get so distracted with everyone else's loneliness that you ignore your own.' She isn't to know that there's only one thought that's been distracting me of late.

'I'm not *that* lonely.' I force a laugh. 'I was just saying that to make you feel better.' I roll my eyes but we both know the truth. Well, that part of it at least.

'Yeah, yeah.' Peggy matches my eye roll with one of her own. 'So what are you doing tonight?'

Staying in, reading my book, trying not to think about Becky and Tom.

'Nothing really.'

'Nothing?' I look up to see Amy standing by the table. She looks really cute with her hair tied back. If Paddy were here, he'd be tongue-tied in no time.

'Nothing!' Peggy confirms for her, incredulous. 'A

225

good-looking young man like that with no plans for a Saturday night. Tell me *you're* out and about, Amy. I need to live vicariously through someone.' She sends a little wink my way.

'Just chilling with a takeaway, I'm afraid.' Amy glances at me.

'So you both have plans to do nothing,' Peggy says. I know where she's going with this. 'Well why don't you plan to do nothing together?'

Oh Peggy, you've done it now.

'I'd be up for that.' Amy suddenly looks shy. 'If you are?'

Am I up for that? Well, it's not like I have any other plans. Tom's busy with Becky and Eve's busy with the kind of stuff I probably *should* be busy with. But right now, I'm struggling to find the energy to do anything other than escape. And Amy, warm and welcoming, is offering me a means of doing just that.

Walking up the steps towards the Dickens Inn, Amy is practically buzzing beside me.

'This is gorgeous.' She gazes up at the fairy lights twinkling from the foliage. 'Thanks for suggesting it.'

She smiles at me, and for a moment I feel pretty awful. I bet she thinks I promoted doing nothing together to a proper date to try and impress her. In reality, I need people around us, a table between us to create some distance that two bodies alone on a sofa categorically don't have. If Amy tries to kiss me, I know I won't have the heart to say no, and right now, I don't need any more complications to add to my list.

'Yeah, I love this place.' I follow her into the bar area, only now realising that it's kind of weird that I've suggested here. I've wanted to come back to this place ever since I set up Tom and Becky's first date. But now that I'm here, my mind is conjuring images of them that I've pictured a thousand times since. But that was just because I was feeling lonely. Now that I'm here with Amy, it's time to forget.

I pull out a chair for her at a table in the corner of the bar. Do people do that in bars any more? Isn't it a dinner thing? Contrary to what Tom thinks, to what I am pretending to be, I'm not actually an expert when it comes to these things. I may have the theory, but I'm sorely out of practice.

'It's so nice to hang outside of work.' Amy beams across the table, taking a sip of her wine. 'I've been meaning to suggest it for some time.'

'Yeah, it'll be nice not to talk about work for a bit,' I admit. I've been hoping we'll have something else in common, but now that we're here, I'm not so sure. 'So what would you usually be doing on a weekend?' I ask, the words sounding a little wooden, as if I'm reading from my own script.

I'm sitting in one of my favourite pubs on a Saturday night with a pretty girl; why on earth does part of me not want to be here? I've spent so long yearning for company, and now I have it. Come on, Max, just be present, just be here, now.

'Not a whole lot, really.' Amy smiles, unabashed. 'I usually work at the care home at weekends, so I try to keep my evenings chilled, but the girls drag me out for drinks every so often. I'm ashamed to say there've been a few hung-over shifts.'

Becky would never go to work on a hangover – her passion is too strong to be diluted by drinking – and her weekends are always as packed as her weeks. Damn it, Max, do not think about Becky.

'I can't imagine that's easy.' I force a laugh at the thought.

'I usually just hang out around Roger on those days; he always stinks of booze.'

That's certainly true – Roger is always on the whisky – but somehow making light of someone else's drinking problem doesn't feel like the right thing to do. I can't help but think of Eve.

'How about you? What do you get up to?' Amy asks across the table.

'I like to get out and about a bit,' I say, knowing I've been doing anything but of late. 'I usually go in search of nature.' I laugh, wondering how living in London can make Tooting Common feel like the Peak District. 'Then I like to have some me time but around other people, you know? Soaking up the vibe whilst soaking up a coffee somewhere.' I'm effectively reading Tom's dating profile out loud.

'So you just sit there in coffee shops alone? That's brave.'

'Is it?' I ask. I thought it was pretty normal.

'Yeah, I hate being alone. Like tonight, I was so glad you were around.'

'Really? I love being alone sometimes,' I say. Well, I did. Before I found someone who enjoys all the same things I do.

'So you just sit there?' Why is Amy finding this so hard to get her head around?

'I usually take a book.' So not really alone: I'm with great authors like Jane Austen, Lewis Carroll and Charles Dickens. 'Do you like to read?'

'Not really.' Amy takes another sip. Well, that's that then. 'I'm a big box-set watcher, though; are you into any?'

'Yeah, I'm loving *The Crown* at the moment,' I beam, recalling the romance, the drama. 'You?'

'*RuPaul's Drag Race*,' she says without pause. A different kind of drama then. I can't help but sigh over my beer, my distracted mind darting to a parallel universe, one where Amy and I are sitting here laughing about films and books and whatever news story has just divided the nation. One where Amy looks suspiciously like Becky.

Her eyes fix on mine and my heart starts to pick up pace. We have nothing to talk about, no common ground, except for work: Peggy and the other patients she cares for day after day. Amy is great. *Amy is great.*

'You're so great at your job, Amy.' I smile across at her.

'Except when hung-over.' She laughs and I force myself to do the same. I glance at my watch, subtly so she won't notice, and my heart sinks when I see how little time has passed. 'But thanks, you're great at yours too. Peggy told me about the walk you're planning; it sounds great.'

'Yeah, it will be. It's just . . .' I sigh. 'Like for a normal sponsored walk you'd need loads of volunteers, right?'

'Yes, and the whole charity and all your partner homes will be on board with this.'

'Thanks, yeah . . . thanks,' I say, honestly touched by the thought. 'But I think we'll need more. Each of the people we're trying to reach might need one-to-one support.' It's only as I say it out loud that I realise what a problem that is. 'And I don't want the people who can't come out feeling like they can't join in, making them lonelier still.' My stomach sinks. I've promised Peggy I'll pull this off without even knowing whether I can. All I've ever wanted is to be a man of my word. And yet here I am again. All the right words, zero follow-through.

'So what are you thinking?'

'I'm thinking of setting up some kind of live stream of the walk and some press coverage so that people inside know they can enjoy it too; maybe get some volunteers to visit those house-bound people and help them log on, sit with them to show them they're not alone . . .'

'That's a great idea.' Amy nods, taking another sip.

'Yeah, but it will need even more volunteers.' Oh God, it will need so many. 'I thought making this about loneliness rather than dementia would broaden the appeal.' Classic Max, dreaming bigger than reality. 'But it turns out I've now got too many people to help and not enough helpers.'

'So this is more about loneliness?' Amy asks, and I nod. 'Well, helping Peggy and the other service users certainly makes *me* feel less lonely.'

'Yeah, me too,' I say. So there's one more thing we have in common.

'So maybe don't think of it as helpers and helpees so much

as helping each other. Have you seen the stats about how volunteering lowers anxiety?'

Yes, Becky talked about them in her messages. I nod.

'So why don't you make the event about fighting loneliness generally, and just get able-bodied lonely people coming alongside those who need a bit more physical help? Pitch it as all of us being a little less lonely together, helping one another, levelling the playing field? I don't know, am I making any sense?'

'Perfect sense,' I say. And it's true. If I can get millennials and different interest groups to see that by helping others they'll help themselves too, we really could be on to something. I could reach out to other organisations with this as well: Loneliness Lab, the Jo Cox Foundation, the Minister for Loneliness. Why didn't I think about it earlier? But then, I've been so distracted. 'Perfect sense,' I repeat. 'Thanks, Amy, you're the best.'

'So are you.' She pauses. 'Max, I've been meaning to ask you something . . .' Oh shit, what? 'What do you think about dating work colleagues? Well, not colleagues, technically, but someone you work with?'

She's watching me intently across the table, but I'm struggling to hold eye contact. I may be shit at signals, but I know she's talking about me. She wants me to say I think it's a good idea. But I don't. Well, not if the colleagues are me and her. She's great but just not great for me.

'I'm not sure it's the best idea.' I sigh as I watch her face fall. Just another person I'm letting down. But it's not her, it's me. Me, who doesn't fancy people the way every other red-blooded male seems to. Who falls for a woman's words rather than her looks. Who wants to fall in love with someone's mind; who worries I already have.

'But there are loads of guys who might think differently. Want me to get you another drink?' I say, as half-heartedly as Tom's offer to join him and Becky this morning.

'No, it's okay.' Amy's smile is a little sad. 'I'm not sure it's the best idea.'

Leaving the Dickens Inn behind, I begin the long walk home. It'll take hours, and yet it's not like I'm in a rush, and I really, really need some time to think. Thanks to Amy, I've got a bit more clarity on Peggy's Walk. With some collaboration, some togetherness, we might actually be able to pull it off. The thought might make me feel better if being with Amy hadn't given me clarity on something else: I like Becky. *Shit*, I actually like Becky.

I've spent years reading about love, experiencing it just one step removed; hiding behind the author's words, enjoying romance from the sidelines. I've spent the last couple of years convincing myself I'll never find my perfect woman online, knowing deep down that I'm just not the kind of man a woman like that would go for. I work for a charity, live in a house share, trying to keep it all together whilst my relationship with my family is falling apart. Messaging Becky brought out the best of me, reminded me it was there. But I wasn't being my best self, was I? I was helping *Tom* be his.

I should have known that trying to write someone else's love story would get me tangled in the most powerful, painful love of them all: one that can never be mine.

Chapter Nineteen

Eve

I fix my eyes forward, mind feeling more settled with every house that blurs by. Running on, my body bosses my heartbeat into place. I swear mid run is the only time its rhythm feels right. Not that even that has worked lately. But the sun's out, the job advert is live and the rumours are rife. *Note to self: it's all moving in the right direction.*

'So it's a shoo-in?' Lola asks, keeping pace by my side. Her impossibly long ponytail bounces behind her, propelling her forward to match my too-long legs.

'I wouldn't say a shoo-in.' Although with each passing day I'm feeling more and more sure that Taren isn't getting the job. And if it's not him, then surely it's me? *It's me.* I savour the thought. After all my confusion with Tom, with my dad, it feels good to remind myself of those two little words. *It's me* who's on the cusp of being promoted. *It's me* who made it happen all by myself.

'Well, that's what Becky says,' Lola pants as we turn the corner towards the flat.

'How does she know?' I say before I can stop myself. The words taste bitter. She knows because she asked me, but only because Tom wanted to know. He was asking after me as me – as Eve, not Becky. He cares about my job, about me.

'Missing her?' Lola asks as I push my burning limbs forward. I wish I hadn't said anything. Lola sees through me – for the most part, at least. She doesn't know about me messaging Tom. Or about my dad's letters. I wouldn't tell her before Becky anyway, but then I told Max, didn't I?

'Yeah, a little,' I sigh, forcing all thoughts of Max and Tom from my mind as my trainers pound against the pavement. *Note to self: your life was perfectly fine before they came swiping into it.*

'I thought she used to distract you?' Lola has a point.

'I guess you always want what you can't have.' I laugh, though it doesn't feel very funny. Becky hasn't been out all the time. It's just that when she's in, it's usually with Tom, his big body and even bigger brain forcing its way into our space.

'It'll pass.' Lola smiles across at me. I really hope it does. At least focusing on the promotion is helping. It feels so close now, almost within reach. 'You know what Becky's like in a relationship. It's how you guys adopted me in the first place.' My mind shoots back to when Becky was with Lola's brother 24/7 so the two of us teamed up ourselves. It was a simpler time. 'The woman goes all in . . .'

'That's true.' I nod. I usually go all in too. Apart from in romance, where I've spent so long sitting on the sidelines that I've practically counted myself out of the game. 'I'm just being silly.'

'You're not being silly, you're just being honest.'

Yes, but not honest enough. For a moment I want to tell Lola about the letters. That since receiving the second one, since chatting it over with Max, I've saved my dad's number in my phone, that I've pulled it up to call countless times before thinking better of it.

'You do know it's okay to sit with your feelings sometimes, to not just run away?' Lola continues. She draws to a halt and I fall into step beside her.

Yes, I know. And I will. But not until I've got what I've been fighting for since I was a little girl: the opportunity to tell real stories. I've told Max my own story, and for now that's enough. I don't need anyone encouraging me to get online, to reach out to my dad, to work on the relationships I've ignored whilst building some stability for myself. No, I'll get the job sorted and then I'll think about sorting everything else. *Note to self: one thing at a time.*

'When did you get so wise?' I throw a sweaty arm around Lola, inhaling deeply.

'Since I started hanging out with you and Becky,' she pants in return.

'Been learning from the best?' I laugh.

'Yeah.' Lola's laugh joins mine. 'Learning what not to do.'

★   ★   ★

I don't need my alarm clock to tell me it's Monday. I've been up for hours, brain in overdrive. It's occupied with the same old stuff: articles, pitches, people I should be thinking about, people I shouldn't be.

But somehow today feels different. Not in a convincing-myself-it'll-be-different way. It feels like something big is about to happen. Reporter's intuition? I've heard colleagues talk about it. Waking up and just knowing the specific location of their next scoop. But as I make my way to the News Building and take the lift to my floor, I know for a fact that I'm exactly where I'm meant to be.

Grabbing the post piled on my desk, I flick through the envelopes at speed. There's nothing out of the ordinary, no sign of the handwriting I was half dreading, half hoping to find. It's only then that I clock that Makena's seat is empty. Ever since I've been putting in the hours at home – pretending to be Becky and then working hard to remind myself who I really am – Makena has consistently beaten me here. But then again, with her lover boy living just across the water, she has no excuse to be late any more. But if that's the case, where is she now?

I head across the office to the break-out area. If I can't find Makena, at least I can find coffee.

'Did you *hear*?'

Moving around the kitchenette, opening a cupboard, pulling out a mug, my ears prick up at the collection of colleagues gossiping over caffeine. Hear what?

'Angela's baby is coming early,' one of them says. 'She's fine but the baby's pretty small, so they've scheduled a

Caesarean for a couple of weeks' time. Trust her baby to be eager.'

'Classic overachiever.' I can almost hear another rolling her eyes.

'So when's she leaving?'

'End of next week. Apparently management have pretty much chosen her replacement. Reckon there'll be an announcement later today . . .'

My heart hammers at the words, hands shaking as I make my coffee. I want to wait, to see what else they have to say, but I know they've clocked me listening in. Turns out it's hard to be invisible when you're over six foot. Let's hope the management team have noticed me too.

When I return to my desk, Makena's still nowhere to be seen. I need to talk to her right now. If the chatter in the break-out area is anything to go by, there are some rumours flying around, and when it comes to office gossip, Makena is the queen.

Eve: Still with lover boy? I need you in the office ASAP. New role. Red alert.

A buzz from her desk draws my attention to her abandoned phone. So she's already here. Okay, it's fine. They won't make the announcement today; surely they need to shortlist and interview first?

Switching on my computer, I scan my emails, but there's nothing out of the ordinary: a stack of messages from PRs, and a few new pitches approved: The Hottest Nail Varnishes

238

This Season. How to Stop a Spot Before It's Begun. Top Ten Online Dating Rules. Just a brief scan of the rules tells me that Becky and I have broken most of them. Although saying that, our message ploy seems to be benefiting everybody but me. But I don't need that distraction any more. I've been far more focused since Becky and Tom have been up and running, and chatting to Max reminded me about what matters most. Using my own backstory as fuel for the fire, propelling me into a purposeful future that is only days, hours, even minutes away.

'I'm here,' Makena says next to me, reading the message I've just sent to her out loud.

'Oh crap.' I press my hand to my heart. 'You made me jump!' It isn't like Makena to be subtle, sneaky. But I didn't hear her slide into the desk beside me.

'Sorry, Eve,' she says, and as I turn to her, she seems a little sad. Like she's sorrier for something far bigger than surprising me. I'm sure it's nothing serious. Between me and Makena it rarely is; our friendship is too tight to sweat the small stuff.

'Did you hear the rumours?' If any question can get her going, it's this.

'No?' She looks like a deer in the headlights. But she usually knows everything.

'Apparently they're making an announcement about Angela's replacement soon.'

'Oh, right.' Why does she look worried? Does she not think I'm going to get it? That they've decided to go with Taren all along? *Note to self: do not jump to conclusions, Eve. One thing at a time.*

'Makena?' She's usually so vibrant. 'Is everything okay?' She struggles to look at me, and when she finally does, her eyes are swimming with tears. What the hell? 'Oh shit, what's the matter? Is it Ajay?' She'll be devastated if they break up.

'It's not Ajay.' She sighs, a single tear falling down her cheek. Then what? 'Eve.' She reaches a hand to rest on my knee, our chairs now just inches apart. 'It's Angela's role.'

'Oh crap, no.' My heart is hammering. They've interviewed already? They've given it to someone else? I take off my jumper, temperature rising. Just breathe, Eve, breathe. 'They've given it to someone else?' I ask, and slowly Makena begins to nod.

Crap, crap, crap.

'But they haven't even interviewed for it, have they?'

'They did some last week.' She's actually crying now. They what? But how did I not know? And if Makena knew, why didn't she tell me?

I can't help the tears that are filling my own eyes. Sweat prickling on my skin. Heart throbbing in my chest. Vision becoming blurrier. My surroundings feeling less and less real. All the symptoms I love when I'm running somewhere feel like dread when I'm fixed to the spot. The same damn spot I've been trying to move on from for years.

'Yeah, I wasn't sure whether you'd got an interview and just wanted to keep it quiet.'

Why would I keep it quiet? But then there's so much else I've decided to keep that way: Tom, my dad. Never this, though. This is the only thing I'd let myself shout from the rooftops.

'And now you think they've filled the role?' *My* role. It was meant to be mine.

'I know they have.' Makena pulls herself together, wiping away a stray tear.

'Taren?' I ask, dreading the answer.

'No.'

No? Not Taren? Then who? It was only ever him and me.

'Me.' Makena's hand on mine burns red hot. 'They gave it to me.'

'Eve? *Eve?*' I can hear Makena hammering on the toilet door along the corridor. The sound fades into the hammering of my heart, throbbing against my too-tight chest. Makena? They gave the role to Makena? But that means she applied for it without telling me. That she interviewed for it without me knowing. That she listened to me chatting on and on about how that position was made for me. And she just stayed silent.

Sitting on the toilet lid, legs shaking, head in my hands, I try to calm my breathing. Breathe in, breathe out. But the walls feel like they're closing in, stealing all the air from my lungs. It was just a job. It was just a job. *It was just a job.*

But it wasn't just a job. It was the step up I needed to validate everything I've built, to show that the single-mindedness I've cultivated all this time was worth it. Worth every mile I've run in the morning. Every article I've written late into the night. Every date I've turned down. Every urge to contact my dad that I've ignored.

Becky thinks I'm a girl-boss, that I'm smashing it at life.

So does Max. Buying my bullshit about taking all my broken bits and using them to build something bigger, better for myself. Tom even fell for the bits of me I managed to bring into Becky. And all this time I've just been lying to myself.

Fumbling in my pocket, I hold my phone in my hands, searching for a lifeline. Headspace won't cut it this time. No app able to fill the void. *Note to—* Oh what's the point? Datespace? It was only ever a distraction. A distraction from fixing my eyes on the prize. From seeing Makena sweep in to take my space. I don't want to see her now. Becky? I can't. She'll be teaching, thriving at work like she's thriving at home. Her parents? They were never mine in the first place.

I scroll to my dad's number, reading the digits. Tears stream down my face and scatter across the screen. I need family right now. Someone to be there to remind me what I know in my heart but have never had the strength to say: yes, I want to write stories that matter, but I want to matter to someone else more.

As soon as I dial the number, I hang up.

To love is to be vulnerable.

I wanted this step up at the newspaper more than anything. And look where that got me. No, I can't let him in. Not until I've got my shit together. Otherwise I'll start building my life on him again just to have him let me down once more. Relationships work for some people. Like Becky and Tom. Man, I want to message him now. To lose myself for a while. The best parts of me and the best parts of Becky bouncing off the best parts of him. Why do I always want what I can't have?

242

Maybe this is my lot. A supplementary woman writing supplementary content. Being supplementary to everyone's lives. Happily enough.

The phone vibrates in my hands: *Dad?* But then the message flashes from the screen.

Max: Hey, Eve. Tom gave me your number – hope you
don't mind. He mentioned it might be a big week at
work for you. Just wanted to wish you luck. M x

I reread the message, longing to wind back time. To unsay all the things I said about this role and the stories and the reason I wanted to rise. None of it matters now. My tears fall into the silence, colliding with Max's message.

Chapter Twenty

Max

Becky: Morning! How were your sessions? Confession: I've not got out of bed yet.

Becky: Sorry, me again. Finally up! Want to do something later on?

Becky: Assuming you're busy but would be good to know if we're on or not. Eve's a bit down and if we're not hanging out I'm going to try and cheer her up.

Becky: Tom?

Yvonne: So good to see you at the gym this morning. Was nice to finally talk. Made me realise how much I've missed it.

Yvonne: And by it, I mean you.

Yvonne: I'm out in Tooting. Fancy a drunk?

Yvonne: DRINK, dammit. Stupid autocorrect.

Yvonne: But I am drunk. So I guess the question still stands.

Yvonne: Oh God. I'm so sorry for the drunken texts last night. Any chance you fancy helping nurse my hangover over a coffee? It'd be good to talk. X

'Fancy doing something today?' I look over at Tom, who is busy typing on his phone, his smile as wide as the first time he and Becky started messaging. Well, Becky and I. I can't believe that was three months ago. Since then, the two of them have been getting stronger. And I've been forcing my feelings for her further inside, nestled in close to my anxiety about the future, my regret from the past.

'I can't, mate, sorry.' He barely looks up. 'Heading out for a coffee.'

'With Becky?' I ask, but I already know the answer. He's always with Becky. But then again, he seems pretty busy at the gym recently. And he mentioned something about Becky's school preparing for SATs, so I guess she's busy too. I've not seen her around the flat since last week, which in part is a welcome relief, though another part of me kind of misses having her here. Damn it. Don't think about Becky.

'Could invite Eve and make it a foursome?'

As soon as the words leave my mouth, I regret it, knowing Tom will latch on to any mention of Eve.

'Sorry, mate,' he says, serious for a moment. Did he not hear what I said? Unless the thought of me dating someone while trying to organise Peggy's Walk is so far-fetched that he isn't even bothering.

'What's up, dude?' I ask, sitting up a little straighter.

'Nothing.' Tom shrugs, stashing his phone and getting

245

up, ready to leave. It's only then that I realise he's been on his work phone. He must be *really* busy at the gym. He only uses that phone to talk to clients.

'I know when you're lying,' I say, hoping he doesn't think the same about me. Haven't I been lying to him about Becky all this time?

'Okay, well don't freak out.' He turns to face me, and for a moment I'm scared of what comes next. Freak out about what? He knows I'm not good at surprises. 'But I'm not meeting Becky.'

What? Then who?

'I'm meeting Yvonne.'

'Yvonne?' I repeat, not meaning my voice to rise an octave.

'I told you not to freak out.' Tom shakes his head, forcing a smile. 'It's no big deal.'

'Dude, it's *Yvonne*,' I say. 'It's always a big deal.' Their whole relationship was a big deal. Massive highs, huge lows, big break-ups, big make-ups. And then the final break-up followed by the worst down I'd seen Tom go through. Until a little woman called Becky came into our lives and made it all better. 'Why?' I ask the one question that Tom's trying not to ask himself.

'She approached me at the gym a week or so back,' Tom explains, like he wasn't asking for this to happen. 'And we just started chatting and I wondered whether there was something there still. But obviously I've been seeing Becky—'

'You've been seeing Becky *a lot*,' I say, not entertaining any downplaying of it.

'So I didn't go chasing it, but then Yvonne drunk-texted

me a couple of times. I've been trying to ignore it, but I think there are still feelings there . . .'

'But I thought you liked Becky?' Otherwise why the hell have I been feeling so awful for liking her too?

'I did,' Tom says, before correcting himself. 'I do. It's just, we've been struggling to keep the momentum going a bit, like we're running out of things to talk about.'

'You could have asked for my help?' I say, not meaning to sound so hopeful.

'Yeah, but you can't keep making me out to be the perfect guy forever,' Tom objects.

'I wasn't—'

'And this is *Yvonne*.' He smiles again and I want to wipe that silly grin right off his face. Not that it was much easier to handle when the woman who caused it was Becky, but she really seems to like Tom. And the thought of him upsetting her now is even worse. 'She likes me for me.'

'Yeah, until she doesn't any more.'

'What's that supposed to mean?' Tom asks abruptly. I've clearly hit a nerve.

'You know what it means, dude,' I say, trying to soften my voice but feeling an anger I've boxed in somewhere starting to rage within me. I'm not sure who I'm more angry at. Tom for threatening what he has with Becky, Yvonne for being the bombshell or me for caring for Becky so much that I'm just too damn invested in making sure she doesn't get hurt. 'Yvonne's great and everything, but she's never been sure what she wants. You thought she was all in last time, until she slept with that other PT.'

247

'Yeah, but that was my fault.' My eyes widen in disbelief. How the hell was that his fault? 'We never put a label on what we were. I thought we were more serious than Yvonne did, so technically it was just a miscommunication.'

'Well how about you and Becky? Where are you guys at now?'

'We haven't discussed it.' Tom sighs. 'But she's been a bit off this week.' No she hasn't. I've seen Tom's personal phone, discarded on our coffee table, lighting up with messages from her all week. I just assumed he'd replied when I wasn't around.

'Okay, great, so you're just going to do to Becky exactly what Yvonne did to you? Play the "we didn't put a label on it" card?'

'I'm not playing any card, Max.' Tom shakes his head, clearly getting more and more frustrated. 'I'm just following my heart. Something that a guy who reads as much romance as you doesn't know all that much about.'

Ouch, that was uncalled for.

'So you've told Becky this? That you're following your heart all the way to coffee with your ex?'

'No,' Tom admits, a flash of sadness darting across his face. I know he likes Becky; they seem happy together, even when it makes me feel anything but. 'But I will.'

I want Tom to be happy. I want Becky to be happy too.

'You're going to regret it, dude.' I shake my head. I might not know much about following my heart, but I sure as hell know what it means to regret not doing it.

'No, I won't.' Tom stiffens, his expression serious. 'Yvonne says she's changed her mind.'

'But she'll change it back again.' I shake my head. 'I promise you she will.' I'm sure Yvonne can be lovely, to her friends, to her family, to a man she's set her heart on. But she hasn't set her heart on Tom, not now, not then. If she had, she wouldn't have broken his in the first place. 'Then when things come crashing down with her, you're going to wish you'd kept it going with Becky.'

'So what are you saying, I shouldn't end things with Becky?'

'Yes.' I nod. 'And you shouldn't start things with Yvonne.'

'Well I'm not doing that,' Tom snaps, shaking his head, defiant and delusional, as he begins to pace the space between us.

'Women like Becky don't come along every day,' I say, and I've never been more sure about anything.

'Well if you like her so much, why don't you go for it?' Tom spits, his clenched jaw, his clenched fists telling me this is far from a blessing. He wouldn't be okay with it. Because he likes her, he really does. He's just blindsided by Yvonne. 'It's your personality she fell for anyway.' He throws his personal phone towards the sofa cushions beside me.

'That's not true,' I say. It can't be true. Because if that's the case, why has she spent the last three months with Tom? Star-crossed lovers are less romantic in real life. Turns out they're just really fucking sad. And if Tom ends this for Yvonne now, there'll be two more broken hearts in the world. 'Please don't do this, Tom.'

'I've got to go,' he says, struggling to hold eye contact, as if even he knows this is a bad idea. Like deep down he knows he's going to regret it. 'If you want to message Becky from me, keep things ticking over until Yvonne *changes her mind*, be my guest.' He looks upset now, upset that I don't have his back. Why can't he see that I do? 'But don't blame me when you end up hurting her even more. I know you're far too high and mighty for anything like online dating, but sometimes letting something dwindle naturally is the kindest thing you can do.'

'Or you can just shag someone else and break their heart instead?' I say as he turns away, his huge frame heading towards an even huger mistake. 'You know what that feels like, right, buddy?'

He turns back to look at me, shoulders squared, eyes filled with fire. For a moment I think I've got him, that he might come to his senses. But then he opens the door and is gone, and the next thing I hear is his phone buzzing with a message demanding to be read.

Becky: Tom, what's going on? I've barely heard from you all week.

Becky: And I really don't want to believe this, but I can't help wondering whether it's because we finally slept together.

Becky: Please tell me you're not just another guy who finally got what he wanted?

I look down at the screen, reading and rereading Becky's messages and wishing I could erase them from my memory all at the same time. What the hell is Tom playing at? This is so out of character for him. But then again, isn't it me who's been playing the character of Tom all along? At least everything I said just now was truthful. Yvonne is going to change her mind. Or cheat on him. Either way, she's going to break his heart. Again. And now Tom is breaking Becky's.

Tom, what's going on? I wish I could tell her. That Tom is brilliant, everything she's hoped for and more, but that even the greatest of guys has weaknesses, every hero an Achilles heel, and Tom's is Yvonne.

My eyes dart around the room, searching for something – anything – to distract me from Becky's messages. Tom is long gone. But eventually he'll come to his senses and he'll want to take her in his arms and never let go. And he needs to, because if Becky isn't with him, she sure as hell can't be with me. Not after everything that has happened.

Please tell me you're not just another guy who finally got what he wanted? So they finally slept together? I'd wondered when they would, ever since Tom had told me the wait had started to mean so much more, though part of me didn't want to know. Becky thought they had a future together, and now *this*? I swear Yvonne has a sensor for these things. For knowing just the right time to come and fuck up my friend's life. And now Tom has gone to her, even though I tried to stop it, to tell him that it didn't need to play out this way . . .

But maybe it *doesn't* need to play out this way. I have his phone. I have Becky's messages. And I have Tom's permission. Well, kind of.

Don't blame me when you end up hurting her even more. His

words spin through my mind. But how is sleeping with her and staying silent any kinder? Tom will come to his senses eventually, but by then, his silence may have stretched for too long. I don't want to see him regret this. And I hate the fact that Becky might get hurt. If heartbreak can be avoided, isn't omission as bad as getting involved? I helped them get started after all; maybe if I can just keep them going until this thing with Yvonne finishes, their love story might still yet have a happy ending.

I look down at Tom's phone in my hands, take a deep breath and begin to type.

Tom: Hey, Becky! I'm so sorry. I lost my phone earlier in the week and I've been trying to contact you. And work's been mad – it's still mad. But I promise you I'm definitely not just another guy. How you been? X

I mean, it's a shitty excuse given all the other ways he could have reached her, but Becky must know Tom isn't a social media guy. And if she likes him like I think she does, then hopefully it's enough. I look down at the message, still not sure whether it's a good idea but knowing for certain that Yvonne isn't, and that in any case, it's too late to turn back now . . .

Becky is typing . . .

Chapter Twenty-One

Eve

'Oh shit, he's messaged, he's messaged,' Becky squeals, and before I know it, she's snuggled by my side, sending Buster scarpering across the room.

'Who?' I look at her through bleary eyes. I've been up for hours, but after dragging myself from my bed to the sofa, I haven't moved an inch.

'Tom,' she says, looking a little concerned. And not just about Tom. About me.

'Oh, right, yeah,' I say.

I should have known. Becky's been talking about him all week. And not in the way she was before, all excited and loved up. No, that kind of chat climaxed last weekend. The second they'd slept together. The post-sex run-through was the most painful I'd had to endure. I knew the moment was coming, but after so long, it kind of caught me off guard. It was Tom, *Tom*. The man who had occupied my mind for all the moments it hadn't been filled with work. And now the work part felt pretty painful too.

Looking around the room, at my closed laptop edging further and further beneath the sofa, my stomach churns. Oh God, I don't want to think about work again. I've gone over and over the same ground with Becky all week. As she's gone over and over Tom's messages since that night. More sporadic with each passing day. 'I'm so stupid,' she said while I stroked her hair and dried her tears. 'I should have known I'd never meet anyone good online.' I tried to tell her otherwise. But misery loves company, I guess.

'He says he lost his phone; that's just an excuse, right?' Becky looks at me, snuggling my elephant cushion to her chest. She needs me to be her stability right now. Eve the elephant; sensible and secure. Who am I trying to kid? Ever since Makena's announcement – or confession or betrayal or whatever else I've called it this past week – I've felt smaller than I've ever felt before. Small, vulnerable, insignificant. Yet here's Becky still looking at me like I have something of worth to say. Like what I have to say matters.

'It is an excuse,' I say, not meaning to sigh. It isn't Becky's fault this is all happening now. It's mine; I should have seen it coming, shouldn't have been so wrapped up in my own success that I didn't see Makena as a competitor. 'But is it a good enough one?'

'I don't know.' Becky sounds on the verge of tears. She cried and cried the first day he didn't call. And I've cried and cried ever since hearing about the job – tears of sadness, tears of embarrassment. I'm surprised that between us we have any left to fall.

'Do you want it to be?' I ask. Becky is happy with Tom, isn't she? And I've been happy spending time with him too. But even if this is the end for the two of them, it could hardly be the start of something for me. That ship sailed around the time I first swiped his profile as Becky. Maybe if I hadn't been so distracted with him, with my dad, I wouldn't have missed all the signals pointing to Makena in the first place. *Note to*— Oh it doesn't really matter now.

'Part of me does.' Becky looks down at his message. She starts to type a reply. Then stops and deletes it. Then starts again. Man, I wish we could start this whole damn story all over again. 'There was a part of me that really connected with him, that thought we had something special . . .' She stutters to a halt, and for a moment she looks like she's going to cry again. Oh God, I hate seeing her like this. I wish there was more I could do to help. But I can't even help myself. 'But another part wonders whether we really had all that much in common, whether he might be better suited to someone like you . . .'

'I'm sure that's not true,' I say, trying to muster some energy. Some hope. For her.

'Come on, Eve,' she says, enough energy for both of us. 'He sleeps with me and then instantly cools off. Suspicious timing, don't you think?'

'Yeah, but that doesn't sound like Tom,' I say, hating the fact that I know him so well. 'And anyway, if he was just in it for sex, he would have ended things ages ago.'

'Maybe he was enjoying the thrill of the chase, or whatever it was you told me about.'

Maybe if I hadn't meddled in the first place, Becky wouldn't be in this situation. She would have been with her usual guys: one date, one night, on to the next. But I'd encouraged her to believe in her happy-ever-after, to invest in something different, deeper – and now what? She'd ended up let down and heart-bruised. Like I had with Makena. And my dad. And well, anyone else I'd let in before.

'Eve?' Becky asks, clearly worried by my lethargy.

I guess Becky has always been here for me. She's seen all of me, repeatedly, and she's never let me down. Maybe I should have told her about the letters from my dad. But that doesn't matter now. I'm not taking any more risks. I'm going to concentrate on helping the one person who has been there from the start. Tom was good for her. And so what if for a moment I thought maybe he'd be good for me too?

'I think you should give him the benefit of the doubt. He makes you happy, and life is really short. So if you want to do something, trust yourself, don't overthink it.'

'That doesn't sound like you,' Becky says before she can think better of it.

But she's right. It doesn't sound like me. It sounds a hell of a lot like Max. Maybe if I'd taken his advice sooner – if I'd sent in my application, forced myself into the right meetings, the right rooms – I wouldn't be stuck in this dead-end job.

'I know, I . . .' I stutter, trying to find the words. I'm crying again. When will I stop crying? It was only a job. And Makena deserves it too. I'll find the strength to cheer her on one day. But right now, it just feels like the finishing line has shifted from beneath my feet. I was working towards it for so long that now I have no idea what's worth fighting for any more.

'Oh Eve. It will get better soon, I promise.' Becky wraps her arms around me. 'Is it just about the job? Not that that's not a valid reason,' she adds quickly. 'I know how much that opportunity means to you.' She pulls away and looks at me, just wanting to make everything okay. And here I am wanting to make everything better for her.

'Meant to me,' I correct, the words catching in my throat. It's over now. But things don't need to be over for Becky and Tom, not if she doesn't want them to be.

'I know, Evie,' she soothes. '*Eve*, sorry.' She knows only my dad calls me that. 'I can't help feeling this is a bit about him too,' she sighs.

'About Tom?' I say, not meaning to sound so guilty.

'No,' she says, confused by my confusion. But then she knows I've not been myself all week, maybe even before then. I guess I've felt a little lost for a while. It's easy to ignore that when you've fixed your eyes in one direction, on one destination. 'Your dad.'

'What's my dad got to do with this?' I ask. She hasn't found the letters, has she? But I know she hasn't. If she had, she would have said something by now. Plus we've been taking it in turns to do the chocolate run all week. If Becky knew there was a secret stash in one of the top cupboards, it wouldn't have survived the past few days.

'I just . . . You haven't mentioned him at all lately, not even a little bit,' she says, treading on eggshells all of a sudden. My heart beats harder in my chest. A run would usually calm it. But I'm knackered. It's as if all the stress and hard work of the last few weeks has come to collect its debt. 'And you've just been so focused on the job, and then so . . .'

'Broken?'

'Not broken.' Becky shakes away the thought, but her hands, still resting on the tops of my arms, squeeze a little tighter. As if trying to hold all the shards of my heart together. 'Just bruised. And I know sometimes you try and run away from family stuff, and I don't know . . . Am I way off the mark?'

No, Becky. You're not. You're bang on the money. And I love you for it. I should have told you about the letters a long time ago. But things are messy with Makena now, messy at work. Messy in my mind. And right now you're the only thing that's right and I can't risk hurting you too.

'I guess I've been too distracted by the job to really think about him.' I smile through my sadness, the weight of his letters feeling heavier still. Not light like they did with Max. Buster springs up from the carpet to stretch across my lap, noticing that I need a lift.

'Okay, that's it!' Becky gets to her feet, sending Buster running scared again just when he thought he'd found some stability. I know the feeling, mate. 'We're going out.'

'We're what?' I look at her as if I've forgotten what 'out' means. And who could blame me? I've been a hermit ever since my heartbreak.

'Going out,' Becky repeats. 'Yes, you're disappointed. Yes,

you're down. And yes, Tom has disappointed me too . . .' Her eyes dart to her phone for a moment, his message still unanswered. She's making him sweat, and I would feel proud if it didn't feel like all my major keys had been replaced with minors. 'But we can't just wallow here, expecting someone else to make it all better.'

Someone else to make it all better is what Becky has hoped for ever since I've known her. A knight in shining armour riding in on his bright white steed. But maybe all my darkness has been enough to prompt some positivity in her.

'But I'm tired,' I say, almost scared at the thought of going out, of putting myself back out there again.

'I know, darling, but you're going to stay feeling tired if you don't move. You're *Eve*.' She says my name as if it's supposed to mean something. But what if all my Eve has run out? All my *notes to self* run dry? What if all my chasing stories and running miles before breakfast was really just me running away?

'Why don't I see if Lola and Makena are free and we can make a night of it, cheer each other up?' Becky looks at me and my face must say it all: why do Lola and Makena need cheering up?

'You go ahead.' I smile at her, now my turn to give her a little squeeze. She's handling this Tom stuff so well all of a sudden. Just another sign that she loves that he's messaged, that a part of her is starting to feel in control again. God, I'd give anything to feel the same. 'I'm just really tired. I think I fancy a night in with my book.' I'm trying to sound more okay than I feel. Turns out I can be a pretty good liar.

'Now that sounds more Eve,' Becky says. 'I can stay with you if you like?'

'No, no.' I shake my head, not knowing why I'm pushing her away. Maybe because I know she needs to blow off some steam too. And unbeknownst to Tom, reading a book is not Becky's idea of letting her hair down. 'You go. You deserve it after this week. Going to message him back?' I ask. She should. Tom is great and Becky deserves the best.

'Do you know what?' She's typing at speed to call in backup: Makena and Lola, maybe Ajay and Benj too. 'I don't think so. Eve, he finally slept with me and then fell off the face of the planet – for a *week*.'

'He said he lost his phone and that work's been busy,' I remind her.

'Work's been busy for me too, and I still managed to message.'

'Yes, I know but . . .' I'm suddenly not sure why I'm defending him. Maybe because I've been so low this week that the thought of losing one more thing hurts like hell.

'I'm done with boys,' Becky says. A sentence I've heard a thousand times before. 'Yes, I liked Tom. Yes, I thought he was a good one, but his actions say otherwise. And *my* actions?' She stands up from the sofa. She's not grown an inch, but somehow she's standing taller. She holds her phone up and I watch her swipe and press the screen. Has she messaged him back? 'Deleted.'

'Deleted?'

'And blocked.' She smiles, but I can see the sadness in her eyes. 'And Max's for good measure. Can you delete him too? Full cull. I know he got your number from Tom.'

It's the simplest of requests. For a second I wish I hadn't told her about Max's text. But I did – and I told her it didn't mean anything. Just like the many other things that don't mean anything any more.

'Oh, I . . .' Part of me doesn't want to delete his number. But why? Maybe because it's my only link to Tom. But with Becky here, waiting impatiently for me to take out my phone, it's not like I have much of a choice. 'Deleted.'

I stare at my book. I must have reread this passage a thousand times, but it's just not going in. It's like my mind is too busy to take any more. So I'm not moving forward at work. And Becky isn't moving forward with Tom. Both dreams deleted, blocked, my almost-friendship with Max just collateral damage. I can imagine Becky now, laughing and joking with Lola, toasting Makena's promotion. And I will too. One day. I'm just not ready for that yet. I guess I'm just not ready for a lot of things.

I turn the page, hoping to turn the thought away. Becky might do a good job of pretending to be okay. But come tomorrow, hung-over and unhappy, I know she'll start to miss Tom. To wonder what might have been. To wonder how things would have unfolded if she'd just decided to message him back.

And then there's Max. Maybe he'll text me again. But

then what? It's not like I can be friends with him if Becky isn't dating Tom. And as for Tom getting in touch with me? He's never knowingly done it before.

Before I realise it, my book is on my lap and my phone is in my hands, hovering over the number I haven't dialled since that moment in the toilet cubicle at work. No, I don't want to call Dad. It isn't about him. Plus, he must have seen the missed call and he still hasn't returned it – surely he must know it's from me? No, this is about so much more than him; this is about a life I've been building for myself that has now veered woefully off script. I've never been a relationship girl. I've been a work girl. A get-promoted girl, a too-busy-for-a-man girl. Until I wasn't.

My finger moves towards the dating app still down-loaded on my phone. I should have deleted it a long time ago. As soon as Becky didn't need my help any more. Something was stopping me. But what's stopping me now? I hover over it, and then click. I was too busy to date before. But if I'm not getting that role, not getting in touch with my dad, maybe I'll have a bit of time for someone. Someone like Tom?

Flicking left and right, I get a few matches, but before long, my finger is drifting to the messages. Only then do I remember that these matches aren't mine, this profile has *never* been mine. That I've never made one about me. Scrolling through my conversations with Tom, I see so much of myself on the page. A part of me I liked. Naturally, the messages are from months ago. Setting up our first date at the Dickens Inn – the one I never got to go on. Messaging

262

before our double date – the first time we ever actually met. It was confusing seeing him in person but chatting to him as me: it wasn't the same. But the man I messaged here? That man I'm really starting to love.

The phone starts to shake in my hands. Oh *shit*. Tom has messaged Becky on the app.

Tom: Hey, Becky. I'm not sure if you got my message or you've blocked my number or something, but I'm honestly really sorry for being MIA. There's been a lot going on but I'd love to talk to you about it if you'll just give me a second chance. If you don't message back, I'll take the hint and stop bothering you, I promise. X

He's asking for a second chance. And I know Becky will want to give him one. She really liked Tom. She was happy with him. She's just had too many bad boys to trust that a good man can exist.

Leave this, Eve, *leave this*. But for the first time all week, the adrenalin pumping around my veins has me up and ready to run. If I leave this and Becky doesn't reply, then Tom might delete the app. Or he might meet someone else. Maybe if I just keep things ticking along, from a distance, Becky will thank me in the long run.

Even as I start to type, I know this is a bad idea. But like an addict trying to resist alcohol, the guilt washes over me before I've taken my first sip.

Becky: Hey, stranger, long time.

Tom: Hey, Becky. I'm so sorry.

Tom: And I've really missed chatting to you.

Becky: I've missed you too.

Tom is typing . . .

For a moment it feels like everything is right with the world. Yes, this is a bad idea. And yes, I'm not in the best place to be making decisions. But I am doing this for Becky. If I don't, she'll be regretting what may have been with Tom for years to come. This relationship started with my help and it sure as hell isn't going to end with an unsatisfactory fizzle. If we can't help each other make our happy endings, then what are friends for?

Chapter Twenty-Two

Max

Max: Hey. You around?

Tom work: No, sorry, mate. I'm with Yvonne today.

Max: Cool.

Tom work: We're just hanging round her house otherwise I'd ask you to join.

Max: It's totally cool.

Tom work: Maybe the three of us could hang out sometime?

Max: Has Yvonne said she wants to?

Tom work: Not exactly.

Tom work: But she can't keep me to herself forever, can she?

No, Tom, she can't. Why can't he see that she's just using him? I look up from my phone to navigate past the people walking by. It's another gorgeous day and yet Yvonne is keeping Tom tucked away inside. Away from her friends, away from his, because let's face it, if you keep your relationship in a box, it's easy to return it just before your receipt runs out.

A group of friends walk past me, almost forcing me off the pavement. Of course Yvonne and Tom aren't hanging out with other people. Once you introduce your significant other to your significant others, things get messy, harder to break apart. Friends make everything complicated. But how Yvonne feels about Tom? She's lonely and he's easy – at least to her. That part is pretty obvious – at least to *me*.

Becky: Good morning.
Becky is typing . . .

And then there's Becky. I reach for Tom's phone with the cracked screen, stashed in my pocket. She still likes Tom too. But not because of his body; because of his brain. A brain that will come to its senses soon and realise that it's Becky he preferred all along, that he never should have let her go. Tom has always had my back, always been there for me – well, before Yvonne came and drew his attention further and further away from his friends. And isn't this – me messaging Becky, keeping things ticking over – just me having Tom's back, being there for *him*? Yvonne will end things soon and there will be one more lonely person in the world. Isn't that what I've spent the past couple of years trying to avoid? Why I'm on my way to update Peggy about the walk? I want to make people feel less alone. And then there's the tiny fact that speaking to Becky makes me feel a little less alone too.

Becky: How did you sleep?

Tom: Good thanks. How about you?

Becky: Yeah, all right. Probably shouldn't have stayed up quite so late, though.

Tom: Who were you in bed with this time?

Becky: Dickens.

Tom: Again?!

Becky: I think your date kick-started some kind of obsession.

Becky: *Our date.

Tom: Ha! So what are you up to today?

Becky: Working still.

Becky: SO.

Becky: MUCH.

Becky: MARKING.

Tom: Bless you!

Becky: You're the same though, right?

Tom: Yeah, patients coming out of my ears.

Becky: Patients?

Tom: I mean clients.

Tom: So sorry I've not been able to see you this last couple of weeks. It's just been mad. Soon, though?

Becky: Don't worry, I'm as busy as you.

Becky: And to be honest?

Becky: After our little wobble, it's quite nice just going back to basics for a bit.

267

Tom: I know, I still feel bad about that.

Becky: It's okay. I forgive you, plus messaging is fun. Feels like the early days, right?

Yes, it feels like the early days. When things were simple. When it was just me, Tom's phone and Becky. Maybe part of me is enjoying it, but that doesn't mean I'm not doing it for Tom. It's like Amy said at the Dickens Inn: don't think of it as helpers and helpees; think of it as helping each other. Helping Tom is helping me feel better. And it's helping Becky avoid a broken heart.

Tom: Yeah, but I feel like I know you so much better now.

Becky: I know. There's something really intimate about messages, don't you think?

Tom: Like modern-day love letters?

Becky: Yeah, exactly like that.

'Dude, are you even listening?'

I look up to see a bearded hipster holding my takeaway mug practically in my face. Somewhere in between messaging Becky, I have managed to drift into the café on the corner near Peggy's care home, order a double-shot flat white and pay for it without even noticing.

'Thanks, man.' I smile at him; it's the guy who's usually here on a Saturday.

He looks down at Tom's phone in my hands and smiles. 'You should get that fixed.' I've been telling Tom that for weeks, but he's got his shiny work phone so he hasn't bothered.

I take the coffee and stash the phone. It's only when I do that I realise that even with Tom's half-hearted blessing, I definitely have something to hide.

Walking back into the sunshine, I stroll the final stretch to the care home, the warm breeze shaking me alert. I take a gulp of my coffee, and then another. I'm going to need this today. Just like Becky, I stayed up far too late last night – well, too early. Sadly, not drifting into Dickens' prose, but drafting some of my own.

Between Paddy, Heather and the rest of the team, we've managed to secure most of the permissions we need for the walk. Amy has hooked me up with multiple partners, and now we just need to nail down the date and start telling people about it. It feels like standing on the starting line looking out at the miles before me. I've been working up to this for so long, and now that I'm finally on the cusp of everything, I feel like I want to jack it in and walk away. But I can't. I've promised Peggy. She's the reason I'm doing it, after all; well, one of the reasons. That part is clear. But still I spent the early hours of this morning tossing and turning, trying to answer the question Heather asked me just yesterday: 'The media don't just need to know *why* we're doing the walk, they need to know why *now*.'

Tom: Hey, sorry. Was just grabbing coffee.
Tom: Much, much needed after last night.

Becky: What was last night? I thought you said you
   slept well?

This is why I shouldn't lie. Makes it pretty hard to keep
up with myself.

Tom: Yeah, to be honest, I slept pretty badly. Just didn't
   want to make it all about me.
Becky: Busy mind?
Tom: You could say that.
Becky: Anything specific?
Tom: Yeah, I guess.
Tom: Peggy's Walk.
Becky: That Max is putting on?

Oh shit, that's right. It's not Tom's thing to worry about.
And I'm being him. But just sometimes, speaking to Becky
makes me feel more like myself than anything else.

Tom: Yeah. Guess I'm just a bit worried about it.
Tom: *Him, sorry. I meant him.
Becky: That's really sweet.
Becky: You're such a good friend.

God, I hope so. That's what I am trying to be.

Becky: So what's been going on with it? Just out of
   interest?
Tom: It's going well, generally.

270

Tom: Well, that's what Max says.

Tom: Just trying to find a hook for media, something that answers the 'why now?' question for anyone looking to sponsor the event.

Becky: Like an awareness day or something?

Tom: Exactly like an awareness day.

It's just a shame I couldn't get it together sooner, too busy feeling sorry for myself whilst Dementia Action Week came and went. And Loneliness Awareness Week is towards the end of the month. There is no way we can pull this off before then. Why is everything I do just a little bit too late?

Becky: Shame Dementia Action Week was a couple of weeks back.

Of course Becky knows that. Sometimes she seems to know everything that is important to me.

Becky: How about World Alzheimer's Day in September?

Tom: That could work timing-wise, but isn't it too exclusive? We're meant to be broadening it out to address loneliness generally, make the whole thing more inclusive.

Tom: Well, that's what Max says anyway.

Damn it, Max. Keep it together.

Becky: Well, it's the cause of about seventy per cent of dementia, right?

Right. Why is Becky always right?

Becky: And it's just a hook in any case, an excuse to get in touch with the media. But if the story's good they should take note of it anyway.

Tom: You sure?

Tom: Could you ask Eve?

Becky: I'm sure.

Becky: Though I'm not up for talking about media stuff right now.

Becky: Eve, sorry. I mean Eve's not up for it.

Tom: Oh shit, why? Is she okay?

Becky: She didn't get that job.

Eve didn't get the job? I look up from my phone as I navigate my way through to the reception area of the care home. Peggy is already sitting in her favourite armchair by the window, looking out across the courtyard, dreaming about places she'd rather be. And now Eve is dreaming about that too? Feeling stuck in a position she wants to move on from. I don't know her that well, but even I know how much that role meant to her.

Reaching into my pocket to pull out my own phone, I gaze down at the two screens in my hands. One cracked and broken and trying to hold something together. The other my own. Man, I want to message Eve. To just tell her I'm thinking about her. But if I speak to her, don't I risk the chance of her finding out the truth about me, about Tom? No, I'll just have to wish her well through Becky and hope that somehow she gets the message.

Tom: Oh God, I'm so sorry to hear that.
Tom: I know how much that job meant to her.
Tom: She must be devastated.
Becky: Yeah, I am.
Becky: For her, obviously.
Becky: But she's keeping her chin up.
Becky: Being kind to herself for once.
Becky: Holding on to the things that give her hope.

'Who is she?' Peggy asks as I look up from Tom's screen, smiling.

'No one.' I stash the phone before bending down to embrace her. She seems to be doing a little better today, the sunlight from outside warming her lined face. Despite the heaviness of her eyes, they have a twinkle in them, the way they do when she knows a secret. Well, when she *thinks* she knows a secret.

'Not buying that for one second. I know that face.' She shakes her head, sending her dangly earrings rattling in the process, still audible over the sound of her cough. Her eyes dart across the room to Amy, who's smiling down at her own phone.

'It's not Amy, if that's what you're thinking.'

'I know that.' She shakes her head. '*She* likes someone else.'

273

She does? I study Amy, who's trying her best to stop her laughter from escaping into the room. I know that face too. It's the face I usually wear when Becky is around – digitally at least.

'*Amy* tells me things.' Peggy raises her eyebrows at me, another cough escaping through her laugh.

'I tell you things,' I object. Lots of things. It was talking to Peggy that prompted this sponsored walk in the first place. But I can't tell her about Becky, can I? There is absolutely no way that Peggy will be okay with me pretending to be someone else. I thought there was no way *I* would be okay with it. But then these are exceptional circumstances.

'That's fine.' She sighs dramatically. 'I'm just an old woman sitting in a care home, staring out of a window at the same old view, day after day . . .' I know what she's doing, but I'm not going to bite. A wicked smile turns up the corners of her mouth, as she waves her fragile arms dramatically. '. . . waiting for something, *anything* from the outside world to entertain her, just wondering who is causing my *favourite* man to smile like that . . .'

'Fine, *fine*.' I put my hands up in surrender. She had me at *favourite*. 'The person who is making me smile is Becky.'

'Tom's girlfriend?' Peggy tries to sit up straighter in her seat, disappointment palpable. I can't let her down, I just can't.

'Let me finish,' I say, before I even know how my sentence is going to end. 'Tom's girlfriend Becky was making me smile . . .' Probably best if Peggy doesn't know the details about this either. '. . . because she was telling me about her best friend, Eve.'

274

Peggy's smile widens, making her whole face shine. '*Eve*,' she breathes.

It isn't technically a lie, is it? Becky has just been telling me how Eve is disappointed about not getting the job and yet is digging deep, finding strength to fight, to be that phoenix rising from the flames all over again.

'Can you tell me about her?' Peggy smiles again, reclining in her chair and closing her eyes, as if getting ready for a bedtime story.

Can I tell her about Eve? I haven't seen her since that Saturday together almost a whole month ago, hanging out in Soho. But I feel like we really opened up to each other then. So yes, I guess I *can* tell Peggy about her, just with a bit of Becky added into the mix.

A little like Tom and I did in the first place.

'Sure,' I say, reaching to rest my hand on hers. She smiles again, still resting her eyes, heavy head nodding. 'Well, she's smart, really smart,' I begin, remembering our first conversations together, the way we bounced off one another as I tried to help Tom keep things flowing at the Fable. 'And super-ambitious, really passionate about what she does. She's a journalist, works on this trend supplement for a newspaper but is fanatical about stories that matter, human-interest pieces about what motivates people to redirect their lives, to fight for a better future . . .'

Even as I say it, I remember how cool Eve is. Trust Becky to have a brilliant best friend; there is nothing not-brilliant about her.

'She loves to run, talk, read . . .' Now that I've started,

I'm somehow struggling to stop. It's nice to share how I feel out loud, even if those feelings are pinned on the wrong girl. 'And she's super-fiery about family being something you build around you rather than something you're born with.' Peggy squeezes my hand tighter at the mention of family.

'And what does she look like?' She smiles again, eyes still closed, ready to conjure my mystery woman. *Well, she's small, brunette, olive-skinned . . .*

'She's tall, really tall,' I begin, knowing I shouldn't be lying to Peggy about fancying Eve, but also sure this is the lesser of two evils: she can't know I've been lying to Becky, even with my good intentions. 'And blonde, and pale . . . but she tans well in summer,' I add, not sure how I know this; I've only seen Eve in spring. 'And she's got this really cool, laid-back look about her, even though she's really not that laid-back at all.' I laugh, and realise Peggy is joining in. She opens her eyes again, taking in the sunshine scattered across the courtyard before turning back to me.

'She sounds . . .' her smile is more alive than I've seen it in weeks, despite her shrinking body and her sporadically fraying mind, 'magical.'

'She is.' I smile back. At least I know that part is true.

'Will she be at the walk?' Peggy asks.

Maybe. I was going to ask her if she wanted to cover the story, but that was before Becky and Tom's dating hiatus. I can't ask now, can I? Not while things are so risky. Eve is too good at discovering the truth for me to be around her with all these lies.

'Maybe,' I reply, forcing a smile. 'I hope so.'

'I hope so too. Any woman who can make you smile like that is a wonder. And Eve sounds lovely.' Peggy doesn't need to know that the woman and Eve aren't one and the same.

She looks back out of the window and sighs. As much as she wants to live vicariously through me, I know it reminds her that her best days are behind her. But not all of them; there is still the walk, her dream, her last chance to see dementia get the attention it deserves. My phone buzzes in my pocket and I know for a fact it's Becky.

'I think we're closer to a date for the walk,' I tell Peggy, and her smile brightens again.

'Is that so?' She struggles to sit up, as if eager to get walking despite feeling so weak.

'September,' I say, thinking of Becky and a media hook magicked so quickly that it stands a chance of impressing even Eve. 'World Alzheimer's Day.' I hear another buzz.

'September? As in three months away?' Peggy looks apprehensive and excited at the same time. 'Well what are you playing at, hanging out with me? Get to work!'

'Don't get yourself worked up.' I pat her on the shoulder, pretending to patronise her. She narrows her eyes, shooting a playful glare my way. 'Remember that you're a hundred and one . . .'

'I'm *eighty-four*.' She rolls her eyes at me before resting a trembling hand on mine and squeezing it gently. 'But on that walk, Max?' Her smile is warm, so full of life. 'I'll be eighteen again.'

Becky: Long day.

Tom: Tell me about it. Chilling now?

Becky: Yes.

Becky: I mean kind of.

Becky: Still doing work so you can't really come over, sorry.

Tom: Marking?

Becky: Huh?

Tom: The kids' work?

Becky: Oh yeah, sorry. I'm busy marking.

Tom: Don't worry, I wasn't inviting myself.

Becky: I know, but it's annoying, isn't it, someone messaging all the time but not wanting to meet up. Isn't that like Dating Rule #1?

Tom: I thought that was don't date twin sisters?

Becky: Ha! Isn't that more like Dating Dream #1?

Tom: Not for me. One woman is enough.

Becky: Well that's a relief. But seriously, I'll see you again soon.

Becky: I promise.

*YOU'VE SHARED 10,000 MESSAGES.
CONGRATULATIONS ON FINDING
YOUR PERFECT MATCH*

I look down at Tom's screen, a digital confetti cannon sending colour through its cracks. Ten thousand messages? My perfect match? I reread the message. The one Becky will be looking at too. Just after her promise to see me again. We aren't the perfect match. We can't be. Her perfect match is Tom. Breathe, Max, breathe. This is okay. This will all be okay.

I look down at the clock in the corner of Tom's screen: it's gone 10 p.m. and he and Yvonne are still out, so I assume he won't be coming back now. But then it can't be long until he's back for good, can it? Until Yvonne has turned her back on him and he wants to pick up with Becky again.

But what if he doesn't? What if he and Yvonne work this time? I guess I'll have to ghost Becky, or worse – for me at least – break up with her via message. It's not like we can keep chatting on the app forever, is it?

I look down at her words, for a moment feeling as cracked as the screen. The problem is, I could. I could keep chatting to Becky forever, if the situation were different. But it isn't. And Tom's right. If I carry on like this for much longer, Becky might get more hurt than she ever would have been by Tom in the first place. What if she sees them, Tom and Yvonne out together, and thinks he's cheating on her? No, I have to stop this. Stop messaging the only woman I've ever sent ten thousand messages to. My perfect match? Dammit, Max. You idiot. Only you could fall into crazy, stupid unrequited love.

Except what if it isn't unrequited? What if she likes the guy on the other end of the phone more than the man in person? Ten thousand times more?

Becky: Oh wow. Ten thousand messages.
Becky: Eve always says I talk too much.

You don't talk too much – well, maybe in person a little bit. When Tom is around and you're trying too hard to be something you're not, the woman he wants you to be. You talk the perfect amount on here, though, about the perfect things, messaging me at the perfect moments when I just need someone to encourage me through my day. Dammit, no. This was a stupid idea. I'm not helping Tom. I'm not helping Becky. I'm just trying to help myself.

I look across the living room to the space on the sofa where Tom used to sit. Without thinking, I fling his phone across the room. It lands safely on the sofa cushions. Not that it would matter if it didn't; it's already broken. Broken things have a way of breaking more; it's a sad but inevitable fact. So isn't it better that I keep breaking rather than Becky?

Without Tom's phone in my hands, I feel empty, eyes searching the room to replace it. Scanning the stacks of books by the sofa, I look for something that doesn't remind me of Becky, but I'm at a loss. She swiped into our lives mere months ago, but it feels like her fingerprints are everywhere.

I don't even bother looking at my own phone: it's late now, and who else would message me? Tom is with Yvonne, and Paddy is dating some new girl, and well, Eve was only ever a friend once removed. Maybe I can work on the walk. Take a leaf out of Eve's book. Although it doesn't sound like she'll be spending her Saturday nights working any more. Sounds like everyone is struggling to be themselves nowadays. Becky's messages seem to demand a reply from the other side of the room, and it's taking all my strength not to run over to her. Come on, Max. Just stick Netflix on and drown out the noise of your mind with the white noise of a screen like everyone else. Everyone but—

My phone begins to buzz in my pocket. Becky? I reach for it, looking at the caller ID. It's only then that I realise that Becky would never call my phone anyway.

It's Amy. My heart sinks to my stomach and for the first time ever I pray that she actually likes me, that this is a drunk dial, that her other man is just a lie. But I know that's not true; the only one lying to Peggy today was me.

'Hello?' I pick up the call, speaking into the ether. Silence greets me at first, and I listen intently, hoping for the faraway sounds of a pocket-dial. But then I hear it: the faint noise of Amy sobbing. No, *no*. What's happened? Has Peggy had another turn? 'Amy?'

'It's Peggy . . . she's . . .' Amy whispers the words in broken shards before breaking herself, her cries raw and ragged at the end of the line, the only words audible through her gulps for air repeated over and over: 'I'm so sorry . . . I'm so sorry . . . *I'm so sorry* . . .'

Chapter Twenty-Three

Eve

'I'm sorry?' I tear my eyes from the television to look across at Becky. Buster is curled up on her lap, her open book resting on his ginger back.

'You heard me.' She smiles. It's strange enough that she is actually reading. But now she is going to take her book out to a coffee shop *by herself*. Maybe she and Tom are the perfect fit after all.

'But you don't like going places by yourself,' I say. I can't believe what I'm hearing. It really doesn't look like she is going to fall apart this time. Every day I've studied her face for signs of sadness, waiting for her to download her dating app again and find all my messages there. But with each morning comes a new strength. A new strength she thinks I am finding too. When really all I have found is Tom. All over again.

'Turns out I do, I'd just never tried it before.' She surrenders her book, waking Buster with a thud: David Nicholls'

One Day. One of the first I ever discussed with Tom. 'One of the downsides of having overprotective parents, I guess.' She laughs at the thought, before stopping herself short. 'Oh Eve, I'm sorry.'

I shake my head to tell her it doesn't matter. Becky still doesn't know about my dad's letters. Maybe she never will. I called him in my darkest moment, and surely after just giving me his number, he'd want to check whether the missed call was from me? His letters claim he wants to be there for me, but maybe even the thought of one missed call from me has sent him scarpering. Buster shoots from Becky's lap and across the room, illustrating the thought.

'Another man leaving me,' she laughs. But it doesn't sound sad like the week Tom didn't message. Where she felt him pulling away. It sounds carefree, content.

A vibration starts up, and I reach for my phone discarded beside me. Becky does the same with hers, and for a moment I stall: please don't be on the app, please don't be on the app. She has never asked me to delete it from my phone. To not use her password. But then Tom hasn't replied to my last message anyway. The one I sent last night, right after that annoying 10,000 messages notification flashed across the screen.

It scared me, sure. *They* are the perfect match. And yet so many of those messages are mine. So much of me on the screen. And Tom doesn't even know. But why would it scare *him*? He likes Becky, and Becky likes him. Or at least I thought she did. I look at her now, concentrating on her screen. If she is heartbroken, she's putting on a better show than me. I read over my last message to Tom: *Eve always says I talk too much*. Why did I bring Eve into this situation? Tom won't have guessed, will he?

'You got the same message?' Becky swings her bended legs around to touch her toes to the floor. I look up from my screen. Shit, no, Becky can't know about these messages. Not yet, not until I've worked out how the hell this story is going to end. 'From Makena?'

I swipe away the app and see Makena's message dancing at the top of our group chat. I still haven't seen her outside of work since the announcement. In the office I've managed to keep things professional in a way they never used to be. Keep our conversations minimal. But I know that the truth will come out over a couple of drinks. And, well, it turns out I am pretty good at avoiding the truth.

Makena: Vintage pop-up shop near the canal. You in, bitches?

'You do know it's not very woke to call each other bitches?' I look at Becky with a little smile, hugging our sparrow-shaped cushion to my chest. It's by far the most outrageous in our collection. Which, naturally, makes it Becky's favourite.

'We're reclaiming it.' Becky moves across the room towards me and sits down by my side on the sofa. 'Heeeey, you told us off for not being woke.' She beams up at me as if to say: *welcome back, bestie.*

I've been far from *woke* since my job dream fell through.

Filling my days with mindless nothingness. Before I started filling them with Tom. And that part, I guess, is making me feel more like myself again. Reminding me of who I am. *Note to self*— Oh piss off, Eve. Well, it did. Before he stopped messaging me back.

'Fancy it?' Becky asks, as I try my best to force Tom from my mind.

The only reason I was messaging him was to save Becky from realising too late that she wanted to give him a second chance. But looking at her now, balanced and content, next to me, anxious and on edge, I know there is only one broken heart between us.

'It would be good for you to see the girls . . .'

'I'm just not really up for it today,' I say, heart hammering at the thought. Messaging Tom made some of the disappointment drift away. But now the silence of my screen, knowing that anything we shared wasn't *shared* at all, is bringing it all back. I can't see Makena, not today. Not while me and my motivation are still on a break.

'You'll have to see her outside of work sometime, Evie,' Becky says softly, my dad's endearment in her mouth making me flinch. 'Eve, sorry. *Eve.*'

'I know, I'm just . . . I've not got the energy,' I say. It's true. I haven't had the energy to do much for the past fortnight. Apart from message Tom.

'Are you sure? Do you mind if I go?'

'Why would I mind?' I laugh. It sounds pretty fake.

'I'm . . .' Becky scans my bare face. Not an inch of make-up, but so much of me hidden. 'I'm worried about you.'

I would ask why. But I'm watching *Sunday Brunch* and showing no signs of going anywhere. The old Eve dead and buried. Momentarily resurrected by Tom. But it's not like that could have gone on forever. I was only doing it for Becky. And she seems fine. Better than fine. Right now, I feel broken. Broken by the goal I have set my sights on for too long. Broken by my dad, who seems to back off when I need him most. Broken by Tom, the only one able to remind me of the woman I was. Before everything became so blurry.

'I've not seen you write in weeks.'

'I've written,' I object, not meaning to sound so mean. 'I wrote a piece on the plight of living with curls just this week.'

'I definitely need to read that.' Becky smiles. She's too kind. She deserves the best. I thought she deserved Tom, but now she doesn't want him, and I do. And oh God, this needs to stop. Right now. Today. 'I mean your articles, the human-interest stories, the ones you love,' she goes on. 'What happened to the column you were developing?'

'Chucked out.' I shrug. 'Like my CV.' I used to laugh at Becky's dramatics. Before I became the leading clown.

'I think you should write anyway. A new job will come up.' Not any time soon.

'Yeah, I'll write again,' I say. But not to Tom, I *won't* write to Tom.

Becky studies my face, as if searching it for the truth. Maybe I will write again. I did love it, didn't I? That's why it was able to hurt me. To love is to be vulnerable and all that.

'You just want to write something that matters,' Becky

says. It isn't a question. She's heard me say it enough times before. And I did. I do. 'I think you should quit.'

'Pardon?'

'I think you should quit your job.' She looks at me, eyes wide with enough hope for both of us.

'Quit?'

'Eve, it's making you miserable. You have so many good ideas, and you deserve to be able to share them.' She squeezes my arm.

I let the thought swirl around my mind. Quit? *Quit?* All my strength is going into *not* quitting right now. But I would love to leave, for that pointless article to be my last. To write the stories I have wanted to write since I was eight. Ever since I stopped believing in fairy tales. My conversation with Max shoots into my mind, the way it often has over the last couple of weeks. He made me feel like I could do anything: rise like a fucking phoenix.

'It's what *I* would do,' Becky says.

Yes, it's what Becky would do. But Becky has parents who will back her to the hilt – emotionally, physically, *financially.* Not all of us are so lucky.

'And live off what?' I finally ask.

'You'll get a new job . . .'

'Do you not think I've looked?' I don't mean to snap. 'There's nothing out there. And I can't *not* have a job, can't not have an income . . .' Now that I've started, I'm not really sure how to stop. Just like with Tom. 'We don't all have *overprotective* families like yours, Becky.' I spit the words back at her, the ones she's already said sorry for.

She looks at me, smile vanishing. For a moment I think she's going to get mad. But she doesn't. She just looks sad, a little hopeless. Like she wants to know how to fix me. She puts her arms around me.

'Are you sure this is just about the job?' she whispers into my hair. 'Like, are you sure there's nothing else on your mind?' Her eyes scan my face before darting to my phone. Tom. Tom. *Tom*. But no, that's over now. For Becky. For me. 'Like, maybe . . . your dad?'

My dad? This isn't about him. It's not always about him. But isn't that better than it being about Tom?

'I guess . . .' I begin. I know Becky needs something to make sense of why the job stuff has hit me so hard. Because I've put all my eggs in that one sodding basket, pushing thoughts of family and love and relationships aside for far too long. 'Sometimes I think it would be nice to have him in my life again.'

Becky's face breaks into a smile and she breathes deeply, like: *thank God she's finally being honest*. If only she knew I was just scratching the surface. There's so much more swirling beneath. His letters. My missed call. My last message to Tom. It's over, and I've been left to pick up the pieces yet again.

'I think he'd like to hear from you too.' Becky gives my leg a little squeeze.

Why is she saying that? I glance at my phone, knowing that I need to bury this thing with Tom, bury my feelings deep down before she can find them out. For a moment it looks like she wants to say something else. Surely not about

288

Tom? There's nothing going on between us, between them, any more.

'Aren't you meant to be meeting the girls?' I ask, subtly changing the subject.

'Oh crap, yeah. Are you sure you don't want to come?'

'I'm sure.' I smile at her. 'Tell them I'll see them soon.'

Soon. It's what I've been telling Tom as Becky all week. Turns out that soon – like sorry – is one of those words that gets worn out pretty quickly without any action to back it up.

As soon as I hear the door shut behind Becky, I allow my tears to fall. Messaging Tom was always a distraction from my feelings, right from the start. It distracted me from work, from my dad, from my disappointments. But what is going to distract me now that my feelings are for *him*?

Through the tears I look down at my last message to him: *Oh wow, ten thousand messages. Eve always says I talk too much.* I always do: just look at the way I spilled my secrets to Max after a couple of coffees, a couple of kind comments. And now I've given myself to the wrong person again. Ten thousand messages that can't lead anywhere. Not that Tom would want them to if he knew they were just me.

It's time to stop this. To delete the app. Just like I should have done the second Becky and Tom met in person. Finger hovering over the app, I press the icon and it begins to shake: *Are you sure you want to delete?*

'Yes,' I say out loud, mustering the courage to push my

finger down and confirm my decision. But then my phone starts to vibrate.

Tom: Sorry Tom didn't reply.
Tom: *I didn't, sorry.
Tom: I don't know why I said that, my head's all over the place.
Tom: Something's happened.
Tom: I really need you.

Shit. What has happened? But this shouldn't be my problem. Tom doesn't need my help. He needs Becky's. Yet he needs someone right now. Just someone at the end of the line. I am so fed up of letting people down. Maybe I can still be here for him. One last time . . .

Becky: I'm here.
Becky: What's wrong?
Tom: It's Peggy.
Tom: She's gone.
Becky: Oh God, I'm so sorry.
Becky: How's Max?
Tom is typing . . .
Tom: I'm devastated.
Tom: *He's. Dammit. Autocorrect.
Tom: He's never felt like this before.
Tom: Doesn't know what to do.
Tom: I thought maybe you'd know what to say.

Oh God. I read the messages, my tears falling faster now. My heart breaking for Max. Breaking for me. Breaking like the promises told to loved ones every day, that we'll always be there, when no one can promise to be there forever. Max will be distraught. I remember our conversation: me telling him my dreams. Him telling me about Peggy's. His own dreams completely intertwined with hers. And now Tom is here wanting to be a good friend to him, whilst I am being such a terrible, terrible friend to Becky. But I know what it's like to lose something – to lose a mother, lose a father, lose a vision, lose yourself.

Becky: Sometimes there's nothing you can say.

Becky: Sometimes you just need to be there.

Becky: To sit with him. Let him cry.

Becky: And then when he does, tell him what he needs to hear.

Tom: What would you tell him?

Becky: I'd tell him that you know it hurts like hell.

Becky: That it's okay to cry.

Becky: That it's okay to not be the hero.

Becky: That he doesn't need to be a knight in shining armour.

Becky: That it's okay to break.

Becky: But that it won't feel this way forever.

I cry harder and harder, just wanting to hold him. Hold Tom, hold Max. I read my messages back. *It's okay to cry. It's okay to break.* Don't I need to tell myself that too? When did

I start trying so hard to be what everyone else needed me to be, to be the perfect best friend? So much that I stopped being a friend to myself.

Tom: I might never get over this.
Tom: *He.
Becky: He will. I promise he will.
Tom: I think maybe it's bigger than Peggy, though.
Becky: How so?

Even as I ask Tom the question, I know the answer. Max told me about his grandma, about the fact that he wasn't there when she needed him. How he felt like he'd let her down, broken his promise to her. And now he's promised Peggy she'll see one last dream become a reality, but it's too late. Again. Feeling Max's grief, even from a distance, makes me feel the full weight of my own. Oh gosh, loving someone is hard. But Max can't beat himself up forever, not for his grandma, not for this. Sometimes things just happen. *Note to self: not everything's under your control.*

Tom: It's stuff with Grandma.
Tom: His grandma. He's been carrying around guilt and regret about her death for a year now, and now this.
Tom: Peggy died before he could do the walk.
Tom: He promised her.
Tom: And he broke that promise.
Tom: And now he feels like it's breaking him.

Becky: It will do.

Becky: Of course it will.

Becky: But Max is strong.

Becky: And he'll mend.

Becky: Even stronger than before.

Becky: Like a phoenix from the flames.

Tom is typing . . .

Chapter Twenty-Four

Max

Becky: So remember what I told you?

Tom: Yes.

Tom: Be strong.

Becky: For Max.

Tom: Yes, for Max.

Tom: Show him that it's okay for him to be sad.

Becky: Yes, but that Peggy wouldn't want him to *stay* sad.

Tom: Right.

Tom: But I still hate myself for not seeing it coming.

Tom: *Max does.

Becky: But he couldn't have done anything different.

Becky: Life has a way of surprising us.

Becky: Sometimes brutally.

Becky: Sometimes beautifully.

Tom: Man, I love your words.

Becky: And I love yours.

Becky: But Max needs your words more than me today.

Becky: Tell him what I've told you. It's not his fault. It never has been.

Becky: And tell him again and again and again.

Tom: And again? Ha.

Becky: Tell him as many times as he needs before he believes it.

I look up from Becky's messages to the crowds of people piling into the church, savouring every syllable. She may be messaging Tom, but her words are meant for me. I don't think I've ever needed them more than I have done this past week, since the moment Peggy passed away. I know I shouldn't have messaged her back, that message ten thousand and one was a mistake. But I can't do this grief thing alone, not again. It will kill me, it will actually kill me. Somehow Becky's words are soothing a pain in me that I'd just got used to living with, finally restoring some hope.

Scrolling back through our messages from the past week, I search for the one I've starred: *Like a phoenix from the flames.* It was what I had said to Eve that afternoon in Soho. Maybe Eve told Becky about our conversation, finally told her about her dad's letters. But either way, reading Becky's words back to me is helping me see things differently.

I was with Peggy on the morning she died. Laughing, joking, telling her about Eve. I was there on the day, that seemingly ordinary day, and nothing could have prepared me for that evening. And even if I had been there with my grandma, it wouldn't have changed anything; it wouldn't have stopped her dying. Life has a way of surprising us: brutally, beautifully. Becky's words are helping me see that. And sometimes you don't need to be there in person to know someone is standing with you. Becky is helping me see that too.

'How you holding up, dude?' I turn to see Tom standing beside me as I slip his phone into my pocket. I can't believe he hasn't asked for it back yet. Things had been frosty between us ever since Yvonne came back on the scene, ever since he thrust his seemingly redundant phone in my direction. But as soon as I told him about Amy's phone call, the ice thawed. I guess he's is always there when I need him.

'Been better,' I reply as he throws a muscular arm around my shoulders.

'Me too.' His smile is a little sad. Tom has been back at ours all week, and he hasn't mentioned Yvonne at all. Hasn't seen her. Maybe things have finally gone south with them? Ended just like I knew they would? But why isn't he telling me? Maybe because I need him more right now.

'Ready to go in?' He squeezes my arm a little tighter.

'Ready as I'll ever be.' I smile back at him, a lump in my throat.

'It's not an open casket, is it?' he says, a glimpse of horror in his eyes.

'No, dude, it's not.' I can't help but laugh at his relief.

'Thank God for that.' He shakes his head, his cheeks a little white. 'I mean, I loved Peggy and everything, but dead bodies freak me right out.' He bites his lip, suddenly realising that he's probably saying all the wrong things, acting insensitively, breaking funeral protocol. But that's what I need right now, I need him to be here, I need him to be *him*.

I laugh again at the horror on his face, and then I laugh harder and harder, tears making tracks down my face until any joy turns to sadness and I sob all the more. Tom pulls me close, and I let my tears fall into his strong suited shoulder. My breath catches, my shoulders heave and I cry hard. I cry for Peggy. I cry for my grandma. And I cry for me, for all the moments when I've told myself I don't deserve to cry.

'It's okay, dude, it's okay,' Tom says, and it's only as I pull away that I see his cheeks are wet with tears too. He's standing with me, saying very little but doing all the right things. Turns out he doesn't need Becky's advice; that's just for me.

Behind us, the two large wooden doors swing open and summer sunshine floods into the church. One by one we leave the darkness of the old stone building and walk out into the light. Sadly, my own darkness comes with me. But as I step into the crowds of people who loved – still *love* – Peggy, something else comes too: hope. I won't feel this way forever. Just like Becky said, one day my broken bits will mend.

Walking further into the church gardens and towards the tables of drinks and cakes, the people mingling together, sharing memories together in a way Peggy would have loved,

I see a familiar figure. Two familiar figures actually. Tom by my side, I catch up with them, walking hand in hand. Amy in her black sundress and – *no way* . . .

'Paddy?' I look at him as he turns around. Appropriately solemn, but still smiling next to her.

'Hey, Maxy.' He throws his arms around me in a tight embrace. 'I'm so sorry.'

'Thanks, dude.' I pull away, smiling at him before throwing my arms around Amy.

'Peggy loved you,' she croaks into my chest, tears tracing their way down her rosy cheeks.

'She loved you too.' I smile back at her, the words catching in my throat. She really did. Peggy was the one thing we had in common. I look at Paddy, weaving his fingers back through Amy's. 'You two.' I never saw this coming, but maybe I should have. They're a good match. Brilliant, even.

'Yeah.' Amy smiles, a little sheepish. 'I know you said you thought dating people you work with wasn't a great idea . . .' I recall her question from that night in the Dickens Inn, the night Peggy tried to force us together before she knew our hearts were both set on someone else. 'But after I came to your offices that time . . . well, Paddy got my number off Heather . . .' Did he now? Paddy shrugs his shoulders: guilty as charged. 'And, well, we messaged for a bit, and one thing led to another . . .' They always do. 'And here we are.' I look at them smiling together, hand in hand. They look so right that I wonder why I didn't see it all along.

But then sometimes it's the things closest to you that are the hardest to see.

Becky: How did it all go?

Tom: As well as can be expected, I guess.

Becky: And Max?

Becky: How was he?

Tom: Gutted, obviously. But I know he's going to be okay.

Becky: Of course he is.

Tom: I think in some strange way, the grief of losing Peggy is helping him let go of some of the grief of my grandma.

Tom: *His.

Becky: That makes sense.

Becky: Sometimes things are easier to get right second time around.

Tom: Learning from your mistakes and all that?

Becky: Something like that.

Becky: Is it still full steam ahead for Peggy's Walk?

Tom: I've not really thought about that.

Tom: *He's.

Tom: I guess Max was always doing it for Peggy.

Tom: For her to see it.

Tom: So in a way, what's the point?

I look down at Tom's cracked screen, up to him sitting in his usual place on the sofa. I'm sure he knows I'm still messaging Becky, but if he does, he isn't saying anything. Maybe he understands that I need this right now. I glance down at the screen again, at Becky typing her reply to my last message: *What's the point?* I was only doing the walk for

Peggy. And now she isn't here any more. The thought hurts like hell. But I know that what I said to Becky is true. I am going to process my grief properly this time, talk about it, not be afraid of it, not carry it around by myself.

'You all right, dude?' Tom must have clocked me drifting off into the distance.

'Not really,' I admit.

'Well you do know you can talk to me about it, right?'

'I know that.' I notice that Tom looks pretty down himself. 'And you can talk to me. Two-way street, right? What's going on with Yvonne anyway?'

I put Tom's phone down. Becky has stopped typing anyway. I imagine her letting herself get distracted by Eve. She has said that Eve is still finding things hard with the job. Of course she is; she put so much into getting that part of her life sorted before contemplating sorting anything else. But are any of us really ever sorted? Aren't we all a work in progress?

'It's over.' Tom looks at me, daring me to say *I told you so*.

I knew this would happen; it's why I carried on messaging Becky in the first place. Well, one of the reasons. But what now? Will Tom want Becky back, just like I predicted? That will be good, right? Becky will be happy. Tom will be happy. I will be . . . well, I'll be okay. I'll be more than okay one day.

'She ended things?' I ask, trying to keep my tone measured.

'No.' Tom shakes his head, smiling a little. 'I did.'

'You did?'

'Don't act so surprised, bro.' He laughs, throwing a cushion my way. It misses.

'I'm sorry, it's just . . .' I choose my words carefully, even though Tom can see right through me, 'not what I expected. Are you okay? What happened?'

'You fucked it.' Tom says the words through laughter. What? What did I do? His phone buzzes by my side, full of Becky's replies. Shit. Shit. Shit. 'Remember when you asked whether Yvonne wanted to hang out, the three of us? Well, I asked her, and she said no, which is cool, right? But then I asked her again, and about her friends, and she snapped and said she didn't see why we had to hang out with each other's friends anyway.'

'Do you think she was trying to keep you at a distance?' I ask.

'Either that or she's really not a friend person, but I can't imagine dating someone who doesn't like my friends. Some of the best times I had with Becky were when the four of us were hanging out together.'

'So do you want to give things another go with Becky?' I ask, not knowing what I want his answer to be.

My heart hammers, palms starting to sweat. If he says yes, I'll have to stop messaging her and hope to God he doesn't hate me for staying in touch all this time; that he understands that I was doing this for him – well, kind of. If he says no, then I'll have to stop messaging her too. Say goodbye to all the late-night conversations and good-morning messages. Who am I kidding? There's only one way this is going to end.

'Honestly?' Tom says as I try not to think about all my lies. 'No, not really. She's an amazing girl, but I don't think we'd have much in common without you helping me.'

Yeah, I guess I knew that too.

'Probably best we let that one go.'

'Yeah,' I sigh.

My stomach sinks, my heart showing no signs of slowing, but this can't carry on, can it? What did I think was going to happen? That a woman like Becky would fall like a guy like me, a guy who lied his way into her inbox in the first place? Tom might need to let this go, but I need to let Becky go too. I never should have let myself fall for her in the first place. The Peggy stuff is so raw, and our messages have got so intense, but what other choice do I have? I'll rest it out for a day, lighten the tone, but then I'll have to let it go, let *her* go too.

Becky: What's the point? Are you joking? Tell Max there's a massive point in carrying on with it.

Becky: Yes, Peggy was the catalyst, but Max has a real heart for lonely people and the walk was always so much bigger than Peggy, that was the point.

Becky: It's sad that she didn't live to see it, but there are still thousands of people living with loneliness and surely Max's passion for helping them hasn't changed, has it?

Tom: No, it hasn't.

Tom: Well, I don't think so.

Becky: So tell him to not lose sight of the bigger picture.

302

Tom: Okay, okay. I will.

Tom: I'll tell him to see it through.

Becky: It's what Peggy would have wanted.

Tom: I know.

Tom: I'll tell him.

Tom: I've been meaning to ask, actually . . .

Tom: Well, Max has been meaning to ask.

Tom: Would Eve like to cover the event?

Becky: I'm not really writing at the moment.

Becky: *Eve's not, sorry. Bloody autocorrect.

Tom: Because of the job still?

Becky: Yeah, she kind of doesn't see the point if she's just going to have to write stupid stories for the next year or so until new jobs come up.

Tom: Yeah, but what about her own stuff?

Becky: She was just writing all that for the job.

Becky: I think.

Tom: Well, I hope you've given her one of the pep talks you just gave me.

Tom: To pass on to Max, obvs.

Becky: What do you mean?

Tom: Like . . .

Tom: Yes, the job was the catalyst for Eve's column, but she has a real heart for real stories and that was always so much bigger than one role.

Becky: Oh, I see.

Tom: And . . .

Tom: Surely her passion for telling real stories hasn't changed, has it?

Becky: Right.

Tom: So tell her to not lose sight of the bigger picture.

Tom: Basically, give all the advice you've just given to Max to Eve and she might just remember why she loved writing stories in the first place.

Becky: Yeah, okay. But what if she's still stuck in her job?

Tom: Tell her to quit.

Becky: But there are no other jobs she wants to apply for.

Tom: She could go freelance?

Becky: With what money?

Tom: Well, maybe she might not be able to go freelance right away, but if she starts charging for stories on the side, then maybe she can start moving in that direction.

Tom: Baby steps.

Tom: Plus, she could always ask for some help whilst she gets started.

Becky: From who?

Her dad? He wants to be back in her life, doesn't he? But then I still don't know whether she's told Becky that. She made me promise I wouldn't tell anyone, and as much as I trust Becky, there is no way in hell I am betraying my word to Eve. Plus, Tom doesn't know about her family, does he?

304

Tom: Her family? Yours? You said they think of Eve as one of the family, right? That they'd do anything for her.

Becky: I did?

Tom: Yes, you did. That with Eve, your family feels complete.

Chapter Twenty-Five

Eve

I look at Becky, sitting in our usual corner of Ciao Becca. It's like one of the first photos I uploaded to her dating profile coming to life right before my eyes. So much has happened since then. For both of us. I barely recognise the woman sitting opposite me now. No phone in hand. No dates planned. Happy just to be in the moment. And I can barely register what I'm about to ask Leonardo and Sofia.

'You're doing the right thing.' Becky turns to me now, still struggling to comprehend what I mustered the courage to tell her last night. That I am actually considering quitting my steady job at the paper to go freelance, to write the stories I know I have within me, and just hope to God someone will be willing to pay me for them. It's not like I could tell her Tom's messages were the catalyst. But after he reminded me of why I wanted to write in the first place, my mind has slowly started to splutter into motion.

Expanding its vision beyond my well-thought-out plans for the first time in years.

'Two spaghetti carbonara for the *señoritas* in the corner.' Leonardo moves his hips in time to the music as he makes his way across the restaurant floor towards us.

'Dad, you're Italian, not Spanish.' Becky laughs, reaching out to accept one of the piled-up plates with glee. I gratefully receive my own, putting it down on the table before me. I'm suddenly less hungry.

'So what did you want to talk to us about, Eve?' Sofia pulls a chair up to our table, coming to join us.

It was Tom's message that planted this thought in my mind. A ridiculous thought but one I couldn't shake, one I finally shared with Becky last night in shards of sentences: if I go freelance . . . need to find money to pay the rent . . . at least for the first couple of months . . . don't want to risk losing our home . . . mould and Matilda and our stupid back-front-door be damned . . .

It was Becky who asked whether I had heard from my dad. Who suggested I reach out to him. The news of his letters was still on the tip of my tongue. From his second one, it sounded like he was financially stable, maybe even in a position to give me a loan. But after years of him coming to *me* for cash, I didn't want to resume our relationship on that rocky footing again – that's *if* we resumed it at all. It didn't take long after that for Becky to suggest the two people I reluctantly had in mind all along.

'I mean . . . it's a bit awkward . . .' I look to Sofia, only now realising that this is ridiculous. I can't ask Leonardo and Sofia for a loan even if Becky says they'll want nothing more than to help me out. And isn't that what Tom said in his messages? That they think of me as one of the family, that they'll do anything for me. I let the memory soothe me as I stare into Sofia's wide eyes. If I ask them this and they take it the wrong way, it could change everything. After all, love had always come with conditions in my life until the moment I moved in with Becky.

'Eve's writing again.' Becky beams from me to her parents, laying the groundwork like the sibling I never had.

'Oh *Eve*.' Sofia puts a hand on her chest as Leo pats my back in support. 'That's wonderful. We've been so worried, *so* worried.' She throws her arms around me, and it's only then that I realise they really have been. Each time I've come into the restaurant or they've been round to ours since the job announcement, they've asked after me, about the job, about what I might do next.

'And she still hates her job.' Becky's eyes widen at me as if to say: *come on, Eve, you can do this. Take control.* But haven't I been trying to stay in control for too long already? *Note to—* No, I don't need to control this, don't need to keep myself in check with mental Post-it notes any more. This is about letting go, taking a risk for once.

'As do we.' Leo nods in solidarity. 'I mean . . . don't get me wrong, we love Makena too, but that role was made for you, Eve, anyone could have seen that.' He smiles at me.

Was it? Or was that just what I'd told them so often, told myself so often, that we'd all started to believe it?

'Makena's doing a wonderful job.' I smile back at him. 'But

I don't really want to stay stuck in my role much longer. I'm thinking of maybe dropping my hours . . .' my eyes dart to Becky, who's shaking her head, 'or even quitting completely.' Becky nods. Her vote has always been to go all in. And like she always used to say, I'm not one for doing anything by halves. Thank God I have her here to remind me of that. Well, her and Tom.

'But that's obviously a little risky financially, until I start making money, and freelance jobs usually pay invoices one or two months after delivery.' Becky rolls her eyes playfully: I'm beating about the bush. 'And I just wondered, if it's not like the cheekiest, rudest thing in the world . . .' I stall for a second. This is crazy. I spent the whole of my adolescence giving my dad money. Why on earth would it work the other way now? With two people who have no ties to me apart from the fact that I'm their daughter's best friend? 'I wondered whether I could ask you for a loan to get me set up.' I say the words so quickly I swear I may need to repeat them. 'I'd pay you back as soon as I'm able to, honestly. It's just I love living where we are, just down the street from you, and with Becky, and like—'

'Yes.' Sofia puts her hand over mine before looking at Leo. 'Yes?'

'Of course, it's a yes.' Leo pats my back again. 'And if it feels right to quit completely, you should quit completely.'

'Isn't that too much of a risk?' I say, looking between them.

'It is a risk . . .' he says slowly. 'But risks are much easier to take when you've got people to catch you when you fall.'

'That's very poetic, darling,' Sofia murmurs, and I swear I see a tear in her eye. But then again, they're starting to gather in my own.

'I'm telling you, Romeo and fucking Juliet.' Becky rolls her eyes again, but it's clear that seeing her parents' love story doesn't make her feel like she's lacking any more. Like me, she's beginning to realise just how much love has been in her life all along.

'Language, Rebecca!' Sofia tuts.

'I'll pay you back soon, I promise,' I say again, hoping to God that's true.

'It's okay, darling.' Sofia's smile is warm and soft. 'We trust you.' It's then that I can't help the tears from falling. They trust me, Becky trusts me. And yet I've still been messaging Tom. I have to stop it now, I should have stopped it weeks ago – maybe I shouldn't even have started.

The Amatos beam back at me, excited for my new adventure, cheering me on, carrying me forward. And for just a moment, I know that regardless of what happens, regardless of what difficulties I'll face, the love of Becky and her family, and writing the stories that matter, will get me through. It's a love that I've built around me, firm and stable, and it will take more than a few storms to break it.

'Your parents are amazing,' I say to Becky for the thousandth time since Sofia and Leonardo agreed to give me the loan.

'I know, but so are you.' She smiles back at me, taking a sip from her third glass of wine. It's nice to have an evening

310

together without either one of us staring at our screens. 'They wouldn't do that for just anyone, you know.'

'I know that.' I smile back.

'You do know they're not going anywhere, right?' she says.

'I should hope not.' I laugh. 'I don't know what I'd do without Ciao Becca at the end of the street. I'm going to need a *lot* of free spaghetti if I'm going freelance.'

'No, I mean . . .' Becky tries again. 'If, say, your dad was back on the scene, they'd still behave exactly the same way. Your part in this family is not dependent on your relationship with your own.'

'That's very poetic, darling,' I echo Sofia's words from before, mostly in an attempt not to cry again. I've been doing far too much of that recently.

'I'm serious.' Becky smiles.

'Well, thanks. But I've told you, I'm still not sure about reaching out to my dad.' And I'll probably never tell you about him reaching out to me . . .

'I know that.' She sighs. 'But I can't help but think . . .'

This again. Why is Becky so convinced that I'm missing him? Though to be fair, I have been doing a fair amount of messaging and moping and drifting aimlessly around the house. But I can't tell her that the reason for that wasn't my dad. It was Tom. But that's over now. He's given me the confidence I need to move forward. Yes, letting go of whatever we almost shared will hurt like hell, but I can't keep risking my friendship with Becky for the sake of a guy.

'I really hope you don't mind . . .' Becky looks at me, a

311

little nervous now. 'But I've invited . . .' She looks behind me, guilt personified.

No, no, no. She wouldn't invite my dad. How would she? They're not even in touch. She doesn't know about the letters.

'What? Who . . .' And it couldn't be Tom, could it? *Max?* No, why on earth would it be Max? But for the briefest of moments, my heart leaps at the thought.

'Hey, bitches,' I hear Makena boom behind me, and I sigh in something like relief.

'You know, it's not very woke to call each other bitches.' I stand up to hug her, and for the first time since she told me about the job, it doesn't feel awkward and weird.

'We're reclaiming it.' She beams at me, her hands gripping the tops of my arms, not letting me go. She must notice that I'm not frosty any more, that I've finally thawed.

'Well, it's not working,' I laugh.

Makena takes a seat at our table and we all watch as Lola is spun around the restaurant by Leo.

'How we all doing?' she beams as she finally, rather dizzily, pulls out her own chair. Leo has handed her two empty glasses somewhere mid dance and she begins to pour wine for herself and Makena.

'We're good, thanks,' I say, realising how much I've missed them, missed this.

'Eve's quitting her job!' Becky may as well shout it across the restaurant.

'Considering it,' I correct, looking at Makena, whose delight has been replaced with concern. 'I'm thinking about going freelance,' I explain.

312

'This isn't to do with me, is it?' she asks, almost in a whisper.

'No, no, I promise.' I reach for her hand across the table. 'And I'm sorry for how the whole job thing went down . . .'

'I should have told you they'd asked me to apply.' She looks genuinely sorry. 'You were so sure the role was for you, and I wasn't even going to apply for the longest time, but then I thought, well, I'll probably not get it anyway . . .'

'I'm glad you did,' I say. Becky practically snorts into her wine. 'Well, I'm glad now, anyway. And going freelance is the right next step for me. I think deep down it's what I've wanted to do all along, I just couldn't imagine it without the stability of a salary . . .' I look at Becky, who smiles knowingly across the table.

She's my stability. This family is my stability. Becky, Leo and Sofia. Lola and Makena. The family I've built around me.

'But I think I'm ready to let go now and kind of just see what happens,' I say as the girls surround me with smiles. And I also know I have to let go of Tom. That I've already messaged him for the very last time.

313

Chapter Twenty-Six

Max

Tom work: Hey, dude, what you up to today?

Max: Currently?

Max: Sitting with a flat white in Mud.

Tom work: Book in hand?

Max: Yep.

Tom work: Looking wistfully out of the window?

Max: Yep.

Tom work: Oh man, I used to love doing that.

Max: No you didn't, ha.

Tom work: Nah, never.

Max: We just made it look like you did on your profile.

Tom work: What were we thinking?

Max: Yeah, I guess that profile was always going to find someone like me.

Tom work: Nah.

Tom work: There's only one of you, dude.

I look up from my phone, my book discarded to one side. There's only one of me. And I guess my being here, in my usual spot in my usual coffee shop, back to my usual weekend activities, is me trying to get back to just being me. But then there was another thing I'd usually do on a Saturday afternoon: visit Peggy.

My gaze drifts out of the window to the weekend wanderers thronging towards the common, my mind drifting into memories of her. I'm not going to keep them in a box like I did with my grandma. I'm going to let myself remember, to feel them, even when it hurts.

An elderly woman walks slowly down the street, and my eyes follow her just to check that she's okay. I'll go and visit the care home again soon, see Amy and the others. Of course I will. Most of them will be joining me on the walk in a couple of months anyway, many more logging in or reading about the event with befrienders by their sides. The press release has gone out, the internet copy is live. A handful of journalists have said they'll be there but I know none of them will capture the story as well as Eve would. Becky said she'd ask, but then it's not like we're talking to each other any more. I look at the lush green trees, summer now in full swing. It's probably for the best that she's not replying, that I might never speak to her again.

Tom work: You heading to the care home this
    afternoon? Want me to come with?
Max: Nah, think I'm just going to hang at home.
Tom work: Cool. You deserve a rest.

Rest. It's probably what I should do. Create better boundaries. Finally achieve that work–life balance that every baby boomer seemed to chase after before we came along. But who am I kidding? I'm a messed-up millennial with blurry boundaries, not content to keep my passions in neat boxes but allowing them to spill out at all hours, every aspect of my life merging into one.

My eyes drift to my phone, always half expecting it to ring. The other managers told me to be careful, that it's too easy to get attached in this line of work. But what's the point in trying to guard your heart from getting hurt? It has a way of bruising anyway. To love is to be vulnerable. I guess if this thing with Becky has taught me anything, it's that. Even behind screens, hidden behind someone else's identity, letting someone in and then letting them go is always going to hurt like hell.

Max: Self-care and all that?
Tom work: Yeah, you been reading Eve's supplement again?
Max: Ha, no.

Well, maybe. I look down at her name on my screen, eyes stalling on those three little letters. Tom hasn't mentioned Becky or Eve in over a week, not since that moment after Peggy's funeral when he told me that he and Yvonne had broken up and that he wasn't going to go back to Becky. One relationship going up in flames, the other just fizzling away, but both ending all the same. I was planning to let

316

my messages with Becky fade out too, but it turns out I didn't have to. It's been nine days since she's been in touch. Not that I'm counting. I've wanted to ask Tom about her all week, about whether she's contacted him some other way. But I guess part of me worries that if I do, he'll ask for his old phone back. That said, he's been marvelling at his uncracked work screen for weeks, wondering why he didn't switch phones sooner.

Reaching into my pocket, I hold his phone in my hands. Can't blame him for not missing it. Not missing Becky's messages, on the other hand? That I'm struggling to comprehend. At least he doesn't seem to be missing Yvonne any more.

Max: Still no word from Yvonne?
Tom work: The odd drunken text.
Tom work: She just wants what she can't have.

Can't imagine what that's like.

Tom work: But I'm over it, dude.
Tom work: Don't know why I didn't see it sooner.
Tom work: I know Becky and I weren't the perfect match.

No, because she was the perfect match for me.

Tom work: But I did like her. And I think spending my time with someone I could potentially have a future with made me see that's what I want one day.

Tom work: Not chasing women I know deep down it
   could never work out with.
Tom work: Thank God for Becky, eh?

Yeah, thank God for Becky.

Tom work: See you back home then, dude?
Max: Yeah. Be back soon.

Just as soon as I've deleted this app. Deleted all trace of
Becky from our lives.

I turn Tom's old phone over in my hands. Just delete
it, Max, delete it. But no, my fingers find their way to
the dating app, the one that got me here in the first place.
Heartbroken to lose something that has never been mine
in the first place.

I look through our messages for the thousandth time,
wondering what it was that made her stop replying. Maybe
it was the fact that Tom hadn't seen her in weeks, that she'd
finally got the message that if his actions didn't match his
words, he just wasn't that into her.

Or maybe she figured, like Tom, that they didn't have
that much in common in the first place. But how could she
think that? Our messages have anchored me through so many
storms: losing Peggy, losing my grandma. In talking to her,
I've kind of found myself again.

I reread our final messages: *You said they think of Eve as
one of the family, right?* And her last reply: *Did I?* Did I say
something she'd never told Tom? Was it Eve who had actually

318

said that to me? I can't remember. In any case, it's not like it matters now. I have to delete the app. But first I just need to say goodbye.

Tom: Hey, Becky, I know it's been over a week and you've probably got bored of waiting for my work to die down, but

'Max?' I hear her voice behind me, like I've dreamed her into reality. Slowly I turn, Tom's phone still clutched in my hands, to look at a face I've imagined before me so many times. Though never once here. Never once looking at me like this: angry, hurt, confused.

'Becky!' Part of me wants to throw my arms around her. She's finally here. But now that she is, her presence jars, and I remember how the in-person Becky never felt like the real thing. It always felt like she was putting on an act. A little like me.

She's dressed too formally for a weekend, like maybe she's about to meet someone. Another date? My heart starts to hammer as I follow her stare down to the cracked screen in my hands, Tom's cracked screen, the one I was just messaging her from. How long has she been standing there?

'How are you?' I force out the question.

'What do you think you're doing?' Her eyes are still fixed on Tom's cracked screen. They're filled with fire, and not in the way I imagined her fighting for feminism or getting passionate about politics. No, right now she just looks really fucking fuming.

'Reading?' I try to hide Tom's phone, replacing it with my book; I know it's too late.

'That's Tom's phone.' Becky's eyes dart to where it's lying face down on the table. 'And you were just messaging me.'

'No, I wasn't,' I say, just wanting to tell her the truth, to make everything okay.

'Max, I've just seen you.' She shakes her head, reaching to grab the phone. Dammit, dammit, *dammit*. It's still open on the app, and now she's scrolling through the messages, reading her words, *my words* on the screen. I watch as her usually flushed cheeks become drained of colour and her mouth twists in confusion.

'Look, Becky,' I begin, voice as shaky as my hands. 'I can explain . . .'

'How long?' She looks at me, too angry to sit down.

How long? Such a simple question, with an answer that right now feels impossible. Since Tom stopped messaging? Since Yvonne got in touch? Since we first created her profile? Began laughing about books and films and articles together?

'Too long,' I say, sorrier than I think I've ever felt before. And just when I was starting to feel better.

'No, Max, I need to know how long.' She shakes her head, her whole body trembling with emotion. I'm sorry, Becky. I'm so sorry.

'About six weeks,' I say, only then realising how bad that sounds, how bad it *is*.

'Six weeks?!' she explodes, and a few heads turn to look at her. 'Six weeks . . .' she repeats under her breath, this time like she's thinking, like she's searching her mind to place it.

'That's . . . no . . . that's just after we slept together, just after Tom cooled off . . .'

'I know, I know . . . I just . . . Tom was going through some stuff and I thought he really liked you . . . he *did* really like you,' I correct before I can hurt her further. 'And I just wanted to keep things going for you both, because I really thought he'd come around. And then my friend died, and I . . .' I can't help my voice from cracking like the screen held in her hands, like my heart hammering in my chest. 'It was selfish and stupid, but your messages were the only thing that made me feel better,' I look into her eyes, not knowing why telling her this doesn't feel intimate like our messages, but just *wrong*, like maybe I've got it wrong all along.

'But I never messaged you,' she says slowly.

'I know, I know, you thought you were messaging Tom, it was stupid . . .'

'No, Max.' Her eyes widen. 'I never messaged you, or Tom . . . not since that week when he cooled off. Whoever was messaging you,' she shakes her head, 'it sure as hell wasn't me.'

A stunned silence stretches between us, pulling us both in. It wasn't Becky? Then who the hell was messaging me all that time? My heart races, my mind in turmoil. I need to say something. Anything. But what am I supposed to say? And who the fuck should I be saying it to?

'But . . . but . . . how . . .' I reach a trembling hand towards the phone and Becky's fingers uncurl, like she's so stunned that at least for the moment she has lost all her fight. I scroll through the app, heart belting out of my chest, sweat prickling across my forehead. These are her replies. Her messages. About Peggy. About the walk. About telling me to carry on . . .

'Shit, *no*,' Becky says, her face like thunder. 'I deleted Tom's number, I made her delete it too . . .' Her eyes dart to me, for a second looking guilty, like just maybe she has some secrets of her own.

'But *who*?'

'Eve.'

'Eve?' I whisper, heart fit to burst. 'Why would Eve . . .' I begin, but my stomach is already sinking and Becky is rushing out of the coffee shop. No, no, no. She can't disappear. Not now. Not like this. Not until I know what the hell is going on here. Without thinking, without even paying, I'm leaving my book and my coffee and the incriminating phone behind and following her out onto the street. Stop, Becky. Just slow down.

'Becky?' I shout behind her. Slowly she turns to look me dead in the eye. 'Becky, please, can we just talk about this? We *need* to talk about this . . .'

'Just leave it, Max,' she hisses. 'This is between me and Eve.'

Eve? *Eve?* No, no, *no*. It can't be. Can it? Rushing back inside, I throw too much cash on the counter before running back into the sunlight. I'm sure as hell in the dark. Becky had no idea it was me messaging her. She had no idea *she* had been messaging me. But Eve? Can it really have been her?

Rushing into the road, I hail a taxi, bundling inside. How the hell has this happened? That night at the Fable. The Saturday in Soho. I shared stuff with Eve. She shared with me. But not our whole selves. I thought that was what I had been sharing with Becky.

'Where to, mate?' The driver turns in his seat. Where to? Who to? I have no fucking clue what's right any more. Eve, Eve, Eve. Her name rushes through my mind. The way Becky's did for so long. How did I get everything so wrong?

Just breathe, Max, breathe. All I know is that Becky is on the warpath. Rushing home to Eve. Angry at her for this. Whatever this is. I need to get to her. To make everything okay.

To find out what the fuck is going on.

But this isn't all about me. I need to make things right between Becky and Eve. Before I mess everything up even more.

'Camden,' I croak. To Eve. This is all about Eve.

Maybe it always was.

Tom: Dude, something's happened. We have to get to Becky's.

Tom work: You're still using my phone?

Tom: Oh shit, sorry. It's a long story. Just get yourself to Eve's.

Chapter Twenty-Seven

Eve

It was all about me. I read the words I have just typed aloud to Buster. He's purring on my lap, happy to be back in his usual spot by my overheating laptop. *Until I realised how much the befriending scheme was helping me.* Buster looks up at me. It's a good ending. Unlike mine and Tom's – or rather, *Becky* and Tom's – which stopped abruptly as if in mid sentence. I just hope this article is good enough. If I'm really going to hand in my notice on Monday, I *need* it to be good enough.

'Right, what should we do now?' I ask Buster, who looks content to simply sit. But I've never been one to sit still for too long – except maybe when I'm lost in a book. Without thinking, my eyes scan our bookshelves for the one story I know will calm my racing mind. It's not there. Maybe it's in Becky's room.

Moving Buster and my laptop, I walk the short distance

to her room and find my thumbed copy of *Far From the Madding Crowd* cast aside by her bed. Picking it up, I turn it over in my hands and can't help but smile at the memory of sharing my thoughts on this story with Tom. Missing him hurts like hell. But I'm still glad he came into our lives. If he hadn't, Becky would still be here, swiping mindlessly, trying to find someone to complete her. Now she's out by herself, alone but not lonely. After all, algorithms rarely lead to love . . .

Except for me, for a moment, they totally had. Sitting on the edge of the bed, I let my tears fall. Heart thumping, breath heavy; my body aches, my heart hurts. Not fast and light, like a fear I have to flee from, but raw and real: I loved, I lost, I let someone in. And I'll do it again, only this time as me. Everyone deserves a second chance.

Walking back into the living room, I find Buster's face buried in my handbag and the memory of my dad's letters floats into my mind. Maybe he deserves another chance too? He says he's changed, but what if he hasn't?

It doesn't mean you're going to go back to square one. Out of nowhere, Max's voice rings through my messy mind as my legs surrender, forcing me to sit on the edge of the sofa. *You're different now, you're stronger.* So what if my dad hasn't changed? I have. And didn't I spend weeks, months, years just wishing that one day he'd get in touch, finally come knocking?

Thud, thud, thud.

I look up in the direction of the door, the one people

rarely manage to find. Buster darts off, scared. My heart beats faster and faster. Who the hell? *Dad?* No, there's no way. But who else would it be? Becky has a key.

Rushing towards the door, I pull it open to see Becky standing there, her cheeks flushed red, hair a little wild. Her tiny body so fit to burst that it seems to fill the paved space outside our flat. What the hell?

'I can't believe you . . .' Her wide eyes fix themselves on me and my heart starts to hammer again, panic rising. Why does she look so mad? Too mad to even find her key. What could possibly have . . . No. *No.* How would she know? 'I know you've been messaging Tom. Pretending to be me.'

'Becky, I'm . . . I can . . .'

'Just because we messaged together at the start doesn't mean it was okay to carry on doing it. Without my permission. *Behind my back.*' She spits the words and I feel my tears starting to rise again.

Oh shit. *Shit.*

'I'm not . . .' I begin, trying to hold it together. But how can I, when I can feel the thing most important to me starting to fall apart? 'I did . . . for a bit . . . but I was doing it for you . . .' Becky rolls her eyes, angry in a way I've never seen her before. 'But then when I realised . . . I stopped, Becky. I stopped, because you're the most important—'

'Oh please. I knew you were enjoying it too much.' She puts a hand up to stop me. It's shaking. So am I. 'But I just thought you were lonely, that you wanted a relationship of

326

your own, that maybe . . .' She looks at my wet cheeks, like for a moment she's scared, stalling on a thought. I swear I see something like guilt fill her eyes. But what does she have to feel guilty about? This is all my fault. Everything. 'But all this time,' she breathes, pushing whatever thought has slowed her to one side, 'you wanted Tom.'

'I'm so sorry . . . I'm sorry.' I say the words over and over. *Sorry gets worn out pretty quickly without any action to back it up.*

But my actions *did* back it up. I stopped. I stopped messaging Tom even though at one point it was the one thing keeping me going. Until I realised that Becky and her family had been carrying me all along. 'I stopped. Honestly, I stopped. That evening with your parents, I came to my senses, realised how much I had to lose.' Hold it together, Eve. Just hold this all together. 'I knew that whatever I felt I had with Tom—'

'You never had anything with Tom.' Becky's words slice through my sentence.

'I know,' I cry. 'I know he only ever liked you.'

'No,' Becky says. 'You never had anything with *Tom*. It wasn't even him.'

'What?' As I speak, I swear I see Becky reaching to touch me. Torn between wanting to rip me apart and wanting to hold my sorry pieces together. *What?* Of course it was Tom who was messaging. I read his name, savoured those three little letters every time they crossed my screen. If it wasn't Tom, then who was it?

'Eve.' I follow the voice up to the top of the steps leading from the pathway to our poor excuse of a patio, tracing it all the way to . . . Max?

'Piss off, Max.' Becky turns around to see him walking to stand beside her. 'This is between me and—'

'Tom?' I say, seeing his broad figure materialise like a mirage against our backyard backdrop.

'No, this is *Max*, Eve,' Becky says, her words dripping with sarcasm.

'No, *Tom*,' I say, nodding towards him as he too comes to join us in the tiny space outside our house.

'Oh shit.' He stumbles into a flowerpot, which falls over as if to make space for him.

'What the fuck?' Becky turns to look at him. Max is staring from Becky to me as I quickly brush the tears from my cheeks. 'What the hell is going on?'

'We can—' Tom starts.

'We can explain,' Max says.

'We?' I ask, eyes fixed on him, heart hammering in my chest.

Becky's eyes dart between the three of us, angry and confused. 'Oh fuck this.' She throws her hands up in the air. 'I don't even care.'

She turns to walk away from our home. But no, she *is* my home. And I can't lose her. Not over this. Not over Tom. Not over *Max*.

Running up the steps, I follow her down the side of the house and onto the street. Heavy footsteps sound behind me. Tom? Max? Who the hell knows? Right now, it doesn't really matter. All that matters is . . .

'Becky!' I shout after her.

'Eve, I can't do this right now . . . I can't . . .'

'Evie?'

We both stop, stunned. Eyes fixed on the man stepping out of the taxi, its door still open behind him. He looks at me, and I start to shake, torn between running into his arms and running away.

'*Dad?*' I whisper. 'What . . . what . . . why . . .'

I look at the taxi, lingering like maybe he won't be staying. I look at Becky, crying now. Hard. No, she couldn't have got in touch with him. There's no way. She knows how complicated things with my dad are. Knows not to get involved. She doesn't even know he contacted me. How could she? The only person I ever told about his letters was . . .

I turn around to see Max and Tom standing behind me. Max's eyes fix on mine, the way they did after the only real conversation we shared. Well, that we shared in person.

Please don't tell anyone what I've told you.

Your secrets are safe with me.

'Your friend got in touch . . .' My dad steps towards me and Becky and Max move closer. No, no, *no*. Max was the only person I told. How dare he take matters into his own hands? I didn't ask for this. For any of this.

The taxi is still pulled up by the kerb, beckoning me in. My getaway car. I need to run. I trusted Max. I let him in. He let me down. Just like Dad.

Run, Eve, run.

And I do. Into the taxi, closing the door. The car, like my mind, pulling away. From Tom and Becky. From my dad. From Max. All the while not knowing why running away from him feels like running away from myself.

Chapter Twenty-Eight

Max

'Eve, Eve!' I shout as she climbs into the taxi and closes the door. No, no, *no*. I hit the back of the vehicle as it pulls away, taking Eve away, and all my answers with her.

God, I need answers.

I turn to look at the three people staring back at me. Eve's dad and Tom look as confused as each other. Becky is crying harder and harder, her shoulders heaving, unable to stop. What the hell has happened between them? Is this about the messages? I need to go after Eve, to make sure she's okay. But her dad is here and Becky is inconsolable. What am I missing? And if I know, will it help me find Eve?

'What's going on?' Eve's dad asks the one question everyone is thinking. 'I thought you wanted me to come here, but then you mentioned the coffee shop . . .' He looks genuinely worried, his words catching in his throat. He's just seen his daughter for the first time in years, all grown up. Becky, what have you done? And where has Eve gone?

'Becky . . . look, I'm sorry how things ended between us . . .' Tom risks a step towards her. Oh God, Tom. No. My eyes attempt to warn him. This isn't about you.

'This isn't about you,' Becky bites back through her sobs.

'Then what *is* it about?' Tom throws his arms wide, exasperated. I knew things would be messy when I messaged him, but I never imagined *this*. I need to work out what the hell is going on, where the hell Eve has gone.

'I'm Max.' I turn to Eve's dad.

'Freddie,' he says, reaching out a shaking hand. 'Eve's dad.' He says it quietly, reluctantly, like he doesn't deserve the title.

'I'm Eve's . . .' I begin. But what am I? How many of those messages were hers? I look at Becky now, the woman I've spent the last few months imagining, in pieces before me. But which pieces of the woman I liked were actually hers? 'Friend,' I settle on. Eve really needs one of those right now. I turn to Becky. 'We need to find Eve,' I say. Her eyes are red, raw, and she looks sorry, so very sorry. But for what?

'I've screwed up,' she whispers.

'Becky,' Tom says again. Stop speaking, dude. You have no idea what's going on. His eyes dart down the street to the small bunch of people gathering on the other side. 'Why don't we all go inside?' Becky nods. Some things are best kept private, but right now I need everything in the open; I need to get to Eve.

We bundle into Becky and Eve's living room. Tom takes a seat on the sofa and the biggest ginger cat I've ever seen jumps on his lap. *Buster.* I walk with caution into the room, the one I've imagined Becky writing to me from so many times.

My eyes scan the bookcases either side of the fireplace. The fireplace looks like it's not been used in years. Unlike the books, which look thumbed and loved. But not by Becky. By Eve. There are traces of her everywhere, an open laptop discarded on the sofa to one side. Carefully I move it, sitting where she has just been, longing to read her words. But she's not here. I don't know where she is, and I need to find out. To find out whether she's the woman I've been falling for all along.

'Becky?' I ask again. 'What's this about?'

'My messages,' she sobs, eyes darting to Tom.

'Messages?' Tom sits up a little straighter. 'You've still been messaging?'

'Yes,' I say slowly. I feel sorry for them. So sorry. But surely even my messages wouldn't have caused *this*. 'I wanted to keep the two of you together, so I messaged Becky for a bit. I know I took it too far. I should have stopped a long time ago, but I really enjoyed chatting to . . . well, to Eve?'

'Eve?' Tom asks, still too confused to be angry.

'Yeah, I think she's the one who's been messaging you back,' Becky says. She turns to Tom. 'At the beginning, we kind of set my whole profile up together. It was stupid, but I wanted to meet someone different and I guess we thought that if *I* was different we might find him . . . and we did, we found you.'

'Oh shit.' Tom looks at me. 'They've been doing the same as us all along?'

'You've done the same thing—'

'Becky.' I interrupt her before she can get started. '*Please.*'

'Okay, well, when you cooled off,' she goes on, 'I was gutted at first, but I kind of realised I hadn't been myself anyway, and you can't really keep that up forever, can you?'

'No, no, you can't.' Tom shakes his head; he couldn't keep it up either.

'So I didn't message back, but *Eve* did,' Becky explains, and Tom's eyes widen, like the penny has just dropped.

'And you did too?' he asks me.

'Yeah, but—'

'It was Eve.' Becky smiles for a second, before it disappears.

It was Eve.

'You have to forgive her, Becky,' I plead. 'It's my fault, I was going to end things and then Peggy passed away and . . . Eve was never trying to hurt you . . .'

'I know,' Becky says, voice cracking. 'And I was never trying to hurt her with my messages either.' She looks at Freddie, perched on the edge of an armchair.

'*Your* messages?' I ask. Just when I thought I was getting on top of things.

Freddie clears his throat. I had imagined bumping into him, trying to smooth things over for them so that Eve could finally admit that she missed him, that a part of her wanted to try again.

'I sent Eve a letter,' he says. 'Two, actually.'

'I know,' I say.

'You know?' Becky's mouth falls open in surprise.

'Eve told me,' I say. If it helps us to find her, I need to tell the truth.

'Well she didn't tell me,' Becky says, but she doesn't sound angry. 'I found the letters and I just knew that Eve wanted to reply but that she was scared that he would let her down again . . .' She glances at Freddie, who looks awkward but understanding. 'So I thought maybe if I could just get in touch, meet him, sound out what his intentions were . . . the way Eve sounded things out with you,' she says, not knowing whether to direct that part of her sentence to Tom or to me. 'I swear I had good intentions, but I shouldn't have done it, shouldn't have meddled behind her back.' She fixes her eyes on me and we both sense the irony, but now isn't the time. Now is the time to find Eve. 'I just wanted her to know she deserves a happy-ever-after as well.'

'Me too,' I say, putting a hand on Becky's.

'Do you think she'll ever forgive me?'

'If I know Eve like I think . . .' I say, and can't help but smile.

'You do.' Becky nods.

'I know she will.' I squeeze her hand, the hand that has held Eve's so many times before – physically, metaphorically. The hand that so rarely messaged me. It was Eve. It had always been Eve. 'Let's go and find her.'

'But where?' Becky says, pushing herself to her feet.

'I don't know.' I shake my head. 'She could have asked that taxi to go anywhere . . .'

'I found her at work,' Freddie says reluctantly, like it still isn't his place to speak up. 'The only reason I was able to write to her was because of her bylines. I sent the letters to her office . . .'

'The office,' Becky says, rushing towards the door. Tom follows, lost in every sense of the word. At least this explains why Becky was never the girl for him. One day he'll thank her for reminding him he can feel something for someone other than Yvonne. But right now isn't the moment.

'You coming?' I turn to Freddie.

'If it's okay with you, I think maybe I should hold back . . .' He looks a little apprehensive. 'Eve's had to wait for me this long; I'm not going to demand she sees me until she's ready. I'm not going to demand anything from her at all.'

I know he's telling the truth. There are some things you just can't fake.

'Right now, she needs her best friend and her . . .' he offers me a smile, 'whatever the hell you are.'

Chapter Twenty-Nine

Eve

The taxi closes in around me as it journeys towards the only destination I can think of. I try to catch my breath. Counting in for three. Out for three. But I can barely hear myself over the sound of my heart beating in my chest.

Scenes of London shoot by, my busy mind trying to capture the images playing in my head. My dad was there, at my house, trying to find me. And then there was Max. The only person I had told about the letters. Standing there staring at me, along with Becky. The only person I could trust. The person I had just betrayed.

I tumble out of the taxi, running the final stretch. How did I think pretending to be Becky would get me my own happy ending? I knew I was only ever destined for *happily enough*.

I look up at the News Building and my stomach sinks. How many times have I looked up like this, thinking that the answers to my questions were waiting inside? That if I could only move forward here, I would be moving forward in life. When all this time I've been leaving parts of myself behind. The relationships that were too real to ever try to control.

I rush into the building. I just need somewhere to hide. Like the many times I've hidden behind my work before. Before Tom – or Max – and my dad's letters came along.

As I run to the lifts, thoughts rush through my mind. I'd trusted Tom's messages like I'd trusted Max when I told him about my dad's letters. When he felt like a safe space. He'd listened, not forcing me to do or decide anything. Promising he wouldn't tell. But he had betrayed me. *To love is to be vulnerable.* But I didn't love Max, did I? I didn't even *know* him.

Emerging onto my floor, I pace across the empty office. The odd discarded coffee cup tells me that I've missed the weekend workers by minutes. But I'm alone now.

On autopilot, I switch on my monitor and load up my emails, looking for something to lose myself in. It worked before, right? Back when trying to move up in the newspaper was the only thing that mattered. Before Makena getting the role I'd marked out for myself made everything else unravel.

Gazing mindlessly at my inbox, my thoughts start to race. I'd missed my dad for years but never once admitted it to my best friend, never once admitted it to myself. Wasn't that why I'd kept any romantic interest at arm's length? Knowing that if I let someone else in, I would have to start being honest with myself.

I click open an email from a PR, scanning the words but

not taking them in. All it had taken for me to fall was one match with someone who was on the same page as me in all ways but one. But no. I didn't fall for Tom – or Max; how could I?

Moving mindlessly towards the window, I look down at the almost silent streets below. How could I love Max when all I had known was his messages? But then of course the Max in person and the Max on the screen were the same. His gentleness, his depth. And then there was the Tom in real life. The one I didn't feel connected to. I had always thought that if we were just left to our own devices, but . . .

It had always been Max.

I move away from the window and turn back to my monitor, my mind still running at a mile a minute. It was Max when I was messaging Tom about Peggy. When Tom was asking after me. But what did that matter now? Given everything I knew about Max – online and off – I never thought he'd be the type to reach out to my dad, to reply to his letters. To break his promise.

I scroll through my emails, just searching for something to hold on to. Maybe he was lying about me having what it took to go freelance too. He thought he was messaging Becky. Maybe he was just trying to impress my best friend. A best friend who now won't speak to me. I was so confident about handing in my notice on Monday. So sure I could take risks with Becky and her family behind me. But now what? I've already risked too much.

I look around the empty room. It's a ghost town. No one here to support me. But that isn't any different when the seats are full. I force my eyes back to my emails, press releases jumping from the screen. At least *hot to trot* lipsticks will never make your heart hurt like hell. But then another subject bar catches my eye.

Meeting?

It's from Richard. Why would the most senior person at the paper want to talk to me? With shaking hands I click the message open and read: *Dear Eve, thank you for your application for the role of features editor (maternity cover). As you know, we have now filled this position but I did want to talk to you about your Human Heroes column idea. As you know, your role on the Thursday supplement is a full-time position, but I was wondering whether you'd consider writing this column outside office hours on a freelance basis . . .*

'Freelance basis.' I breathe the words out loud. After today, I'm in no rush to pin too much meaning to a message, but somehow this one feels like a sign. So what if what Max said wasn't true? Or was just meant for Becky? I know my stories are good enough.

I read on: *Real stories are what it's all about: vulnerability, people making mistakes and finding the strength to get up again, being knocked down just to come back fighting, being burned just to rise from the flames. Letting people into the mess even when the story is far from complete.*

I read the words over and over, eyes welling with tears. *Letting people into the mess even when the story is far from complete.* That's what I thought, right? This morning. Before Becky came knocking on the door, before Max was there too. That I was ready to let someone in, not keep them at

340

arm's length, even when it hurt. But if that's what it's all about, why am I here hiding from two people who claim to love me? One more person who *could*. But Dad has broken my trust so many times. And now Max has too. The only person I can trust is . . .

'Becky?' I look up from my monitor to see her running across the office towards me.

'Eve!' She draws to a halt at my desk, doubling over, hands on her knees.

'How did you find me?' I ask, heart beating hard.

'I had some help.'

'How did you get *in*?'

'I had some help with that too,' she pants.

'Look, Becky, I'm so sorry about messaging Tom.'

'Max,' Becky corrects.

'Whoever,' I say. 'It doesn't really matter.'

'Except it totally does.'

'Yes, maybe – a bit.' I try to force Max and his messages from my mind. 'Either way, I messaged as you, without your permission, and it was wrong. I never should have risked letting a stupid boy come between us.' I'm crying now. So is she. 'And not that it makes it any better, but I'm never going to talk to him again.'

'But the two of you are great together.'

'Tom?'

'Max.'

'Whatever.' I shake my head. 'All that matters is . . .'
Having a dad. Having a relationship one day. Telling stories that make a difference. Being myself. Turns out there are a lot of

things that matter when you let yourself care about more than just one thing. 'Well, all that matters *right now*,' I correct myself, 'is making things right with you.'

'I feel the same way,' Becky says, still crying. 'Eve, I forgive you . . .'

'Oh thank God,' I breathe, flinging my arms around her. 'I'm so sorry. Honestly, I can't say it enough times. I was so scared you'd—'

'I'm just not sure you'll forgive *me*.' She cries harder, her shoulders heaving against my chest. What the hell do I need to forgive *her* for? She's always been there. She always will be. Won't she?

'What do you mean?' I say.

'I'm so sorry, Eve.'

'For *what*?' I repeat, heart racing.

'For contacting your dad.'

Instinctively I pull away. What? *Becky* contacted my dad? But how did she even know where to *find* him?

'I know I shouldn't have, and I'm so sorry . . .'

'You messaged my *dad*?'

I sit back down again, legs buckling beneath me. She comes to perch on the side of my desk. Cautiously. Afraid. I want to run into the toilets, pull out my phone and message someone.

But it would usually be her.

Or Tom. Or Max – *whoever*.

'I don't understand,' I say.

'I found your letters.' She breathes the words, like she's been holding on to them for too long. 'And then you seemed to let your guard down when we first started messaging Tom on the app together and I knew things being unresolved with your dad were holding you back and that a part of you wanted to reach out to him. I just thought, if you didn't reply and he moved house or changed his number or something, you might miss your chance to reconnect with him forever, and I didn't want you to live to regret that . . .'

Isn't that what I tried to tell myself about Becky and Tom? That I didn't want her to regret letting him go.

'Then when you were so down about Makena getting the job, I didn't know how to be there for you, didn't know what you needed, so I called him. And I thought if I just met him for a coffee, I could see what his intentions were, whether he was telling the truth, and then if he was in a good place, I don't know, I thought I might try and stage a meeting between the two of you, like *Parent Trap* style or something . . .' She struggles for breath. Struggles for the words. Breathe, Becky, just breathe. 'It was so stupid of me and I know I shouldn't have done it, but then you're just so involved in my family and I guess I thought maybe I had a right to be involved in yours . . .'

'You should have told me the truth,' I say, but on my tongue, the words taste wrong.

'I know,' Becky cries. 'But I swear I had good intentions.'

'So did I,' I say.

'I know.'

'And I should have told you the truth about my dad's letters. About Tom's messages.'

'Max's.'

'Whoever,' I say, and I can't help but smile. We both should have done so many things differently. But I guess that's the thing with family: you can make mistakes and then go again. Be different this time. Stronger.

'Can you ever forgive me?' Becky finds the strength to stand, and I do the same, looking down at her. Becky the Bird. The one who defended me all those years ago still trying to defend me now. 'Can you?' she repeats, scared by the silence stretching between us.

'Of course I can,' I choke, throwing my arms around her. 'You weren't completely wrong either. I was thinking about reaching out to my dad . . .'

'Just not today.' She fills in my blanks, the way I've done so many times with her.

'No, not today.' I nod. 'Bet he's run for the hills by now anyway.'

'He's at ours.' She smiles cautiously, not quite sure what I want to hear, but hopeful that this is a good thing. 'With Tom,' she adds.

I can't help but laugh. What on earth would they have to talk about? I have no idea. Because it turns out I haven't really spent all that long talking to Tom either. I've been talking to Max, and I've really, really enjoyed it.

'And Max?' I whisper, mind in overdrive. But I'm not going to run away from it this time. I'm going to stay and wait. Like my dad.

'Waiting downstairs.' She must see the confusion on my face, because she adds, 'He's the reason I was able to get to your floor without a key card. They're holding him hostage.'

344

She can't help but laugh, even though her face is still stained with tears.

'So he didn't tell you about the letters?'

'Eve, you left them behind my chocolate stash.' She rolls her eyes. 'For a while I even convinced myself you *wanted* me to find them.'

'But Max?' *Just answer the question, Becky.*

'No.' She shakes her head. 'He didn't tell me. He didn't tell anyone.' Her face risks another smile. 'It's been him all along. All the bits of Tom's profile you liked – the books, the films, the adventures, the ideas – it was all Max.'

'It was all Max,' I repeat under my breath, my mind shooting to that night in the Fable, to our afternoon in Soho. The connection we shared in person, sparking off a screen like magic. It was Max. It was all Max.

'Yeah.' Becky grins.

'This is a lot to take in.' My mind is racing. The column idea. Max, Tom. Becky. My dad. 'How do I play this?' I look at her. 'Help me?'

'Your life isn't a game, Eve.' Becky rests her hands on the top of my arms. 'What do you *want*?'

'I think I want to see my dad,' I whisper, new tears forming in my eyes.

'Great, let's start there. One step at a time.' For someone who Becky once claimed didn't believe in doing anything but completing the whole circle then lapping it ten times before breakfast, I was finally taking things slowly. Somehow, though it didn't feel like doing it by halves.

'But what about Max?' I ask, even though I know the

only person who can answer that is me. But I need to let today settle. To let this whole damn situation settle. In my mind. In my heart.

'What about Max?' Becky echoes back to me.

'I think I need time, but . . .'

'Say no more. Give me ten minutes,' Becky says, my own personal bodyguard. Except I don't need to guard myself from Max, or anyone, any more.

'But what if he—'

'Evelyn,' Becky says, already beginning to walk towards the lift. She turns around to smile at me. 'You're an ending worth waiting for.'

I smile back at my best friend, tears in my eyes, ready to talk to my dad for the first time in years. I don't feel like an ending right now. I feel like a new beginning.

Chapter Thirty

Max

I search for a new beginning, scrolling through my Kindle app trying to find a story strong enough to distract me. Turns out the only thing strong enough to distract me from the thought of Becky and Eve coming down the escalator beside me is the security guard breathing down my neck.

'They shouldn't be long now.' I look at him towering over me.

'For your sake, I hope so,' he laughs. 'This your girl?' and I turn my head so quickly I swear I've given myself whiplash. Looking at the lifts, heart leaping out of my chest, I see Becky.

'No, no it's not.' My heart sinks. She was never my girl.

My eyes search for Eve, but I know she's not coming down. Not while I'm here. Eve was never my girl either. She's her own woman. Individual and unpredictable in a way the protagonists confined to the pages of my books never could be. And that's a good thing. I'd rather have a relationship off script anyway. I know that now.

'Hey, Max,' Becky says, her smile soft and kind. She looks calmer now. Lighter for having been able to sort things out with Eve. But what about me? When will I be able to sort things out with her? 'I'm sorry, but—'

'How is she?' I interrupt. I don't give a shit about me right now. I just want to know how Eve is feeling.

'She's okay,' Becky sighs. She deserves to be better than okay. To know how wonderful she is. Just as her.

'And the two of you?'

'We're going to be fine.' Becky can't help but beam. My eyes dart behind her, still not knowing whether Eve is going to materialise, what I'll say to her if she does. 'Max . . .'

'I guess this is my cue to go home.' Becky nods slowly. My heart sinks like my stomach. I'm not sure what I was expecting. Sure, her messages meant a lot to me. But she thought she was messaging Tom. Now that she knows she wasn't, that I don't look or talk or act like him, I should have realised she'd want to move on.

That it was too good to be true.

'She just needs some time.' Becky smiles.

'Time?' My stomach flips and my heart flutters with hope. 'Time for what?'

'She's going to go and see her dad.' Her smile vanishes. She never should have got in touch with Freddie without Eve's permission. But people make mistakes. Just look at me. 'She needs a bit of time to process everything.'

If I was Eve, I'd need some time too. Even if my

messages have got into her head, her dad has been on her mind longer. She owes it to herself to sort things out with him first.

'I get that.' I nod, giving Becky a little hug, not meaning to grab her so tightly.

'I'll send your bestie back to you.' She laughs a little. To think I ever thought her heart was set on him.

'Thanks,' I say, knowing I'll need Tom's strength to pick me up tonight.

'Oh, and can I have your number?' Becky grins. 'For Eve? She asked me to ask you. My friend thinks you're pretty cute.'

'Well I think your friend is pretty cute too.' I can't help but laugh. After all this time, it feels like just the beginning. I tap the digits into Becky's phone.

'It might take her a bit of time to work everything through,' Becky explains again. 'But she wanted to have it for if she wants to get in touch.'

I smile back at Becky before turning to leave her behind. And with her, I leave Eve behind too – an Eve who might just message me.

Emerging from the Tube station, I blink in the last of the evening light. I'm back south of the river – the right side of the tracks – but Eve's 'if' has made its way across the border with me. My phone buzzes in my pocket: Eve? My heart leaps in my chest.

Tom work: Hey, dude. Back home. You on your way?

Max: Yeah, just walking back now.

Tom work: Great, dinner on the go.

Tom work: Strange day, eh?

Max: You can say that again.

Tom work is typing . . .

Max: Don't say it.

Max: How was Eve's dad?

Tom work: Freddie?

Tom work: He's a G.

Max: Huh?

Tom: A gangster, like proper cool.

Max: Oh Tom, you can't pull 'G' off.

Tom work: Hey, you tried to pull off being me.

Tom work: You can at least let me have this.

Max: Never again, dude.

Tom work: Never again.

I look up from the screen, gazing across the common as I walk the long way home. Eve will be back by now. Back with Becky. With her dad. Starting from where they left off? Maybe even better.

If. If. *If.* Those two little letters circle in my mind with every step I take towards home. But when it comes to how I feel about Eve, I'm pretty sure they don't apply. I like her. Maybe even more than that. It was Becky's words – Eve's words – that had me hooked.

I look down at my phone. I want to hear from her, to start again. Or start from where we left off. That part is clear. Whether I'll actually hear from her? That part isn't clear at all.

Putting one foot in front of the other, I walk on. I have no idea what happens next. Just like I had no idea what was coming with my grandma, or Peggy. When grief would hit or loneliness would lift. Life has a way of surprising you like that.

As I turn onto our street, the sunset lights up the sky: reds bleed into pinks and oranges fade to yellow as the sun kisses the ground. Whatever happens with Eve from here on in, we'll both be okay. We'll make mistakes. We'll pivot. We'll turn. But the sun will always rise. Reaching for my phone again, I pull up her number and delete it. I'm not going to force things this time. It's time to let go and let the rest just happen.

Walking into our living room, I see Tom lying in his usual space on the sofa, beer in one hand, book in the other.

'Tom Hardy?' I laugh. 'Who are you trying to impress?'

My eyes search the room, but he's dateless. The days of Ruby and Yvonne and Becky are long gone. Now it's just us. But there will be others for Tom. When the time is right, maybe even when it isn't. I guess there's some kind of magic in the mystery.

'*Peaky Blinders* himself.' Tom laughs, looking up. 'It's actually pretty good.'

'I've been telling you that for years.'

'How you doing, buddy?'

'I'm all right,' I sigh. Been better. But I'm all right. And I'll be better than all right soon.

'Good.' He smiles. I know that when I want to talk about it, he'll be there, but right now, he knows what I need. Distraction. And not the dating kind. 'Is there a film version of this?'

'I knew you weren't enjoying it.'

'I am, I am.' He throws his hands up in protest. 'Just not enough to read it all.'

'There is,' I say, reaching between the sofa cushions, feeling for the remote. I scroll through the film options, pretty sure that with these apps we'll always get a match.

'Tom?' I say over the flickering of the TV.

'Yeah, mate?'

'Thanks for being there today.'

'What I'm here for.' He shrugs.

I reach into my pocket, pulling out his cracked phone, the one that got me into all this trouble – with all this promise – in the first place.

'Won't be needing this any more.' I throw it onto the sofa beside him.

'Thanks, dude,' he says, rolling it over in his hand. 'Barely works anyway, good for nothing . . .' His sentence fades into the opening scene of the movie.

It was good for something. I smile as my eyes drift to the screen, remembering all over again why I love this story. The writing. The romance. The fact that the guys are willing to fight for the heart of one girl. That they know what it's like to find something worth putting it all on the line for.

I guess sometimes that's a cause – like loving those with dementia or sharing stories that matter. Or it's the family you're given or the family you choose. And sometimes, just sometimes, there's that one special person who's worth the wait, worth putting it all on the line – or taking it all offline – for.

Epilogue

Unknown: Hey, Max. I'm a journalist hoping to cover Peggy's Walk today. Could I grab you for a quick interview?

Max: Hey.

Max: Yeah, sure, that's great. Who you with?

Unknown: I'm freelance.

Unknown: But I'm a regular contributor to lots of the nationals.

Max: Great. I'm at the finishing line party on Carnaby Street.

Max: You're welcome to join.

Unknown: Brilliant. I've actually just arrived there now.

Unknown: How will I recognise you?

Max: I'll be the one in the orange and pink tie-dye T-shirt.

Unknown: Bold look.

Max: Official merch.

Max: Which thinking about it isn't that helpful for finding me.

Max: I know, why don't I find *you*?

Max: What are you wearing?

Unknown: Bit cheeky.

Max: Oh God, sorry. No. I didn't mean anything by that.

Max: I just don't know how to spot you in this crowd.

Unknown: Chill out, Max. I was only joking.

Max: Oh, right.

Unknown: Okay, I'm here.

Max: Great. What am I looking for?

Unknown: You're looking for a tall woman.

Unknown: Like, really tall.

Unknown: Long blonde hair.

Unknown: Recently resolved daddy issues.

Unknown: Often seen with small friend in tow.

Unknown: Very available.

Max is typing . . .

Max: Eve?

Unknown: And if that doesn't work . . .

Unknown: I'm standing behind you right now.

Unknown: Waiting to kiss you.

Max: Eve?

Unknown: Just turn around and kiss me, you idiot.

Acknowledgements

This story would not be in your hands without two incredible women: Sallyanne Sweeney and Jess Whitlum-Cooper. From the very beginning, you have both been the greatest champions of this book and it has been a pleasure bringing this story to life with you.

A huge thanks must of course go to the entire team at Headline Review. Not only have you published this book with diligence and determination, but during a global pandemic no less!

This book is ultimately about friendship, and I've been blessed to have many a friend show me the meaning of the word throughout my relatively short time on this planet. From dancing in the playground at Holymoorside and lounging in free periods with the Brookfield lot, to drinking in Nottingham, adventuring in Sydney and laughing around London, you all know who you are. For this particular story, a special thanks must go to all the friends I have lived with over the years: you have all felt like family. And Nick, thanks for supporting me in a thousand little ways during the writing of this book.

Then of course there is Mum, Dad, Thomas and Rachel – I love you all so much. To the O'Hagans, thank you. And 'to him who is able to do immeasurably more than we ask or imagine' thank you for setting my sights on a story bigger than me.

KEEP IN TOUCH WITH
LIZZIE O'HAGAN

© Juliet Trickery

 @LizzieOHagan1

 @lizzie_ohagan

Bookends

When one book ends, another begins...

Bookends is a vibrant new reading community to help you ensure you're never without a good book.

You'll find exclusive previews of the brilliant new books from your favourite authors as well as exciting debuts and past classics. Read our blog, check out our recommendations for your reading group, enter great competitions and much more!

Visit our website to see which great books we're recommending this month.

Join the Bookends community:
www.welcometobookends.co.uk

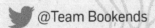 @Team Bookends   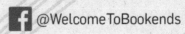 @WelcomeToBookends